MW00878663

DARKEST NIGHT

JESSIE NIGHT THRILLER BOOK FOUR

EMBER SCOTT

BURNING EMBER PRESS

Copyright © 2024 by Ember Scott

All rights reserved.

No part of this book may be reproduced in any form or by any electronic or mechanical means, including information storage and retrieval systems, without written permission from the author, except for the use of brief quotations in a book review.

For my Family

1

Pain Beyond Agony

Agony ripped through her like a dull knife as another contraction tore mercilessly across her swollen belly. She screamed until her throat was raw, back arching off the filthy pallet she had been placed upon. The air grew thicker, the stench of her own filth was quickly being replaced with that of fear.

She wasn't afraid for herself. She had long ago realized she was never leaving this dirty shed. The fear was for the child growing inside her that was determined to make their way into the world this night.

She gritted her teeth and tasted copper. Her blonde hair was plastered to her head and her body was wet with sweat. In between contractions, her body shook as she cried and called out for someone – anyone – to help her. She knew it was in vain. She couldn't scream any louder now than she had ten months ago when she was first dropped into the decaying shed.

Even in the throes of contractions that were increasingly less spread out, she couldn't scream any louder than the night the first of them had shown up and forced themself on her.

That screaming had stopped after the fifth night. At that point, she had resigned herself to the nightly assaults, lying there in the dirt, the grunts and huffs of foul breath covering her face. At least it was always quick.

Her mind disassociated and she took herself elsewhere. Someplace clean and warm and happy.

Despite her situation, she was always thinking of what she would do once she was back home. She was going to escape this hell eventually. And hell was exactly where she intended to send at least one of her captors when she escaped.

While at first she had refused the meager gruel, with bits of chewy, fat meat in it, she realized she would need whatever strength she could manage when the time came. No matter how small.

After a while, time had no meaning. There were slight openings between the wood that framed the decaying shed where she was locked. But when she looked out, her vision was blocked by a black material draped on the outside of the building. Light couldn't get in, and the only time she could see anything was when they came for her, carrying a small lantern that always illuminated whichever corner of the shed she was hiding in, hoping she could make herself so small they wouldn't find her.

It never worked of course. They would find her and drag her into the center of the small room and have their way.

She wouldn't move, even after they left. Always afraid that a second might come in. But thankfully that never happened. After a bit, she'd crawl into the corner opposite the one she had used to relieve herself, and curl up, praying for God to make her a stone.

Time lost all meaning for the woman. Every chance she got, she crawled on her hands and knees, feeling around in the dark for something – anything – that could be used as a weapon. A nail, a piece of metal, a broken chain link. But there was nothing. Still, she knew her time would come, and she knew she had to be ready.

But that determination vanished when she felt the first signs. She knew what was growing inside her and she felt a terror that eclipsed any she had experienced since that first night when the large, misshapen shadow had torn into her tent, hit her so hard across the face that her whole body went numb, and then proceeded to drag her by one foot across the wooded terrain and threw her into the shed.

That was when the assaults stopped. She also noticed there was more slop in the large bowl they fed her from.

She wasn't the only one who knew what was happening.

In the darkness, the only company she had was her thoughts. She kept thinking back to what she should have done differently. She shouldn't have gone hiking alone. She certainly shouldn't have made it a weekend trip where she would camp outdoors alone – even though she had done so many times before. She should have kept a weapon on her, not just the bear spray that she kept under her sleeping bag at night.

She should not have been alone in the woods. Maybe she shouldn't even be alone in life. If she had a partner, maybe they would have accompanied her and she wouldn't be locked in some backwoods shed with only her splintering mind for company.

Time passed. She stayed in her corner as a couple of them would lumber in. She kept her face turned away, pressed into the wood of the wall as she heard the sounds of wood being thrown around close to her. Once they left, she crawled around until she felt the splintered pallets and realized they had made her what amounted to a bed. There was also something soft and musky on top of it and for the first time since her ordeal started, she felt something familiar.

It was her sleeping bag, and for what seemed like hours, she sealed herself inside the cotton and wool cocoon, only venturing out to eat from her bowl as it was refilled.

The night her water broke was the first time she had heard her own voice. It was a scream followed by pleas for help. Help she knew was not coming.

That was when the real fear started. The kind of fear that took hold inside her and broke the core of who she was. All rational thought fled, replaced by a primal need to call out in the darkness.

As time passed, and her contractions grew more intense, she heard the door open and the smell of body parts that had probably never known soap washed over her. She cried. She begged. She pleaded. Whoever was in the dark with her didn't speak or move. But they were there. She knew they were there.

Her mind raced. She didn't know anything about delivering a baby. All she could do was trust whatever instincts she prayed would show themselves as she managed to climb onto the pallets and lay there, panting between screams.

All she could think about was the horror stories she had heard about the dangers that came with giving birth. Complications that could lead to the death of both the mother and the infant.

And that was in a hospital, filled with the miracles of modern technology.

She was in a blacked-out shed, covered in months of her own filth, what little strength she had nourished with only the questionable contents of a bowl of slop.

Still, she found strength she didn't know she possessed. She gave in to the pain, riding the waves until every fiber of her being told her it was time to push.

And push she did.

Until finally, with one last Herculean effort, she felt a new life slip out of her.

Her head dropped back onto the hard pallet as she breathed. She cried out as she felt rough hands at work between her legs, pulling and prying.

"No, please..." she said, trying to push words from her raw throat. She reached out in the darkness, only to have her hand slapped away.

She heard the whisper of metal, and the tugging at the umbilical cord as it was cut. Then, the door opened and closed and she was alone once again.

Weakness seeped into her as she felt blood leaving

her body. She cried. More for what had just been taken from her than for herself.

She knew it was over for her, and she begged whoever might be listening to forgive her for not fighting harder.

Those were the last thoughts she had as she lapsed into a sleep she would not wake from.

2

Worse Fates

The girl told herself to follow their orders and not cause trouble. Actually, that's what they had told her. Keep her mouth shut and don't be a pain in the ass. If she did, things would go easy for her. If she didn't, she'd be punished. She learned quickly what those punishments were—having food withheld, being soaked with cold water and left to shiver through the night.

Not being fed was manageable. The food was always some unidentifiable mush, and she could rarely do more than push it around in the dirty bowl they fed her from. But the water was different. The first night they doused her, her teeth chattered so violently she feared they'd break.

Yet, what terrified her most wasn't the cold or the hunger. It was the visits.

Sometimes there were two men, sometimes just one.

They never spoke or touched her physically, but their eyes roamed over her, lingering in ways that made her skin crawl. Screaming had earned her the soaking on the first night, so she learned to stay silent. She'd curl into the corner, wrap her arms around her knees, and try to make herself as small as possible, praying this time they wouldn't do more than stare.

The only one who ever spoke was the man with cruel eyes. He had laid down the rules on her first night. When she defiantly told him who she was, he laughed, saying he knew exactly who she was. Then, he said something that chilled her more than the freezing water.

"I've got special plans for you."

Days bled into each other. She used the faint light filtering through the cracks in the wooden walls to search for anything that could be a weapon or aid her escape. She found nothing. At night, she didn't know what scared her more—being alone or the thought of the man with cruel eyes coming to enact his plans.

The isolation had begun to fray the edges of her mind. She lost track of time, tried counting days, tried not to think about her family. She remembered the day she was taken—broad daylight, at home with her parents. The door to her bedroom had burst open, and an impossibly large man grabbed her, shrugging off her kicks and scratches. He threw her over his shoulder and carried her downstairs. She had looked around frantically, calling for help, but her parents were nowhere to be seen.

She had screamed, as the horror of what was happening settled in. The man had thrown her down long enough to shove a foul-smelling rag into her mouth.

Her eyes widened in terror as he drew back a massive fist. She whimpered and stopped struggling. He covered her head with a rough cloth and threw her into a van. She could sense she wasn't alone but was terrified to speak up. She stayed still, listening to the rumble of the engine. They drove for what felt like an hour before stopping. She was hauled out and marched blindly across rough terrain, then tossed into the wooden structure that became her prison.

Hopelessness settled in over time. She thought she was going to die here, alone and far from home. But then she heard it—faint, muffled, unmistakable. A woman's scream, pleading for help. But not for herself.

For her unborn child.

Fear gripped her anew as she shrank back into the corner of her wooden cell, sinking to the cold, hard dirt. She had resigned herself to dying in this place, but the desperate cries outside told her there might be a fate worse than death waiting for her.

3

Not Always a Serial Killer

The kitchen in the Pine Lake Bed and Breakfast hummed with vitality. Large windows streamed sunlight across the butcherblock island that held a kaleidoscope of colorful fresh fruits. The space smelled of the enticing mingle of ripe strawberries, tart raspberries, and sun-kissed peaches.

Jessie Night leaned over the island, closed her eyes, and breathed in the intoxicating aroma of fruits.

Mark, one half of the husband duo who owned the bed and breakfast smiled at her. "You just going to stand there admiring them? Or do you want to get those berries rinsed and into the pot?" He plucked one of the strawberries and popped it into his mouth with an appreciative grin. "The key is to gently heat them so they release their natural pectin."

"I only exist to learn from the master," Jessie teased. She then carefully transferred the crimson berries into a saucepan, reveling in the way their plump skins yielded under her fingertips. As the fruit heated, bursts of jammy sweetness began to waft through the kitchen's airy space.

Mark pointed to the bowls where she had previously measured out lemon juice and sugar in just the right ratios. He nodded as she slowly added them to the berries. "Don't over-stir them. We want the fruit to hold its shape."

Jessie nodded, her face a mask of concentration as she rhythmically folded the jam with a wooden spoon, completely transfixed as the mixture shimmered crimson. She found the motion strangely soothing as tendrils of berry-scented warmth steamed across her face. "Next, you have to show me how to make those flaky croissants you have."

Mark lowered his head, arching an eyebrow at her. "Easy there, Sara Lee." His tone was far more playful than mocking. "I know I'm making this look easy, but let's just tackle one thing a time for now."

Heavy footfall announced Eric's arrival in the kitchen, and Jessie looked up to see the taller of the two men stride into the room.

"I wondered what was smelling so amazing this early in the morning." He proceeded to stride over to Jessie and took an exaggerated smell. "You better be quick with that...the aroma has already spread to the upstairs. The guests will be down soon wanting an early breakfast."

Mark made a tsking sound at his husband. "The dining room is all set with everything they need, including fresh coffee. This is Jessie's treat. She's a natural and will soon be outshining me in the kitchen." He did his best to keep a straight face but couldn't help but burst out laughing. "I'm sorry, I tried."

"Ha, ha," Jessie said, going along with the fun. "You know, maybe in exchange for your cooking lessons, I'll teach you self-defense. Let's see how many jokes you have on the gym mat."

"Oh, now that I would pay money to see," chided Eric.

Mark grabbed the dishtowel he had slung over one shoulder and snapped it playfully at his husband. "Yeah, I think we both know that is not going to happen. But given everything we've been through over the last year, it might not be such a bad idea for both of us. You go a couple of rounds with her first though."

Eric laughed, throwing both hands up and stepping back. "Hey, I've seen her in action. No thanks." He looked at his watch. "I've got to head into town. The special deadbolts that I ordered to reinforce the doors should have arrived at the hardware store yesterday. If I hurry, I can get them all installed before lunch." He gave his husband a quick peck on the cheek and gave a two-finger salute to Jessie as he left the kitchen.

"You two are so cute together," Jessie said. "You're lucky." She didn't mean for her tone to sound remorseful, and quickly went back to stirring the jam. She could feel Mark's eyes on her and prayed he would just let it drop.

"Well, you know you aren't the only single person in Pine Haven, right?"

So much for prayers. "Yes, Mark. I am aware of that."

Thankfully, he turned his back as he went about scrounging for something in the refrigerator. "Because, I think you and the town's newly minted detective would make a gorgeous pair. Like a perfectly grilled lobster dinner and a wonderful chardonnay."

Jessie grimaced. "And who gets to be the lobster in that situation?"

Mark popped his head above the refrigerator door and winked at her. "That's on you. Far be it for me to tell someone how to roleplay."

This time she couldn't help but laugh at his banter. "But in all seriousness, I'm happy for you guys. I'm not sure that I'm built for what you have, but after growing up in a single household, and being around nothing but military families for so long, it's good to see something so real." She stopped stirring and looked his way. "No, that's not right. I shouldn't paint that life with a single, negative brush. It was more the aspects of it that mirrored my own life. Keeping things to myself, not wanting to involve others in the gray areas that my work took me to. The life I led was more about breaking bones than breaking bread."

Mark laughed as he closed the door with his hip and placed a tray of uncooked biscuits on the island. "Well, these are for you. You can take them with you and freeze them if you want or bake them up. I thought if you like these, it can be the next thing we tackle on your culinary education."

Jessie smiled, thankful for the biscuits and the fact that he didn't prod her to continue down the path of self-reflection she had somehow veered onto.

Mark came and looked over her shoulder. "See that consistency? It's just what you're looking for. We can start prepping the jars for canning. It's always hard to resist eating this straight from the pot but..." He went to the cupboards and took out a couple of decorative bowls before returning to ladle a couple of spoonfuls into them. "Luckily, we are adults and can do what we want. As soon as this cools, I say we give it a taste test. but in the meantime, let's line the jars up and have them ready. Canning them is a whole other process from cooking."

Together, they prepped the jewel-toned mason jars, sitting them in a row in preparation for what was to come. Jessie could feel her stomach doing somersaults just smelling the jams. She took in more of the sweet aromas, suddenly very grateful for the few hours where she was able to be fully present amidst the simple joys of fresh fruit, laughter and camaraderie. She couldn't remember how long it had been since she felt so at ease.

She glanced at Mark and he must have sensed what she was thinking. "See, anytime you're not tripping over dead bodies, or fighting serial killers, feel free to stop by and hang out. I'll have you whipping up world-class cuisine in no time." He bent down to give Blizzard's head a quick rub. "And you can even bring this furry monster with you."

Jessie pulled the wooden spoon out of the pot she had been stirring, blew on it a couple of times, and then ran a finger through the sticky goodness before popping it in her mouth. She closed her eyes, releasing a small sigh. "Damn. This is so good, Mark." She turned to face the man. "And thank you. For everything."

"Well, I think you're a natural at this. Welcome to the world of jamming."

Jessie's phone buzzed and she dropped the spoon

into the sink and fished in her pocket. She frowned at the screen before flicking at it and held it to her ear. "Hello?" Her face brightened. "Oh, hi Aura. No, this isn't a bad time at all. How can I help you?" She listened intently, only nodding to herself occasionally. "I am so sorry, Aura. I tell you what, why don't we meet and discuss this in person?" She nodded again, listening. "Of course. I'll see you there in an hour." She swiped at the phone once more before it slid back into her pocket.

"Everything okay?" Mark asked.

She shook her head. "Not really. That was someone I only recently met here in town. She's the sister of Terry Blackburn."

Mark's eyebrows shot up. Everyone knew about what had happened with Terry. Or at least they knew what the papers had printed.

"She's pretty upset," Jessie continued. "It seems that her best friend was found dead up in the mountains. I didn't get the details, but Aura wants to discuss something with me."

Mark moved slowly over to stand next to her as he inspected the array of jars laid out before them. "Is it...?"

Jessie gave him an annoyed look. "Not everything is the work of serial killers, Mark." Her tone was reassuring and confident, even if she didn't exactly feel that on the inside. "But she's understandably upset. I'm going to meet her at Angela's to talk about it." She looked around the kitchen. "But that means I won't be able to stay and help clean up."

Mark sighed. "Not my problem. I cook, Eric cleans."

He gave her a wicked grin. "This will still be here when he gets back."

Jessie laughed and eyed the tray of biscuits. "Umm, if you happen to cook those up for me, I wouldn't be mad."

Mark rolled his eyes and ushered her from the kitchen. She laughed again and nodded for Blizzard to follow her out.

As they walked out into the warmth of the morning sun, she felt the joviality leave her. She didn't get the details about what happened with Aura's friend, but she didn't have to.

Someone was dead. And someone else needed her help.

First case

JESSIE WAS thankful the bakery wasn't as bustling with activity as usual. She was able to get her normal seat at a table next to the large picture window overlooking Main Street and large, open greenspace that ran through the center of town. It was midday, and there were only a few people on the green enjoying an early lunch, or just lounging on one of the benches.

Inside, Jessie wasn't used to seeing the bakery so empty. Especially on such a beautiful day. The air was filled with the aroma of fresh baked bread and strong coffee. There was the slightest overlay of sweetness from the homemade pastries that added to the overall ambience of the shop.

A tinkle from the bell hanging over the doorjamb

caught Jessie's attention, and she looked up to see Aura Riley step into the bakery. She looked around and Jessie half stood from her chair and waved her over.

Aura pulled out a chair and dropped into it. Her face was puffy and her eyes red-rimmed. She ran a hand through disheveled hair and let out a deep sigh.

"Aura," Jessie said, as she reached a hand across the table to grasp the other woman's. "I am so sorry to hear about your friend. I can only imagine what you must be going through."

Aura expanded both cheeks, holding her breath for a few heartbeats before letting the air out. "I just...I can't cry anymore, Jessie. My body is bone dry at this point."

Jessie gave the woman a moment to compose herself then pushed back from the table and stood up. "What can I get you?" She nodded towards the counter.

Aura started to protest but then gave in with a smile. "Just a coffee. Black, please. Oh, and decaf if they have it."

Jessie smiled, gave her a nod and walked away, only to return a few minutes later, a steaming mug in each hand. She sat one in front of her friend and then slid back into her seat. "So, tell me about your friend."

"Her name is—" she caught herself, her tone flooded with barely held back emotions, "—*was* Marley. She was my cousin but also my best friend. And I...I just can't believe she's gone, Jessie. It just feels like some awful nightmare." She was getting flustered, her hand trembled, tapping at the tabletop until her fingers settled on the paper napkin in front of her and began tearing it into ribbons.

Again, Jessie reached forward, laying a hand over

hers, and waited for the woman to look up at her. "It's okay. Take your time and start at the beginning. When did you find out about your cousin?"

Aura let out a sigh and gave a tiny nod. "Two days ago. I got a call from the sheriff's office up in Bidonville. Marley lived just on the outskirts of town there. He said he had some bad news to report. He said Marley's body had washed up on the river bank inside one of the parks." Recounting the story overtook her and she buried her face in her hands for a moment before taking another of the napkins from the table to dab at her eyes. "He said it looked like she must have slipped in upstream somewhere and drowned. But I'm telling you, that makes no sense, Jessie. Marley was an excellent swimmer. And she was smart. She was always hiking or doing overnight camping. She was at home in the woods. There's no way she slipped and fell in the river. And even if she did, there is no way she drowned."

Jessie watched as Aura went back to fiddling with the napkin. She took out her phone and rested her hands on the table. "Do you mind if I ask you a couple of questions and take some notes?" Aura nodded her approval, and Jessie swiped at her screen, opening one of the apps. "First, tell me the names of who you spoke to in Bidonville about this."

"The call came from a Sheriff Michael Cormac. He said they had found her phone at her campsite and she had me listed as her next of kin in her contacts." She sniffed hard before blowing her nose.

Jessie's thumbs were flying across her phone screen. "When was the last time you had contact with Marley?"

Aura looked up, eyes wide. "That's the weird thing. We've been texting each other constantly. The house she bought is in the middle of nowhere. She gets very bad cell reception but would text me all the time. She never went anywhere without texting me. And anytime she was in cell range running errands or something, she would call me. I haven't gotten a call from her in months, but I got regular text updates and we'd chat that way almost daily." She pulled out her cell and pushed it over to Jessie. The last message she had received was two days ago.

Jessie frowned. "This was sent to you two days ago? The same time her body was found?"

She was nodding hard. "Yes. And that's what's so strange. She never even mentioned she was going camping or hiking or anything. There is no way she would have done that without telling me. I feel so guilty. This is all my fault." She started to cry softly again.

Jessie stopped taking notes and gave the woman a second to let her emotions run, before softly asking another question. "Why do you think this is your fault?"

Aura took a deep breath. "My mama's sister— Marley's mother—died four years ago. And on her death bed, she gathered me, Marley, and... Terry together. By then, we were all that was left of our little family. And Marley's mom made us all swear to take care of, and look out for each other. And that's what we did...for a time. But then, all that happened with Terry, and, well...I was dealing with that, and all the bills with his arrangements as well as trying to claim his estate, and, well, I just didn't keep in touch with Marley like I should have. I should have made it a point to go up there and make sure everything was okay. I just had a feeling that her only reaching out by text was weird, and I swear I was going to go see her in person as soon as everything was straightened out with Terry." She looked up at Jessie, her eyes going wide. "Oh my...I'm sorry. I didn't mean to bring that up..."

Heat crowded Jessie's features and her throat went dry. When she spoke, her voice wavered. "Aura...I am sorry about what happened to your brother. If I could have handled things differently, I would have."

Aura looked up, her brows dipping as she reached for Jessie's hand. "Don't. Had you handled things any differently, then you would probably be dead and so would Angela's mom. No one made my brother do the horrible things he did. And you did what you had to in order to keep everyone else in town safe and alive."

Jessie didn't answer. She couldn't tell the woman she had lain awake at night wondering what she could have done to get Terry the help he needed. Something she might have been able to do that would have kept him alive. The truth was, she had never confronted the family of anyone she had to put away—either in jail or into the ground—and doing so now made her question her instincts. But no good would come from going down that road.

Her instincts were what kept her alive in many situations.

"I know what you're going through; as weird as it may be for me to say that." She couldn't meet her friend's eyes.

Aura stiffened slightly. "I know. I haven't lived in Pine Haven for long, but I'm pretty sure everyone knows about...that. And that's why I know you did everything in your power for my brother."

Jessie met her eyes. "How is Andy doing?'

Aura sighed. "As best as can be expected. He really worshipped his uncle. But he's coping. Thank you for asking."

"Alright. I need to ask a few more questions. Are you up for that?" When Aura nodded, she continued. "Can you tell me if Marley was seeing anyone?"

Aura shook her head. "No. She got burned pretty badly by a guy a few years ago, and even though she was starting to come back around to the idea of dating, I just don't think she was ready."

Jessie was nodding along as she spoke, and then looked up. "And what was your cousin's mindset lately? Are you aware of any depression or stress she might have been under?"

Aura frowned, drawing back from the table a bit. "Marley was the most positive, upbeat person I knew. She treasured her solitude, but she wasn't depressed. She just liked being out in nature, as she put it."

"What about her finances. Did she have a job?"

"She designed and painted murals. But what she really wanted was to paint her own art and sell it. That was why she originally moved out to the boonies up in Bidonville. She sold her mama's house and had enough to rent that place for a year. That's how long she gave herself to build up enough art that she could try to get a gallery showing somewhere. That's why she wanted to live out on her own...to get away from distractions." Again, she broke down in tears. "She kept telling me it was just going to be for a year and then she'd be heading back. I should have known something was off when... when she said she couldn't make it down for Terry's funeral."

Jessie swallowed hard but kept taking notes. "I know this is hard, but just a few more. How many times have you spoken with the police department in Bidonville? And have you told them your concerns around the circumstances of your cousin's death?"

She gave Jessie an exasperated look. "I've tried. But they said it was very cut and dried and they consider the case closed. But I'm telling you, it just doesn't feel right. Something is wrong."

Jessie sat for a moment, deep in thought. "Can I have your permission to reach out to this sheriff and ask to receive a copy of Marley's case file? I may need to tell them it's on your behalf, as her only next of kin."

Aura nodded emphatically. "Yes, of course! Do whatever you need to do. And look—" she lifted her purse to the table and took out her check book, "—I don't know what your rates are, but Terry left his life insurance policy to me, so I can pay whatever it takes."

Jessie held a hand up in protest. "Let's just table that for now. Let me make a few calls and see what I can find out, alright?"

Aura nodded and pushed back from the table, sticking out her hand. Jessie ignored the gesture and, instead, walked around the table to engulf the woman in a hug. She pulled back and smiled. "I can't guarantee you anything other than the fact that I am going to do my best to get you and Marley the answers you deserve." Aura, nodded her thanks, biting down on her trembling lip.

As they stepped out into the sunshine, Jessie placed a hand on her friend's arm. "Oh, one other thing. Can you text me the most recent picture you have of Marley, as well as her address?"

"I'll do it as soon as I get home," Aura promised.

They parted ways and Jessie made her way to the Jeep parked along Main Street in the shade of a large oak tree. Blizzard hopped into the back seat and curled up, eyes already drifting shut. A buzzing in her pocket grabbed Jessie's attention and she reached for her phone, swiping to unlock it.

It was a text message from Zoe Knox, the FBI agent who had arrived in Pine Haven to clean up the mess created by Terry Blackburn and Jessie's own aunt—who was quite possibly more than just her aunt.

Though she was expecting it, the message still squeezed the oxygen from her lungs.

I'm sending you the link in thirty. You got four minutes with her. That was all I could manage.

Jessie let out a breath and climbed into her Jeep. Four minutes wasn't a lot. But it would have to do.

4

Bad Things Happen

She made it home just in time to put down a fresh bowl of water for Blizzard, then sit down at the kitchen table and open her laptop. She fidgeted with her hair, unable to decide if she wanted to leave it up in a ponytail or let it hang loose, before slapping at the tabletop with both palms. "Oh, for God's sake, Jessie, she is not going to care in the least what your hair looks like."

Then, as if on cue, the computer dinged, and a security box popped up on screen. She recognized it for one of the highly encrypted ones used by the military and the government for end-to-end communication. She clicked the blue acceptance button and waited for the split second it took to open the private channel. Then, filling the screen of her computer, was the face of the woman who had tried to kill her.

The woman Jessie had only known as Aunt Gina looked directly at the camera and gave a sarcastic grin.

"And they said I'd never speak to another living soul again."

Jessie bit back the emotions she felt, willing her face to remain stone. "Hello, Gina."

The woman narrowed her eyes, her lips pressed together in a thin line. "I take it this isn't a social call you somehow convinced them to let you make. Which means that you probably don't have a lot of time."

Jessie took a deep breath. "I want you to know I forgive you. For the things I know you did, like shooting me. And the things I probably never want to know you were involved in."

Gina frowned for a moment before both eyebrows shot up and she erupted in a fit of laughter. She lifted handcuffed wrists and wiped her eyes. "You forgive me? That's rich. Little girl, what I was doing needs no forgiving. What I was doing would have led to a safer nation for generations to come." She sat back smugly in her chair. "You need to be making peace with what *you* did. You destroyed something that would have had a lasting positive impact on our great country."

Now it was Jessie who smirked. "You mean creating a stronger nation by creating a more obedient assassin— excuse me, asset—that you could then sell to the highest bidder?"

Gina scowled at her, a red blush creeping up her neck. "I would not expect you, a turncoat, to understand. But it doesn't matter. I was merely a cog in a wheel that will keep turning. In the end, you have really accomplished nothing in stopping me."

Jessie fought to suppress a smile. "Oh, I'd hardly say

you were just a cog in the wheel. My brother kept some very...very, detailed records of his time working for you and a few other highly placed individuals within the government and military."

Gina's facade cracked just a bit, and Jessie wasted no time in widening the crack in the older woman's armor. "And in case you're wondering, he also provided the key to decode the names of the buyers inside the human trafficking ring that I am sure prosecutors will be able to link to your network as well. That, combined with the identities of those funding your little experiment on children to brainwash them...should make for a very interesting time in Washington over the next year." She saw the muscles in the older woman's jaw tighten. "And yes...I handed it all over to the FBI. So, you see, I may forgive you, but I can't say the government will do the same."

Gina relaxed, her shoulders dropped, and she seemed to regain control of her facial features. "You know, if that's true, you've signed my death warrant."

"Don't be dramatic. Maybe a few years in a black site will do you some good."

Gina threw her head back and laughed. "I'm not on the government's payroll. I'm not military. I'll be thrown into a jail someplace very far away, and one day...probably in the second week of my incarceration, I'll have an accident. And then be buried somewhere in an unmarked grave. I know how these things work."

Jessie didn't speak, just stared at the woman.

"You know, it's ironic. You sacrificed everything for your father in a situation very similar to this. But you wouldn't consider doing the same for your—for me. Not that I would ask, of course."

Jessie hesitated. The opening was there. The thread was dangling. All she had to do was tug on it.

The smugness returned to Gina's face. "You look like you want to ask me something, dear. Go ahead."

Jessie bit her tongue before finally speaking up. "Why? Why did you do all of this? Why disappear from my life for so long only to come back as...this?"

Gina narrowed her eyes. "We all have a boss, dear. I was just doing as I was told. And your father came along for the ride. Unlike me, no one had to order him to do anything. As much as he hated the thought, he and your brother were far more alike than he wanted. He always wanted you to be more like him...but you take after someone else..."

Jessie flinched. It took all the strength she had to quiet the anger that boiled inside her. "You're right. There is more that I wanted to say to you. But, sitting here now, seeing the look in your eyes, I realize something. I don't care. I'm tired of trying to figure out the why behind people's actions. I've spent my entire life doing that. And what did it get me? Betrayal on so many levels. So yeah... whatever I may have wanted to know, is just not that important in the grand scheme of things. I have a new life and a new destiny. Far from you and people like you. And I'm done living in the past. What's ahead of me is so much brighter than the darkness behind. I'm truly sorry that you can't say the same. Enjoy whatever time you have left. I have a feeling we will never see one another again."

The old woman's upper lip quivered in barely contained rage. Then, she smiled. "No. We won't see one another again. But I have one last parting gift for you, Jessie." Her smile twisted into a sneer. "I just want you to know that I am your—"

Jessie cut her off by slamming the laptop shut and severing the link. Her heart raced and she struggled to control her rapid breathing. Tears welled but she refused to let them fall. Something warm nuzzled at her palm and she looked down to see Blizzard's honey-colored eyes looking up at her. He pushed forward, resting his head on her hand.

"Thank you, boy." Her breath was ragged and her tone pained. "You always know what I need."

The phone lying next to the laptop buzzed and she flipped it over, looking at the screen before picking it up. "Hello?"

"I just wanted to check in on you. Make sure you were okay." It was Zoe Knox on the other end.

Jessie drew in a deep breath, thankful for the warmth of the voice on the other end of the call. "I will be. I needed to get that out. I feel like I can finally close this chapter of my life. And thank you, for making that happen."

"Hey, it's the least I can do. You pretty much single handedly solved a couple of cold cases for us."

Jessie felt herself blush. "Well, I wouldn't say it was single-handed. I had some help."

There was a moment of silence then Zoe cleared her throat. "She was right, you know. She doesn't show up on any official military or government employee lists. But they are very interested in taking custody. Whatever she did...she's definitely going far far away. I'm sorry."

Jessie swallowed the lump that had formed in her throat. "Don't be. You didn't make her do the things she did. No one made her do all that, no matter what she says. So, were you listening in?"

"Only at the end. I had to stay logged onto the server that was used for communication. It's private, but because it was under my credentials, technically I had to be there."

"Oh, I understand how that works. No problem at all."

"Look, Jessie, it is absolutely none of my business... but some of the stuff she laid on you. If you need someone to talk to..."

"Thank you, Zoe. Really. But I've dealt with a lot over the last few years. I can handle this as well."

"Understandable. Just know I'm here if you need anything. But hey – before I go, how are things with the PI thing?"

Jessie smiled, thankful that the agent had dropped her previous line of discourse. "Well, as of two weeks ago, I am an official private investigator licensed in the state of North Carolina. And, I just may have gotten my first cast today."

"That's excellent. So happy for you. And what about your cute little police officer friend? How's that going?"

Jessie felt another blush creep up her neck. "I don't know that I would describe him like that...but Alex is doing just great. He passed his detective exam and is now Pine Haven PD's first official police detective."

"Well. That's excellent news as well. Sounds like the

two of you are on your way to becoming Pine Haven's first power couple."

"Ha flipping ha. Our relationship is strictly professional. And that's why it works so well."

"Well, I'm happy for you both. And glad that you were able to officially put the past behind you. I gotta run... time to turn Miss Gina over to the men in the black cars that showed up this morning to collect her. Have a good one, Jessie, and call me if you need anything. Don't forget, that offer to join the agency is still on the table."

Jessie grinned. "Thank you. But I think I'm ready to explore some things here in Pine Haven first."

"Uh huh. I bet. Talk to you later."

Jessie sighed as the line went dead. She looked down at Blizzard and rubbed the space between his ears as she checked the time. "Looks like I'm going to have just enough time to take you for a quick walk before Alex comes over."

She stood, stretching her arms overhead. She could feel her mind start to drift back to the conversation she had just had with her aunt. Specifically, the way it ended. She refused to let herself wonder about what the woman was about to tell her. At this point, it didn't matter. It would not have changed the past or Jessie's memories of the life she had led up until right now.

Armed with that knowledge, Jessie did what she did best. She pushed it away, deep into the dark corner of her brain, and locked it away.

She opened her phone, double checking that Aura had sent her the information she requested. She had other things to concentrate on.

Blizzard led the way as they left the house and headed for one of the trails surrounding the lake. The fresh, mountain air did wonders for clearing her mind, and she began to formulate a plan for tackling her first case as a private investigator.

She hoped the case would be open and closed. Even though she realized it wouldn't be what Aura wanted to hear. The woman had lost so much recently and was trying to find a way to blame herself for her cousin's death.

Jessie knew what that felt like and could only hope she could spare her client's feelings by giving her the truth.

That sometimes, bad things happen to really good people, for no reason.

5

Not So Cut and Dry

Jessie made it back from their walk just in time to put Blizzard's food down and jump in the shower. Once she had toweled off and changed clothes, she printed the notes she had taken from her meeting with Aura and splayed them across the coffee table. She had just poured herself a glass of wine when a soft knock at the door distracted her. Blizzard looked up briefly from where he was sprawled out on the fireplace hearth, his tail wagging quickly. His lackluster response told Jessie it wasn't a stranger at the door, and she pulled it open to see Alex standing on her porch.

"Well, hello, Detective Thompson."

He gave her a faux bow. "And hello to you, Private Investigator Night." They both laughed at their private joke as Jessie ushered him in.

"I don't think that will ever get old," Jessie said.

She watched as Alex bent over and slapped his

thighs at Blizzard, beckoning the big dog to him. Standing on his back legs, the shepherd was nearly eye to eye with the detective as he nuzzled his big head into the man's chest.

Alex playfully pushed him away, sending him back to his spot in front of the fireplace. "What are you feeding him? I feel like he gets bigger every time I see him."

Jessie laughed, her eyes flitting from one to the other. "Want some wine? I just opened a bottle."

Alex tilted his head to one side as he thought about the question. "Why not. I'm off duty and it's been a quiet day so far. How about yours?"

Jessie poured him a glass and walked it over. "It's been interesting. I think I got my first case today." She jutted her chin in the direction of the papers on the table. "You remember Aura?"

He nodded. "Hard not to. She okay?"

"Not really. Her cousin died. She was reported drowned, yet Aura seems to think there is more to the story. She wants me to find out what I can about it."

Alex glanced in the direction of the paperwork. "May I?"

"Please do. I was hoping you'd offer." She took out her phone while he made himself comfortable on the couch and gathered up her notes. "While you do that, I'll order the pizza. White with caramelized onions and mush-rooms okay for you?"

"Sounds perfect," he replied.

A few minutes later, she plopped down next to him on the couch and sipped at her wine until he looked up. "What do you think?"

He took a deep breath and exhaled, puffing out both cheeks. "Honestly? I'm not sure there's anything here."

Jessie sighed, raking a hand through her hair. "As much as I want to help Aura get answers, what if this really is just a tragic accident like the sheriff suggested?"

"Then that's what you tell her. Don't sugar coat it. Your job is to get the answers to questions your clients ask."

"True. But what if those answers aren't what they want to hear?" Jessie shrugged, chewing her lip pensively. "It's possible there is nothing more to this, I guess. People do have hiking mishaps on mountain trails all the time. Maybe there's nothing more to it."

"But you're still feeling some doubt about the official story? If your gut is telling you to look into this, there's usually a good reason."

She took another small sip. "Or maybe it's just me. I'm so used to there being monsters in the shadows, that maybe I thought they would still be there as I start this new life."

Alex slowly placed the papers back on the table in front of them. "You know, ninety nine percent of your cases will probably be nothing more than catching cheating spouses and spying on injured workers for insurance companies."

Jessie gave him a horrified look. "If that happens, then I want back on the payroll as a consultant with the police department."

Alex gave her a grin. "Wait. They paid you for that gig?"

The doorbell rang, and Jessie jumped to her feet.

"That will be the pizza." She snatched some money from her purse and handed it to the young delivery driver, before returning to the coffee table with the box.

"So, what are your next steps in your first official case?" Alex asked, opening the box.

Jessie folded herself into a sitting position at the end of the coffee table. "Well, I have put a call into the sheriff up in Bidonville. I'm going to see if I can get a copy of the case file on Marley's death." Alex had a mouthful of pizza and was about to answer when Jessie's phone buzzed. She looked down at the screen and her eyes widened. "Well, speak of the devil." She cleared her throat and raised the phone to her ear. "This is Jessie Night." She listened for a moment before interrupting. "Sheriff, before we go any further, may I put you on speaker phone? I'm here with my friend Alex Thompson and want to be able to make some notes as we are speaking. Would that be okay?" She waited for his answer and then swiped at the key and placed the phone on the table next to the pizza box.

The sheriff could be heard clearing his throat loudly. "Can you hear me?"

"We can hear you, sheriff. Thank you for the call," Jessie said.

"Well, I got a message at the department saying you called and asked for call back. How can I be of service?"

Jessie exchanged a quick glance with Alex before speaking up. "Sheriff Cormac, I'm a private investigator here in Pine Haven, and a client of mine reached out after receiving word that her cousin had passed away in your town." She paused, letting her words sink in. "Is that ringing a bell with you?"

"Hmm. Seems like I do remember making that call here not long ago."

"Good. Well, as I'm sure you can imagine, my client is in a bit of shock over losing her only remaining family member." She hesitated, her breath catching on the next part. "She just lost her brother a few months ago, and Marley Stillwell was her last relative."

"Well, I am mighty sorry to hear that. I spoke to your client personally, and she didn't relay that bit of information to me." Jessie was glad to hear his tone was one of genuine concern. Hopefully that would make her job a little easier.

"I think she is still dealing with her brother's death," Jessie continued. "But, as you can imagine, having another death occur has thrown her into a state of disbelief. I believe it would give her peace of mind to know what exactly your findings were regarding the events around her cousin's death."

She could hear the sheriff's breathing get a bit heavier before he answered. "Well, I don't know what more I can provide. As I told the young woman, her cousin died from drowning. A tragic accident. I can imagine that in your client's current mood, it must seem quiet shocking, but I can assure you, ma'am, it was an accident."

Jessie frowned, glancing over at Alex. "I understand, Sheriff. But my client would feel better knowing that she had all the details of her cousin's...accident. I'm sure you understand. Sheriff, is there any way I can get a copy of the autopsy report for my client? Along with a copy of her case file?" Her question was met with silence from the other end. Finally, Jessie cleared her throat. "Sheriff? Are you still there?"

The man cleared his throat. "Yeah. I'm here. Look, the issue is...well, we didn't do an autopsy on the woman."

Jessie's mouth dropped open, and out of the corner of her eye she could see Alex had a similar reaction. "I'm sorry. Did you say you did *not* do an autopsy?"

"That's right. It was pretty cut and dried. Her body washed ashore and was found by a couple hiking. She hadn't been in the water too long, and when we found her campsite upstream, it was pretty much undisturbed. We could tell where she had waded into the shallow part of the river and must have lost her footing. Poor thing fell in and then couldn't get out."

Jessie swallowed her dismay, taking a deep breath. "I'm sorry, but is that typical operating procedure when you find a body, Sheriff Cormac?"

His tone changed slightly when he answered. "Under the circumstances, yes. I mean, if we find the remains of a bear attack, which is very rare, we assume it was a bear attack. No need for an autopsy then either."

Jessie's mind was racing at his words. Actually, there was. But she wasn't going to accomplish anything by antagonizing the man further.

"Besides, when I spoke with the family member, she did not indicate that she wanted an autopsy performed."

Alex threw his hands up in the air and mouthed the words 'is he serious' at Jessie.

She gave him a concerned look before turning her attention back to the conversation. "I understand, sir. I would never presume to question how your department does things."

Her attempt to de-escalate the situation seemed to work. "No. And I didn't mean to come across so gruff. We don't run into these types of situations a lot up here. We just focus on doing the best we can with what we have. We don't have a medical examiner nearby. Whenever an autopsy needs to be performed, we send the body off to the nearest one, about a hundred miles away."

"Oh, we are familiar with situations like that as well," Jessie said, continuing to work her way back into the sheriff's good graces. "And, like you said, I don't even know if my client needs that done. But, what about her personal effects? Will my client be able to retrieve those?"

"Of course. You can tell the young lady we will have everything for her at the station whenever she wants to retrieve them. She didn't have much on her or at her campsite. A cell phone, wallet, a few camping supplies... things like that."

Jessie perked up. "You have her cell phone?"

"Yep. It was in her pocket. One of those nice, water-proof ones. Weren't nothing on it though."

Jessie frowned. "What do you mean? She hadn't made any calls or texts?"

"No, ma'am. We checked because we were looking for contacts to notify. But she hadn't made any calls or texts from it recently."

"Thank you, Sheriff. I'll speak with my client about retrieving her cousin's belongings. One last thing. About that case file. Could I get a copy of it? Sounds like the case is closed if it's ruled an accidental drowning. So, if it's not an ongoing investigation, and there is no foul play suspected, my client should be able to see it, right? Just for closure."

The man on the other end of the call hesitated briefly before answering. "I suppose that would be alright. If you give me your email address, I can have one of my deputies send it over to you."

"That would be great, Sheriff. And thank you for all your help. I'm sure my client will rest much easier knowing that you did everything you could to get her the resolution she needs." Jessie gave the man her email address, thanked him again, and closed the call.

She sank back against the couch and looked at Alex.

"What are you thinking?" he asked.

"I'm thinking that maybe Aura was right. Something is off here."

"You mean aside from the fact that they found a body washed up on a riverbank and didn't think an autopsy was needed?"

"That. And the fact that he said her communication log on her cell was blank. She had been texting back and forth with Aura. A lot. I saw some of them myself, including one right up till the day she died. So, something is definitely not right."

"What are your next steps?"

She smiled and looked over at Blizzard. "I think that it's about time me and Blizzard got to know a little more about these mountains. I think it's time for a road trip."

Alex frowned. "Jessie, if you're thinking about going up to Bidonville, I'm not sure that's a good idea. The communities up around Yancy county can be very closed off to strangers."

She stretched, locking her fingers behind her head. "Oh, I'm not worried about that. Look how I've won everyone over here in Pine Haven. How much harder could it be?"

Alex cast a sideways look at her. "Well, at the very least let me call ahead and speak to one of the deputies in charge up there. At least that way you can have a contact waiting for you. Better yet, I can probably see about getting a couple days off and—"

She held up a hand. "Not necessary. I'll be fine. Once I get the case file, I'll have a better idea what I'm working with. And don't worry. If I need you, I'll call."

She reached for a piece of pizza and hid her apprehension behind a big bite. Maybe this first case as a private investigator wouldn't be so cut and dry after all.

6

—————

Road Trip

The next morning, Jessie was up early, gathering everything she needed for a couple days' road trip to Bidonville. After everything was loaded into the Jeep, she took a quick walk to stretch Blizzard's legs before ushering the big shepherd into the vehicle. She called Aura and asked if she could meet her at the Pine Haven police department in an hour. She was waiting on the steps leading into the building with two cups of coffee as Aura pulled up.

"Jessie, is everything okay? Have you found anything out?" Aura asked.

Handing her the cup, Jessie smiled reassuringly. "Everything is fine so far. I apologize for asking you to meet me so early this morning, but I wanted you to know I'm taking a road trip up to Bidonville to look into some things."

Aura frowned as she reached for the cup. "You've

already found something, haven't you? I knew something was off."

"Nothing like that. But I want to do as thorough a job as possible for you, and to do that I need to check on a few things up there." She motioned for Aura to follow her into the station. "But I need a favor, if you're willing to do it."

"Anything. Just name it."

"Well, I think it will make my job a lot easier if I can get a statement from you saying I have the right to act on your behalf as far as collecting your cousin's belongings and seeing any medical files as may relate to the case. I'd need it notarized of course, so that's why I brought you here."

Together, they made their way to the reception area, and Jessie smiled at the young man at the desk. "Hi, Rick. How are you?"

The man had been scrolling on his phone and quickly shoved it into his pocket. "Well, hey, Jessie. Nice to see you." He looked over her shoulder at Aura and nodded. "Alex isn't in yet if you're looking for him."

"Actually, I'm here to see Doris, down in records. She's expecting us."

"Oh, okay. Well, you know your way around," Rick said with a smile.

Jessie nodded and led Aura past the desk and down the corridor to a small office at the back of the building that was crammed full of file cabinets and open shelving displaying multiple, large bound notebooks neatly arranged by date. There was a small desk sitting in the center of the room, with only a laptop and a curved desk lamp atop it. Behind the desk sat an elderly woman, wearing thick glasses that hung from a string around her neck. She looked up and smiled.

"Hello, Doris," Jessie said.

"Hi, Jessie, good to see you," she said. Despite her diminutive stature, her voice was strong.

"And you as well. Doris, this is my friend Aura, the lady I was telling you about."

Doris extended a hand in Aura's direction. "Nice to meet you. I trust you both have everything you need?" Bending over, she opened one of the desk drawers and retrieved a leather pouch.

Jessie reached inside the pocket of the lightweight denim jacket she wore and took out a folded slip of paper. "This is a declaration allowing me to act on Aura's behalf on any matter I deem necessary in investigating the death of her cousin. It also acknowledges that Aura is also the only living relative of her cousin, so hopefully it won't be challenged." She laid the paper before Doris and waited as the older woman examined the document.

"Looks in order to me. I'll just need to see both of your driver's licenses and then have you sign." She took out her notary and waited until the two women produced their identification and signed their names where indicated. Doris then added her own signature before clamping the paper with her official notary seal and handing it back to Jessie.

"Thank you, Doris. I owe you one," Jessie said.

Doris waved her off. "Don't even think about it. After all you've done for this town recently, it's the least I can do."

Jessie and Aura waved their thanks again as they headed out of the records room and then the station.

"When are you going up there?" Aura asked.

Jessie pointed to the Jeep. "All loaded up and ready to hit the road."

Aura stared at the vehicle and then Jessie. "I can't thank you enough. I really would go with you, but I just can't. Andy is having such a hard time with things here... I can't drag him away for something like this and I wouldn't feel right leaving him with someone else just yet."

Jessie put a hand on the woman's arm. "Don't even think about it. You take care of your child and let me handle this. I should be back in a couple of days with answers for you. But keep your phone with you and on until I get back. If I run into something I have a question about I'll give you a call." She gave Aura a quick hug and made her way to the Jeep. The seats squeaked as she slid behind the wheel and turned to give Blizzard a quick rub. "Hang on, boy. We are going on an adventure."

JESSIE GRIPPED the steering wheel tightly as her Jeep climbed higher into the rugged mountains of western North Carolina. The two-lane road twisted and turned, each curve revealing more towering peaks and plunging valleys cloaked in dense forest. Sheer rock faces lined the road, their slick, gray surfaces briefly interrupted by the occasional stubborn bush that managed to push through the rock. Wisps of fog clung to the highest elevations, obscuring the mountaintops from view. Alex's words flooded Jessie's mind. It really was a whole different world.

The trees grew thicker the higher she climbed—gnarled oaks, towering firs, and twisted maples blocked out most of the sunlight. Undergrowth pressed in from both sides of the road, leaving just enough space for her Jeep to pass. Some turns were so tight, sharp branches scratched at the paint.

As the sun moved past the highpoint of midday, long shadows were cast across the winding road. The air cooled rapidly, carrying the musty scent of damp earth and decaying leaves. She adjusted her grip on the wheel, her eyes scanning in front of her for large pieces of rock that might have broken off from one of the towering shale summits that could be squatting in the middle of the road around one of the many blind curves.

She breathed a sigh of relief when she saw a sign for Burningtown Gap. She had written down instructions for the route to Bidonville, not fully trusting that she would have cell signal the entire way for navigation, and it was one of the places where she had seen that she could stop and gas up. She looked in the rearview mirror at the dog curled up behind her. They could both use a good stretch of their legs, so the stop couldn't have come at a better time.

She veered the Jeep off the road, following the weather-worn sign. Burningtown Gap was just a handful of buildings clustered where two streams converged in a tight hollow. She slowed to a stop in front of a beaten-down building with a handwritten sign across the top of the door that stated 'GAS'. The 'town' was blanketed on all sides by swathes of unbroken wilderness. This was the last stop on the map she had studied before entering the million-acre expanse of national forests that covered the mountains. The next step would be Bidonville proper and she didn't want to risk running out of gas before arriving.

As she killed the engine, she was met with just how quiet the place was. The forest around her was so dense, it swallowed any signs of life. For a moment, Jessie thought about Marley and the fact that she willingly ventured into such desolation as a form of relaxation and escapism. It didn't appear that someone with that kind of mindset and bravery could accidentally fall into a river.

Climbing out of the Jeep, she took a look around. The place looked like it hadn't seen an upgrade since the seventies—weathered wooden siding, a rusted Coca-Cola sign, and a single analog pump that still had spinning dials. She walked around to the back and unfastened Blizzard's safety harness, motioning for him to hop out as well. He stretched languidly, wagging his tail happily as Jessie placed his water bowl on the ground and filled it. As he lapped at the water, an older man appeared in the doorway of the gas station and stared at the two of them.

He shuffled out of the small office. His gait was labored and slow, burdened by a prominent limp on his left leg. Jessie nodded and smiled as he approached.

He stopped and eyed the big German Shepherd that lifted its head at his approach. "Do he bite?"

Jessie shook her head. "Only if provoked." She meant the remark to be lighthearted, but immediately saw a change in the man's body language. She nodded to Blizzard and then the Jeep, and the dog immediately abandoned his water and leapt up into the back seat.

The old man nodded sternly and took a white rag from his overalls and wiped at his hands. "How can I help you?"

"Fill her up with regular, please." Jessie said.

The man nodded, his craggy face betraying no emotion. "Cash or credit?" His voice was a gravelly drawl, the words unhurried.

"Credit, thanks." Jessie handed over her card, watching as the man studied it for a long moment before shuffling to the pump.

As the numbers on the pump crept up at a glacial pace, Jessie watched the man closely. "I'm headed up to Bidonville. Any idea how much farther?"

The man paused, his weathered hand resting on the pump handle. He squinted at her. "Bidonville, huh? What's a young thing like you want with that place?"

Jessie bristled slightly but kept her tone even. "Just exploring the area is all. Meeting up with a friend there."

The man grunted; his expression unreadable. "Well, I'd watch my step up there if I was you. Folks in Bidonville... they ain't right. Keep to themselves mostly, don't take kindly to outsiders poking around."

A chill crept up Jessie's spine at the ominous words. She tried to sound casual. "Oh? Why's that?"

The attendant shook his head, lips pressed into a tight line. "Best not to ask too many questions. And the ones that run that town... well, let's just say I mind my business as long as they mind theirs, if you catch my drift."

Jessie wasn't at all sure she caught his drift but got the feeling that further questions wouldn't lead to anything useful. "I see. I'll keep that in mind. So, how much farther did you say?"

"'Bout an hour up the road. Just follow the signs for Blue Ridge Parkway, then turn off on Old County Road 12. Can't miss it." He replaced the pump handle with a dull clunk. "I'll run the card inside. Might take a bit. Need to turn the machine on and all that."

Jessie frowned. "You know, I think I have cash." She fished through the glove box before handing the man a bill. "You can keep the change."

He stared at the money for a second before giving her a nod. "Much obliged." He started to walk back to the station but stopped and turned to face her. "You're smart to have that dog. Keep him with you."

And with that, he lurched back into the station, and Jessie pulled back onto the two-lane road, making a quick U-turn to head back the way she came. She steeled her nerves and tried to put the old man's words out of her mind as she turned right, following the signs into the Blue Ridge Mountains.

7

Not In Pine Haven Anymore

As Jessie rounded the final bend on Old Country Road, the town of Bidonville began to unfurl before her. After the conversation with the gentleman at the gas station, she wasn't sure what to expect. But whatever she had in mind, it definitely did not gel with the reality she now faced.

The community was nestled in a valley, sheltered on either side by mountain caps that were hidden by late-day mist. She slowed the Jeep as she made her way into the town, the neat grid of streets lined with charming houses painted in cheerful colors, laid out in front of her. Blizzard perked up in the back seat, his keen eyes surveying the new surroundings. Jessie reached back to quickly ruffle his thick fur. "Looks straight out of a story-book, doesn't it, buddy? Let's hope the welcome is as warm as it seems."

Truthfully, it reminded her of Pine Haven. But as she

turned onto their version of Main Street, she noticed one glaring difference. There were hardly any people out. It was a cool evening in the mountains, but Pine Haven would be bustling at this time. She strained to make out the names of the business to either side, noting an absence of coffee shops, restaurants, ice cream shops... the kind of places that invited the townsfolk to come in and sit a spell, as they were fond of saying in Pine Haven. There was an abundance of hiking gear stores and what looked like organic food markets, all closed. Bidonville certainly catered to the outdoorsy types—probably the only thing keeping the town economically afloat in such isolated wilderness.

Following the directions she had scribbled down, Jessie steered the Jeep onto a quiet side street and pulled up to a small, picture-perfect Craftsman home. Its sage green exterior and white trim fit in perfectly amidst the wooded setting. A hand-painted sign proclaimed it the "Lost Ridge Bed & Breakfast."

Grabbing her weathered duffel from the backseat, Jessie clipped Blizzard's leash to his collar and made her way up the flagstone path leading to the house. As if on cue, the front door swung open, and a woman who looked to be in her mid-fifties flashed them a smile. Her hair was silver-streaked and piled in a bun on her head. Her eyes crinkled at the corners as she smiled and reached out a hand. Her grip was firm as she gave Jessie an enthusiastic shake.

"Welcome to Bidonville! You must be Jessie. I see you made good time getting up here," the woman said warmly. "I'm Caroline, your host during your stay. Come on in, you must be exhausted from the drive."

The woman's genuine friendliness melted some of the apprehension Jessie had built up coming up the mountain. She returned the smile, nodding. "I did, thank you. It's great to meet you, Caroline." She looked down at the shepherd sitting at her side. "This is Blizzard. I hope it was okay to bring him. I promise he is very well behaved."

Caroline waved a dismissive hand. "Of course it is. We are very dog friendly around here. Such beautiful eyes. Reminds me of our lab, Ranger. He passed after giving us fifteen glorious years."

Jessie felt a wave of sadness begin to flood her. Even though he had only been with her for a short time, she couldn't imagine her life without Blizzard. "I am so sorry for your loss."

The woman held out the back of her hand for Blizzard to sniff before she scratched between his ears. "Oh, thank you. He is missed, that's for sure. So yes, I am glad you brought your little Blizzard with you. Although, he's not really so little now, is he?" They both laughed, and the woman led Jessie to the tiny living room that doubled as the reception area. There was a small, wooden desk sitting in one corner and Caroline moved around behind it. She opened a large, leather-bound ledger and turned it to face Jessie. "You're the only guest here, so that makes this very easy. Just sign in and pay the deposit."

Jessie handed over her credit card before taking the pen from Caroline. The older woman slid the card into the reader and waited for it to spit out a receipt. She handed the small slip of paper to Jessie and closed the book. "That's it. You're all set."

"Well. That was easy," Jessie replied.

"That's how we like things around here. Now, do you need some help getting your things up to your room? My husband is around somewhere. I can get him to carry it—"

Jessie held up a hand. "I wouldn't think of it. Besides, all I have is this bag. I can manage."

Caroline escorted her to the bottom of the steps. "Top of the stairs, turn left and your room is the last door at the end of the hall. You're in the Bluebird room. Key's in the lock. And when you're done freshening up, feel free to come on down and grab a slice of banana bread. It's just about to come out of the oven."

Jessie took a deep breath and was greeted by the comforting aroma of warm nutmeg and bananas. "That sounds delicious."

"Well, in the morning, I'll have a pot of fresh coffee on and my world-famous wild berry muffins ready for you. Say, are you in town for anything in particular? You don't look like you packed for a long stay."

Jessie had one foot on the bottom step as she turned her face to the woman. "I'm actually here on business. I'm a private investigator and am looking into something for my client."

Caroline's eyes grew almost comically wide. "Well, how exciting! I've never met a private investigator before. Didn't even know they had female ones."

Jessie gave her a puzzled look but opted to let the woman's remark slide. "Yes, well, here I am." She started to take the stairs but stopped. "Maybe you could help me. How far from here is the police department?"

"Just a few streets over. You can walk there from here. I can point the direction to you in the morning, if you like."

Jessie smiled. "That would be very nice of you. Oh, one last thing. Does the name Marley Shaffer ring a bell with you?"

The woman frowned. "No. Should it?"

"Don't worry about it. Thank you again for your help. That banana bread smells amazing. I think I will come back down for a slice in a bit."

Caroline cocked her head to one side, sniffing the air. "Oh, goodness. It's almost ready. I better go check it." She gave Jessie a quick wave and shuffled off towards the kitchen.

Jessie made her way up the stairs and found her room. A brass key with a tiny Bluebird dangling from it stuck out of the lock. She opened the door to reveal a charming bedroom with a plush, queen-sized bed adorned with a handmade quilt in various shades of blue and green. Delicate lace curtains framed the large window, offering a breathtaking view of the mist-covered peaks that framed the community.

She let out a long exhale, sinking onto the plush mattress. Blizzard hopped up beside her, his warm weight pressing in against her. Wrapping an arm around him, she gave him a squeeze, rubbing along his side. She thought back, remembering how many steps she had taken to reach the landing. How many feet she estimated it to be from the front door to the landing. Later, before heading down to the kitchen, she knew she would have to check the other side of the landing to see if there were any balconies or other ways to access the second floor of the house.

She shook her head. Some training was almost impossible to shake.

As she began to unpack her bag, she thought about what her next steps would be. First thing in the morning meant heading over to the police station, followed by a trip to the river where the body of Marley Shaffer was found. Despite the way the case had been mishandled by Sheriff Cormac, she had a feeling that he might be right.

A tragic accident.

But she had been wrong before. If she had learned anything from her time in the military, it was not to take anything at face value. She looked at Blizzard. "Time to start peeling back the layers of this town and see what we can find."

Twenty minutes later, she had freshened up, checked the second floor of the house for any potential security concerns, and then headed down to the kitchen for a slice of banana bread. On her way to the kitchen, she passed the front room where she had checked in. The door was closed and she could hear voices speaking in a low, hushed tone. They were speaking too softly for her to understand, but she could make out Caroline's tone and that of a man. The rapid-fire pattern told her they might be arguing, so she quickly stepped away and followed her nose to a fresh loaf of warm goodness.

When she was finished, she rinsed her plate and placed it in the dishwasher before looking through the pantry to find some foil and cover the bread. She was about to leave when she noticed the back door that led out to a small, cement patio. What caught her eye was not the fact that the door was locked, but the number of locks. She counted five different bolt locks as well as a slide lock and a chain.

Darkness was setting in, and she was unable to make out much beyond what little illumination the overhead kitchen light cast. Part of her was happy to see how seriously the owners took their safety, but another part of her wondered just what it was they were trying to keep out.

8

Better Safe Than Sorry

Jessie woke with a start, her heart pounding in the unfamiliar darkness. She lay still for a moment, trying to pinpoint what had jolted her from sleep. The old house creaked and settled around her, each groan of the floorboards setting her nerves on edge. Curled at her feet, Blizzard lifted his head, ears pricked and alert. He sensed Jessie's unease and his keen senses went on high alert for any sign of potential threat.

Jessie reached for the nightstand and grabbed her phone. It was barely past dawn. She sighed, knowing there was no chance of falling back asleep now. Her mind was too unsettled for any deep rest. The few details of Marley's death she knew, combined with a first night in a strange house, was too much. With a grunt, she swung her legs out of bed and found her running gear. Since she couldn't quiet her thoughts, she might as well put the restless energy to good use. Plus, after a day of sitting behind a wheel, a little run would be good for her body. Blizzard's tail thumped eagerly against the floor as she laced up her shoes, ready for their morning ritual.

The crisp mountain air was a welcome slap as she stepped out of the house. The sun was just beginning to crest the eastern ridge, streaking the sky orange and pink as she took her first steps off the porch. She stepped through the mist that clung to the valley floor, enveloping the cozy cottages that lined the street. She set off at an easy jog, Blizzard trotting along effortlessly at her side. The rhythmic pounding of her feet against the pavement and the steady cadence of her breathing helped to clear the cobwebs from her mind. Everything faded into the background, as she took in the rugged beauty of the mountains.

She spotted a trail that led into the woods and turned right to follow it. The sudden change in atmosphere reminded her that she wasn't running on her usual trails around Pine Haven Lake. The well-manicured lawns and tidy cottages of Bidonville gave way to a realm of untamed wilderness, the path quickly narrowing to a mere sliver of packed earth unwinding before her. The air grew noticeably cooler as she ran farther into the dense canopy.

Beneath her feet, the trail was uneven, littered with gnarled roots and loose rocks that threatened to trip her up. She glanced down to her side and saw that Blizzard was having no trouble navigating the terrain as he bounded effortlessly beside her. As they delved deeper into the woods, the trail began to slope upwards, the incline growing steeper with each step. Jessie could feel the burn in her calves and the quickening of her breath as she pushed herself onward.

Then, she stopped dead in her tracks. Her head tilted slightly to one side before she slowly turned her head to focus on the woods to her left. Blizzard drew in close to her, the hair along his back rising slightly as he lowered his nose, sniffing hard. Neither of them moved as Jessie studied the woods. She held her palm out in front of Blizzard, indicating that he wasn't to move from her side.

Something had been moving with them as they ran.

She looked back to see how far they had come since leaving the main sidewalk, but the harsh undergrowth made judging distance all but impossible. She glanced down and saw that Blizzard's gaze was locked on the area she had been sweeping. The muscles along his body were corded, ready to pounce if needed.

"No, not today, boy. Whatever is out there won't bother us if we don't bother it."

Or would it? What if it were a mountain lion? Or a wolf? Were there wolves in North Carolina? Her eyes widened. What if it were a bear? She turned around on the trail, motioning for Blizzard to follow as they slowly started back towards town.

She heard a low growl from Blizzard as he picked up the pace. Though she still couldn't see anything, she had the distinct impression that whatever was in the woods was following her, keeping step with her as she ran. A crack of a branch caused Blizzard to bark a warning and Jessie increased her pace even more.

By the time she came into a small clearing and could see the path ahead that would lead back to the sidewalk, she was all but sprinting. She stopped to catch her breath, hands on her knees, and glanced to her side. Maybe it was the pounding blood flow in her head, or the hit of adrenaline, but she thought she saw a shadow move behind the trees, retreating into the more heavily wooded sections.

She motioned for Blizzard to follow as she made for the sidewalk and headed back to the bed and breakfast. She scolded herself. This definitely wasn't Pine Haven, and she had to remember that. She realized she was more concerned for Blizzard than herself. Had whatever animal that was confronted her, she knew the dog would have fought till its last breath. There was no way she was putting him in that situation again.

Her breath was heavy as they approached the bed and breakfast. Climbing the stairs, she looked down at Blizzard. "Well, no more runs for us. At least not until we get back home."

The smell of fresh coffee was a welcome relief as she opened the door and stepped inside. Caroline was at the stove in the kitchen when Jessie walked in.

"Good morning, Jessie," the woman said, bending over to retrieve a tin of muffins from the oven and placing them on the butcher block counter. "You're up early. These will be cooled in a couple minutes, but in the meantime, feel free to help yourself to some coffee."

Nothing sounded better at the moment, and Jessie helped herself to a mug. "Don't mind if I do. I got up early to go for a run. It helps to organize my mind and burns some of Blizzard's excess energy off."

Caroline was bending to retrieve a second tin of muffins. "Oh? Did you see the town? Or what little there is of it. It's not much, but we all love our little community."

"I didn't get to see much of it. There was a trail a couple streets away that led out through the woods, so we decided to take that."

The second tin of muffins dropped onto the counter with a clang as Caroline whirled to face Jessie, her eyes wide. "You went into the woods? Alone?"

Jessie frowned. "Well, I wasn't alone. Blizzard was with me." She sipped at the coffee, thankful for the warmth that coated her throat. "But now that you mention it, are there any dangerous animals around these parts? I swear there was something in the woods watching us."

Caroline turned her back, busying herself getting the muffins into a basket. "Well, there is all kinds of wildlife in those woods, Jessie. This ain't like where you're from. The animals here...they ain't scared of people, because in a place like this, there are things in those woods that might not have ever seen people before. To them, we're just another source of food."

Jessie frowned. "Then why are there so many hikers and tourists attracted to the area? I didn't see any beware of bear signs or anything like that."

Caroline fretted with the basket as she sat it on the table next to the coffee dispenser. She wiped her hands on her apron, not meeting Jessie's gaze. "Oh, it's fine. I'm just saying...be careful. Those tourists know what to look out for. Just don't go wandering alone too far from town."

"Yeah. I got that impression. Well, I'm going to go shower and then I'll be heading out. But thank you for the coffee." She walked over to the muffins and placed one on a napkin. I'll have this delicious-smelling morsel in my room."

"I have to run out as well. But the police department is just off Moore Street. Go three houses down to the left and you'll see Moore. Take a right and you can't miss the department," Caroline said.

Jessie thanked her and headed for her room.

Once inside, she pulled off her shoes and sat on the bed. The conversation in the kitchen replayed in her mind. A bed and breakfast in a mountain town that undoubtedly relied on nature and tourism for money. And the owner of the bed and breakfast telling a guest not to go into the woods?

She shook her head, relegating the conversation to the corners of her mind as she bit into the sugary, warm muffin. Whether it was truly world famous or not she didn't know. But it definitely deserved to be. She finished it off in record time before heading for the shower. On her way into the bathroom, she paused at her bedroom door.

For a second, she thought she saw a shadow shift under the doorjamb. She listened but didn't hear any footsteps walking away.

"Get it together, girl." She shook her head and headed into the bath. She paused and turned to the dog curled up on the bed. "Guard."

Blizzard immediately jumped down from the bed and sat at attention facing the bedroom door. Jessie felt better seeing him there. There had been many times where her paranoia had kept her alive. Despite the welcome and comfort the bed and breakfast exuded, it was still foreign to her.

Better to be safe than sorry.

9

Death is Bad for Business

As Jessie neared the Bidonville Police Department, she kept a tight grip on Blizzard's leash. While she was confident that he wouldn't leave her side, she had to remind herself this wasn't Pine Haven. She wasn't aware of what the leash laws were in Bidonville and unlike in Pine Haven, people here didn't know them and might not react well to a one-hundred-pound white German shepherd off leash.

She made her way down Moore Street and did a double take at the police station. She had expected something modest and small, but still in keeping with the rest of the town's architecture. Instead, she found herself facing a squat, nondescript structure that looked like it had been plucked straight from the pages of a 1950s pulp novel.

The facade was a dull, weathered brick that had seen better days. There were a few small windows set high up on the walls, and a faded green awning hung over the entrance, the words "Bidonville Police" stenciled across it in peeling white paint. She looked around as she walked through the nearly empty parking lot. Even the lone squad car parked out front looked like a relic from another era with its boxy frame and black-and-white color scheme.

With a wry shake of her head, Jessie made her way past the squad car and up the cracked concrete steps. She pushed through the heavy wooden door, its hinges creaking in protest, and found herself standing in a cramped lobby that smelled faintly of stale coffee and dust. The interior was just as dated as the exterior, with scuffed linoleum floors and wood-paneled walls that had gone out of style decades ago. A battered metal desk stood against one wall, its surface cluttered with stacks of paper and an ancient computer monitor that looked like it belonged in a museum. Behind the desk sat a young man in a deputy's uniform, his feet propped up on the corner as he stared at a folded magazine in one hand. He looked up as Jessie approached, his eyes widening slightly as he took in first her appearance, and then the giant shepherd at her side.

"Can I help you, ma'am?" he asked. His voice carried a slight drawl.

Jessie noted the way he straightened up in his chair when he saw her, and the way his eyes kept flitting between her and Blizzard. "My name is Jessie Night. I'm a private investigator visiting from Pine Haven. I'm here to meet with Deputy..." She fished in her pocket for the note

Alex had given her. "Deputy Hardin, about a case I'm working on."

The deputy nodded, his expression turning serious. "Right, Deputy Hardin mentioned you'd be coming by. I'm Deputy Briggs, by the way. Let me just go grab him for you. Oh, and if you don't mind signing in..." He shoved a clipboard in front of her as he pushed back from the desk and disappeared around a corner.

A few minutes later, Deputy Briggs returned, followed by an older man in a sheriff's uniform. His graying hair was cropped short, and his weathered face bore the look of someone who had seen more than their fair share of tough cases. Jessie also noted the tiny broken blood vessels around his red nose and wondered how long the man had been drinking.

"Sheriff Cormac," he introduced himself, extending a hand. His grip was firm, his palm callused. "We spoke on the phone earlier." He thumbed over his shoulder. "Hardin will be here in a minute. He's just finishing up some paperwork."

Jessie nodded, meeting the sheriff's gaze. "Sheriff Cormac. It's nice to meet you in person. I'm sorry it has to be under these circumstances."

Sheriff Cormac's expression remained neutral, but Jessie thought she detected a flicker of something in his eyes—wariness, perhaps. Or annoyance. "Well, I am glad to meet you as well. Though I'm not thrilled about the circumstances it's under. But I do understand the family's need for closure. Deputy Hardin will assist you with whatever you need, within reason, of course." He fixed Jessie with a stern look.

"Just remember, Miss Night, this accident happened within our jurisdiction, and we handled it the way we would any other. I expect you to keep me in the loop at all times with any requests and findings. We're a tight-knit community here, and folks don't take kindly to strangers causing a ruckus."

Jessie sensed that last bit was more of a warning than a threat but nodded her acknowledgement. She held up her hands in a placating gesture. "I understand, Sheriff. I'm not here to step on any toes. I just want to give my client some peace of mind."

Sheriff Cormac grunted, his expression softening slightly. "Fair enough."

A second deputy came around the corner and approached the group. He was tall with a lean build. Jessie guessed he was in his early forties, but his salt and pepper hair made it hard to tell. He nodded to the sheriff and then Jessie.

"This is Deputy Lane Hardin," Sheriff Cormac said by way of introduction. "We got a call from your friend, Detective Thomas, and he asked someone be assigned to help. I thought it would be a good idea, especially if it helps expedite your time here." And with that, he gave her another stiff nod and walked away.

Jessie turned to the deputy she had been assigned. "It's nice to meet you, Deputy Hardin. I'm Jessie Night and this is Blizzard. Thank you for taking the time to help me out. I promise not to take up any more of your time than needed."

He gave her a smile and held out his hand in greeting. "It's nice to meet you, ma'am." He had a deep drawl that drew each word out. "And as you can see, there is not much going on around here today. Actually, that's every day. So, I was very excited when your friend called asking for someone to help you out." He looked down at the large shepherd sitting obediently at her side. "And if you don't mind my saying, that is one fine looking fella there. I keep telling the sheriff we need a K-9 unit, but so far, it's fallen on deaf ears."

Jessie laughed and shook the man's hand. "It's always nice meeting a fellow dog lover. Deputy, what would you like me to call you?"

"Oh, everybody just calls me Hardin. That will work just fine. Now, Ms. Night, where would you like to start?"

"Well, first, call me Jessie. And second, I'd like to take a look at the case report, if that's okay. Later, maybe we could take a drive out to where the body was found by the river."

Hardin seemed to contemplate her words, his brows dipping towards one another. "We can do that. But if we're going out to the site, we need to be leaving by midday. It's a bit of a hike to get to where the body was found, and we'll need to be out of there by nightfall." His tone told Jessie there would be no discussion about that and she nodded her agreement. "Come on. I was pulling the case file when you arrived. It's at my desk."

As she followed Deputy Hardin down the narrow hallway, the worn carpet muffling their footsteps, Jessie thought back to her introduction to the sheriff. "Seems like the sheriff is ready to put this case to bed."

Hardin hunched his shoulders up then dropped them. "We don't get a lot of crime up here. Every now and then a hiker has an accident or something, but nothing like a dead body. I think he sees it as bad for business."

Jessie thought about his words as they rounded a corner and found themselves in an open room with two desks, a couple of bookshelves fastened to a wall, and a small table with a single-cup coffee machine. She followed Hardin to one of the desks that had a small folder resting atop it. "I can see how he might think that. But the town I come from also relies on tourism to a large degree. I guess that's the way of the mountain. But...accidents can happen. And most hikers and backpackers are aware of that."

The deputy seemed a bit sheepish as he pulled out a chair for her before taking his own seat at the desk. "Yeah, maybe. But we don't like that here." He opened the folder and spun it around so Jessie could read. "Everything about the case is here. Feel free to ask any questions you might have."

Jessie began reading through the files and looked up at the officer. "You were on scene?"

"I was first on scene. Was out on patrol and got the call from a couple of hikers that were looking to drop their kayaks into the river. They found her, lying face down on the bank."

"And the hikers didn't touch anything? Didn't mess with the body?"

Hardin frowned. "One of them turned the body over, I think. But that was it."

Jessie arched an eyebrow. "You think?" She rifled through the first few pages in the folder. "It isn't mentioned here in your account. How do you know that was all they did?"

He looked perplexed. "Well, who would want to mess with a body? What else could someone have possibly done with it?"

Jessie took deep breaths, steadying herself. "Oh, I don't know. Go through the pockets looking for money. Take selfies with it to post online. All kinds of weird shit."

He looked at her with an expression of genuine confusion. "Why would someone take a selfie with a dead person? And why would they try to post it online? I mean, there isn't even any cell service out there. They had to hike back to an open meadow just to get enough bars to call it in." He shook his head sadly. "I can't imagine the kind of stuff you must have seen to make your mind go there first thing."

Jessie let out a breath. "No. You can't imagine." She pinched the bridge of her nose with her thumb and forefinger. "How many cases like this have you worked?"

"You mean involving a dead body? One. This one."

Jessie nodded. "And how many cases like this have there been in Bidonville?"

Hardin thought for a moment. Jessie saw something flash across his features, but he quickly tamped it down. "Well, there were a couple of accidents with some fishermen that got careless, and then a boater that was found. But that was years ago. Before I was on the force."

Jessie stared at the man. "These were all water-related deaths?"

He thought for a moment. "Looks like."

"And that doesn't seem odd to you?"

"Why would that be odd? Last I checked, humans can't breathe under water. That river is a lot stronger than people give it credit for. You're not careful, it will pull you right under. Then there are all kinds of branches and sunken roots to get tangled in and held under the water."

"Very true. But don't most of the people who have experience with rivers know to watch out for that?" She didn't mention the fact that Marley Shaffer was an excellent swimmer.

"Well, I don't know about all that. But I do know that a lot of people come up here thinking they can master the mountain. A lot of them find out the hard way that this area doesn't care about your intentions or past experiences."

Something in his tone told Jessie that he may have been speaking from personal experience. She didn't pry; time was of the essence here and her focus needed to stay on Marley's case. She read through more of the file, unable to believe some of what she was seeing. As she pored over the case file, her frown deepened with each page. The sheer number of glaring missteps and oversights in the handling of the investigation was staggering. It painted a picture of a police department woefully ill-equipped to handle a case involving a potentially suspicious death. There were basic procedural errors that spoke volumes about the department's inexperience.

The photographs of the scene were blurry and poorly composed, making it difficult to discern important details. The sketches and measurements were similarly haphazard, lacking the precision and attention to detail that Jessie was used to seeing in professional investigations. The documentation involving findings at Marley's campsite was just as bad. There were several instances where pieces of evidence, such as Marley's backpack and water bottle, were moved or disturbed before being properly documented and collected. Jessie sighed. This kind of contamination could compromise the integrity of the entire investigation.

And then her eyes froze on a particular line.

There was an autopsy report. Or what attempted to pass for one. The findings were summarized in a scant few paragraphs, lacking the detailed analysis and medical terminology Jessie was used to seeing. It was as if the coroner had simply gone through the motions, checking boxes rather than conducting a thorough examination.

She looked up at Hardin. "I thought Sheriff Cormac said there was no autopsy performed?"

Hardin tilted his head in confusion. "I can't imagine why he would say that. I mean, it says right there one was done. He's been under some stress lately, so, maybe he wasn't thinking clearly."

"It's dated yesterday," Jessie said, eying the date stamp. "Why wasn't it done right away?"

The deputy shrugged. "Maybe because the doc comes in from out of town for these. Plus, I think he was about to leave for vacation, so he came in and did us a solid so we could release the body to the family. I mean, it was obvious she drowned."

Jessie bit her tongue, trying to remind herself she was in a completely different world. Then she looked up at

Hardin. "What stress? You said the sheriff was under stress lately."

"Oh, it's just his personal life. His younger sister, who has a habit of drug abuse, took off with some man she met on the internet. She left her teenage son with the sheriff and I'm not sure that both of them are getting along the best. The sheriff and his wife aren't the best with children and now they're saddled with his nephew for who knows how long. So, I know that is playing in his mind. Wondering when...and if... his sister is coming back to town." He shook his head sadly.

Jessie looked down at the folder. "I am really sorry to hear that." She hoped that would explain part of the bad reasoning behind everything she had read. Again, she reminded herself that she was in Bidonville on a singular mission. It wasn't for her to make changes to protocol, or reprimand anyone for how they conducted their own business. "Okay. Next steps. I need to see the site where the body was found and her campground, and then the body itself."

Hardin looked at his watch then slapped his thighs. "Well, then like I said, we need to get a move on. Can't be caught out in the mountains after dark."

He stood and gestured for Jessie and Blizzard to follow him. As they made their way out the back of the police station to the waiting patrol cars, Jessie thought back to her potential encounter with something in the woods during her jog. Judging by officer Hardin's tone, maybe she had downplayed it a little too much.

10

Not in Town Anymore

The winding mountain road seemed to go on forever, each hairpin turn revealed yet another dizzying vista of craggy peaks and plunging valleys. Jessie gripped the handle of the deputy's SUV as Hardin navigated the treacherous curves with a steady hand, the vehicle's powerful engine thrumming beneath them.

"I guess four-wheel drive is a requirement for this area, huh?" she said.

"It helps," Hardin replied, taking his eyes off the road long enough to shoot her a smile. "But people only come up here during tourist season. In the winter, these roads are impassable. Most of them are closed, even to us locals." He gripped the wheel and adjusted his body in the seat. "Only thing worse than getting caught up here at night is getting caught here in the winter."

Jessie studied the man. "Alright, that's about the third

time you've made reference to these mountains being dangerous. Why do I get the feeling it's not just the natural beauty of the region I need to be worried about? You know, I was out on an early run this morning with Blizzard and I could swear there was an animal trailing us."

He looked over at her, face stern, before white-knuckling the wheel. "Where was this?"

"Just up one of the trails behind the bed and breakfast. Maybe a half-mile into the woods or so."

"Yeah, you need to be careful doing that. Thankfully, you had Blizzard with you."

She glanced at him out the corner of her eye. "So, what is it? Animals? Is it bears? Cause I had a feeling it was something large watching me."

He shifted his weight uncomfortably in the seat. "Bears don't really come this close to town. But you never know."

Jessie looked out the window at the scenery flying past. "Yeah, so I've heard."

"Was probably a coyote. They won't mess with you if you've got a dog around. Just, maybe don't go out there again though. Just in case."

"Well, I've learned my lesson. Plus, I don't think I'll be here long enough that I'll be going running again. How much farther?"

Hardin leaned forward, craning his neck to look out the top portion of the windshield. "About another half-hour drive and then a half-hour hike into the river."

The higher they climbed, the more forbidding the landscape became. Towering evergreens crowded the road and steep drop-offs appeared at each curve that could swallow a car whole if one ventured too close. Jessie felt the same way she had when she first pulled into Pine Haven.

Small and vulnerable.

But unlike Pine Haven, these mountains were desolate and uncaring. There was no warmth that she could sense. It felt like the mountains were warning her to turn back.

She shook her head and pushed those thoughts aside, focusing instead on the task at hand. She had promised her friend that she would find out the truth about her cousin's death, and she wasn't about to let a little discomfort stand in her way.

Finally, after what felt like hours of twisting, turning roads, Hardin pulled the SUV to a stop at a small trailhead. The path ahead was narrow and overgrown, disappearing into the dense forest only a couple of feet off the road.

"From here, we walk," Hardin said, his voice seeming unnaturally loud in the stillness of the mountains. He moved around to the back of the vehicle and opened the tailgate. Jessie moved to stand next to him as he pulled a semi-automatic rifle from its secured mount on the inside wall of the vehicle. He looked over at her. "Are you carrying?"

She shook her head. "I just got my concealed carry permit but haven't purchased a gun yet."

He nodded, reaching back into the SUV. "A PI that doesn't carry a gun? Alrighty then. Take this." He handed her a Glock 30 nestled in an appendix carry holder.

Jessie frowned, looking from the Glock to his rifle. "I thought you said there were no bears here."

"I said they don't come close to town. We aren't in town anymore." He stretched his hand out again with the firearm. Jessie took it from him, checked the security of the holster release, and clipped it to the front of her jeans' waistband.

"Ready?" Hardin asked. He looked down at Blizzard. "Do you want him to stay with the truck?"

"Absolutely not," Jessie said, steeling herself for the trek ahead. As they set off down the trail, the towering trees blocked out the sun and cast everything in a dull, gray light that made judging rough terrain even more difficult. The only sound, other than the occasional noises from nature, was their footsteps and labored breathing. Before long, Jessie could hear the sound of the river growing louder with every step.

Every rustle of leaves, every snap of a twig, made her heart skip a beat. She scanned the undergrowth, half-expecting to see a pair of eyes staring back at her from the shadows. At her side, Blizzard would look up, taking in his human's posture and reading her emotions before mirroring Jessie's heightened sense of awareness.

Ahead of her, Hardin seemed oblivious to the atmosphere, his strides long and sure as he navigated the twisting path. Jessie envied his calm demeanor.

As they rounded a bend in the trail, the sound of rushing water grew louder, and Jessie caught a glimpse of the river through the trees. They broke out of the undergrowth, and she stared at the rushing water, churning and frothing as it crashed over boulders and fallen logs.

They walked along the steep banks until finally reaching a small area of sand and rock that flattened out next to the raging waters. There were rocks jutting upward all around and masses of tree roots protruding from the soft earth.

Hardin pointed at the small landing patch of sand and rock. "That's where they found her. She was tangled on some of the roots sticking out."

"This is pretty remote. Why were the hikers here?"

"They carried their Kayaks down. This is one of the few places along the river you can launch from."

Jessie studied the muddy water as she walked closer to the beach. The river was broad and the water moved very swiftly, swirling around unseen rocks that no doubt littered the bed. "How deep is it?"

"Over your head towards the center," Hardin replied.

Jessie nodded. This was no leisurely flowing body of water. No matter how competent a swimmer Marley might have been, she would probably not be a match for this. Jessie bent down, looking at the sand. She took out her phone and took pictures from various angles before turning to Blizzard. "Track." Immediately the dog ventured to the edge of the river and began sniffing at the ground, then slowly made his way to the undergrowth to either side of Jessie and Hardin.

"What's he doing?" the deputy asked.

"Familiarizing himself with all the scents that have lingered over the last few days. It's something I have him do. You never know when he might hit on something later on."

The shepherd raised his head, sniffing the air, and

made his way over to Deputy Hardin and began sniffing around his boots.

"Yeah, we know he was here," Jessie said, motioning for Blizzard to move on.

"Impressive," Hardin said. "And you trained him to do that?"

"Kind of. He is so intelligent that it really didn't take much work. He picks up on commands incredibly fast." She looked around the site again. "And what about where she was camping? Can I see that as well?"

He nodded over his shoulder. "It's a little ways back through the woods towards the fork in the river."

Together, they headed away from the water and back towards the darker forest. As they picked their way through the wooded area, Blizzard ranged ahead, his nose to the ground as he sought out any lingering scents. After about ten minutes of hiking, they emerged into a small clearing where the remnants of a campsite could be seen. There was an indentation in the center where a tent had been erected, and in front of that, a blackened firepit with a bundle of wood lying next to it.

Hardin gestured towards the river roughly a hundred feet away from the site. "This is where we think it happened," he said, his voice raised to be heard over the roar of the current. "The victim was probably down by the water's edge for some reason—maybe filling a canteen or washing up. We figure she must have slipped and fallen in, and the current just swept her away."

Jessie frowned as her eyes took in the scene. Something about Hardin's explanation didn't sit right with her, but she couldn't quite put her finger on it. "That's a lot of 'we think' and 'probably' when it comes to someone's death." She made her way to the water's edge and studied the embankment. It was steep with just a narrow path to the water. "I just can't see an experienced hiker, someone who had been camping and trekking in the mountains for years, just happened to slip and fall into a river that is obviously very dangerous." She made it a point to keep her tone curious and not skeptical.

Hardin shrugged. "Looks like. That's what we were able to piece together. People get complacent, let their guard down. And these mountain rivers, they're unpredictable. One wrong step and you're at the mercy of the current."

Looking at the water, Jessie agreed with his statement. It was moving too swiftly for anyone to fight. Still...

She kneeled by the river's edge, studying the rocky bank. The stones were slick with moisture, but they were also firmly embedded in the earth, providing stable footing for anyone that approached cautiously.

Pointing to a patch of disturbed gravel a few feet from the water's edge, she turned to Hardin. "Look at this. If she had slipped and fallen, there would be signs of a struggle—scuff marks, displaced rocks, maybe even some torn clothing snagged on the branches. There are plenty of strong vines and roots sticking out of the embankment, but none are broken. Surely, she would have grabbed onto them." She pointed to the gravel area. "But these look more like drag marks."

Hardin's brow furrowed as he examined the spot Jessie was indicating. "I don't know," he said, sounding uncertain. "It's possible that the current could have smoothed things over, erased any signs of a struggle."

Jessie straightened up, her gaze drifting towards the abandoned campsite. "What about footprints? Were there any that didn't match Marley's?"

Hardin looked confused. "She was camping alone. No sign of anyone else."

Jessie sighed. "So, there was no forensic evidence collected from the site?"

"Well, we gathered up everything that belonged to her. It's all boxed back at the station for her next of kin."

Jessie bit the inside of her cheek to keep from responding. "What about her home? Did anyone check out her house?"

"For what?" Hardin seemed genuinely confused. "It was a rental. The owner said she will clean it out and send her personal effects to whomever wants them."

Jessie whistled for Blizzard and the shepherd trotted over. "Track."

His nose hit the ground near the riverbed and he began to sniff around. His body stiffened as he hovered over the drag marks on the gravel. Quickly, he back-tracked, smelling his way around the camp site before making his way over to an area of the woods that was a few hundred feet away from where Hardin had led them out of the forest.

"What's he found?" the deputy asked.

"Not sure. But if I had to guess, he's hit on the same scent that was at the river."

"Well, yeah. Marley's, no doubt," Hardin said.

Jessie walked over to where Blizzard was and examined the small break in the underbrush where he sniffed. It looked more like a small game trail than a path one could walk on. Still, it led away from the water and off towards one of the foothills. "What's up there?" She pointed in the general direction the trail seemed to follow.

Hardin hurried over to where she stood and stared. She could see the muscles in his jaw tense before he answered. "Nothing. Just more mountains."

Jessie looked at Blizzard, noting the intensity of his stare. "You sure? Maybe we could follow it just a bit. See what we run into?"

"Absolutely not." Hardin's reply was fast and clipped. He seemed to catch himself and softened his tone. "I mean, remember what I said about getting lost up here after dark. As it is, it will be close to dusk by the time we get back to the car."

Reluctantly, she agreed. She walked back to the campsite, took a few more pictures with her phone, and then joined Hardin for the trek back to his SUV. She patted her thigh, signaling for Blizzard to stay at her side as they backtracked through the woods.

They reached the vehicle just as the sun was starting to disappear behind the mountain range, casting an eerie, orange glow through the canopy.

They opened the back of the vehicle to secure their firearms when Jessie looked down at Blizzard. His tail had stopped wagging and the hair along the ridge of his back was slightly on end. He put his nose to the ground and began smelling around the SUV, emitting the lowest of growls. He stopped at the passenger side, huffing in air.

"What is it, boy?" Jessie said, moving to his side.

Hardin finished putting away the guns and walked over. "What is it?"

Jessie examined the ground near the passenger door. "There's a partial imprint here in the dirt." She pointed to the ground in front of Blizzard before squatting to get a closer look.

"Probably an animal," Hardin said.

Jessie looked up. "Only if an animal is wearing a size thirteen boot. And judging from the depth of this heel imprint, I'd say that animal is nearing three hundred pounds." She looked around, noting the wet puddle directly in front of the partial print. "It also looks like this animal relieved itself right here as well." She stood up. "Do you have something we can collect this dirt in? An evidence baggie or—"

"No. I don't have anything like that. And if I did it wouldn't matter because the nearest lab that could analyze anything is over an hour away. And our department doesn't have the money to pay for the service anyway. It was probably just a hunter that stopped here to check out our vehicle and then moved on. And we need to be doing the same."

Jessie started to argue but thought better of it. She opened the back door and motioned for Blizzard to get in. Then she settled herself in the passenger seat and buckled in. Hardin turned over the engine and pulled away. He expertly made a three-point turn and eased them onto the roadway, heading back down the peak.

"The morgue holding Marley's body is a shared one

for the county," he said, not looking in Jessie's direction. "We should be there in just over an hour."

Jessie only nodded and continued to look out the window. She had seen how nervous Hardin was when she pointed out that it wasn't an animal outside the car. While she wasn't entirely sure what was going on, there was absolutely one thing she did know. She was going to need help getting to the bottom of this case. And she knew just who to call. The hard part was going to be convincing Sheriff Cormac to let her make that call.

11

What the Dead Can Say

The drive to the county morgue was a somber one. Jessie sat in the passenger seat of Hardin's SUV, her gaze fixed on the passing landscape as she mentally reviewed the details of the case for the umpteenth time.

Hardin was uncharacteristically quiet, his usual easy banter replaced by a pensive silence. Jessie hoped that her doubts about the accidental nature of Marley Shaffer's death were weighing on him, challenging the tidy narrative that someone had built in his mind. Whatever his thoughts on the matter, he kept them locked tight, the only sounds he made during the drive was the occasional clearing of his throat.

They pulled into the parking lot of the morgue, a low, nondescript building on the outskirts of town. Jessie had seen more than her fair share of these places, but it never ceased to be unsettling. With their blank walls and shuttered windows—these houses of the dead radiated nothing but pain and sorrow.

Hardin killed the engine, and for a moment they sat in silence, staring at the building's facade. Finally, he turned to Jessie, his expression serious. "Look, I know you have your doubts about what happened to Marley." His voice was low and earnest. "But if you're suggesting this wasn't an accident, then...well the other option is not something we deal with here."

And there it was. If this were foul play, then he and his co-workers were woefully out of their depth. If this wasn't an accident, then it meant they were dealing with the worst kind of animal. One that didn't live in the wild.

Jessie met his gaze and chose her words carefully. "I hear what you're saying, Hardin. And believe me, I get it. I've been where you are right now. I know you want to believe this was an accident; and so do I. But the only way to prove that is by following the evidence and letting it provide the conclusion. Evidence doesn't care what we hope the outcome will be. It can't lie or mislead us. But to do that, the case has to have been handled correctly from the jump. And I'm not so sure this one was."

Hardin sighed but nodded in understanding. "Alright then," he said, opening his door and stepping out into the chill air. "Let's see what the dead might be able to tell you."

Jessie stepped out and looked back at Blizzard. "You stay here, boy."

Together, they made their way into the building, the automatic doors whooshing open with a pneumatic hiss. The interior was just as stark and uninviting as the exterior. Fluorescent lights cast a harsh glare over the linoleum floors and cinderblock walls.

"That's odd," said Hardin as they stepped up to the reception area.

"What is?"

"Peggy. She is the receptionist and Dr. Miller's secretary. Even though he's off on vacation she should still be here." He looked down at his watch. "Maybe she decided to call it an early night. I can't say I blame her. I wouldn't want to hang out in this place." He leaned over the desk and triggered the electronic lock that opened the door leading to the morgue proper. The door clicked and he pushed it open, letting Jessie walk ahead of him.

They walked down a narrow hall that led to another set of double doors. Stepping through, they walked into a large, chilly room lined with stainless steel refrigeration units. Jessie grimaced at the heavy scent of chemicals and the underlying tang of decay.

A man wearing a long white lab coat stood at the far end of the room, his back to them, as he looked over a clipboard. One of the refrigerator doors was slightly ajar as Jessie and Hardin approached.

"Well, hey, Doc. I thought you was headed out of town," Hardin said. The doctor turned slowly, his eyes still cast down on the paperwork in his hand. "I want you to meet someone. This is Jessie—"

Hardin stopped mid-sentence, reaching for his sidearm.

The man bolted forward, knocking Hardin to the ground before he could draw his gun. He raised a foot to slam into the deputy's face, but was stopped as Jessie slammed into him, knocking him off balance. The attacker whirled, slicing the clipboard through the air at Jessie's face. She stepped back, just out of range of the attack. His momentum carried him forward and Jessie stepped in to meet him.

She struck out with the knuckles of her first two fingers, striking a nerve cluster in the man's forearm. He grimaced, letting go of the clipboard just as Jessie struck with her other hand, catching him under his chin and causing his head to snap up and back.

The blow sent him sprawling backwards against a small, rolling medical table. He reached behind him and grabbed the first thing his hand closed around. It was a glass bottle, and he heaved it in Jessie's direction. She ducked, and the bottle shattered against the far wall. Immediately, the area around the broken glass began to fill with a caustic vapor, stinging at Jessie's eyes.

She covered her nose and mouth with one hand while running to Deputy Hardin's side and helping him to his feet. Coughing, they ran from the room and headed for the outdoors.

Once outside, Hardin was doubled over gasping. "Did...did you see which way he went?"

Jessie shook her head, rubbing at the tears that spilled down her face. "No. I have no idea. Are you okay?"

Hardin was nodding his head. "What was that stuff?"

"I don't know. But better we stay out here until we find out."

Hardin went to his car and clicked the radio, speaking into the handheld microphone. He took a deep breath as he walked back to Jessie. "I radioed for the fire department and an ambulance. Without knowing what that was, we should probably be checked over."

Jessie agreed, taking deep breaths to try and clear the remaining vapors from her lungs. She could make out sirens in the distance, and before long found herself sitting on the back bumper of an ambulance, a scratchy wool blanket thrown over her shoulders as a medic placed a blood pressure cuff around her arm and a pulse oximeter on the end of her finger. Beside her, Hardin was undergoing a similar examination, his face pale and drawn in the flashing red and blue lights of the emergency vehicles.

The scene outside the morgue was nowhere near as chaotic as Jessie had imagined it would be. There was a police car, an ambulance and a fire truck, but that was it. No one had cordoned off the area. There were no hazmat teams entering the building to assess the chemical spill. The acrid stench of the fumes still clung to Jessie's hair and clothes, but it was not as noticeable as before.

"Can you tell me what happened in there?" the paramedic asked, his voice muffled behind the respirator mask he wore.

Jessie cleared her throat and filled the medic in on what had happened.

"And this bottle. You don't know what was in it? Was it one bottle or multiple ones?" the medic asked.

Both Jessie and Hardin shook their heads. "Not sure, but it smelled like ammonia, or bleach maybe. It was hard to tell with all the other chemical odors in the room," Jessie added.

The medic nodded, taking the medical equipment off

her arm and finger. "Based on your symptoms—the coughing, eye irritation, and difficulty breathing—it sounds like you were exposed to an inhalation irritant. Possibly chloramine gas, which can be formed when bleach and ammonia are mixed."

Jessie felt a surge of panic at the word "gas". Her mind conjured images of chemical weapons and permanent lung damage. "Is it dangerous?" she asked, forcing herself to control any tremble in her voice.

He gave her a reassuring smile. "In high concentrations, chloramine gas can be toxic," he said. "But based on your exposure time and the fact that your symptoms are already improving, I don't think there's any lasting harm. We'll give you some oxygen and monitor your vitals for a bit, but you should be fine."

Jessie nodded, feeling a wave of relief wash over her as she accepted the oxygen mask slipping over her face. She noticed Hardin doing the same and taking large draws of oxygen. "You okay? How's your head?"

He frowned, rolling his eyes. "A little sore, but I'm fine. Just mad at myself for letting that guy get the drop on me."

"Did you get a look at his face?" Jessie asked.

"No. Not really. I just knew as he was turning around that he wasn't the doc. What about you?"

She shook her head. "It all happened too fast. Dark hair and eyes, stubble...but that was it." She saw the deputy's brow drop. "What? Does that sound familiar?"

"What...no. I was just thinking back to anyone that works here that might fit that description."

There was a flurry of commotion at the front doors as

two medics wearing respirators rushed out pushing a stretcher. Hardin whipped off his mask and rushed to their side, followed by Jessie.

"Oh no," the deputy said. The body of a woman lay on the stretcher, her frail chest barely rising and falling. "That's Peggy, doc's receptionist. Is she—"

One of the paramedics took off her own mask. "No. She's alive, but we really need to get her to the hospital."

They started wheeling her past and Hardin called after them. "Where was she?" But they didn't seem to hear her over the commotion of the firetruck's engine and police car as they continued rushing her towards the waiting ambulance.

"She was in the break room. Knocked unconscious."

Hardin and Jessie turned to see a firefighter walking out the door. He was tall, a little on the heavy side, with a full head of red hair that jutted out in all directions from under the hard hat he wore.

"Kerry," Hardin said, reaching out a hand to greet the fireman. "Nice to see you. Wish it were under other circumstances."

"I hear you." His voice was harsh and deep as he gave Jessie a critical eye. "And who's this?"

Jessie stuck her hand out. "Jessie Night. I'm here on business."

Kerry turned to Hardin. "And what business did the two of you have inside a morgue?"

Jessie was a little put off by the man's tone as well as the fact that he seemed intent on not addressing his questions to her. She started to speak but was interrupted by

Hardin. "She's a private investigator and is here looking into something for one of her clients."

The fireman arched an eyebrow at her, but then turned his attention back to Hardin. "Maybe not the best of ideas, but hey, what do I know. The area's all clear. Those fumes evaporated almost immediately it looks like." He nodded to Hardin and walked away without casting a glance at Jessie.

She stared after the man. "What was that about? Maybe not the best idea..."

Hardin took a long breath, his gaze focused on the fireman as he climbed into his truck. "No idea. Maybe he was referring to going into a morgue. Whatever. But I need to go fill out an incident report and we shouldn't go inside until Sheriff Cormac hears about this and gives us the okay to continue."

Jessie thought for a moment. "Agreed. But there is one thing I need to see, if you're okay with that. It will be quick, I promise."

Hardin hesitated for a moment but finally agreed. Together, they walked back to the refrigerated room where they had met the intruder. Jessie looked around before heading to the back of the room.

"What is it?" the deputy asked.

Bending down, Jessie retrieved the clipboard from the floor and showed it to Hardin. "This. The attacker was going over this information, and—" she walked over to the in-wall unit the intruder had opened, "—this was the unit he opened. Anything stand out?"

Hardin looked from the clipboard to the refrigerated

drawer identification number. "Forty-seven. It says here that's where Marley Shaffer's remains are kept."

12

Request Granted

The next morning, Jessie and Blizzard walked into the Bidonville Police Department with a large tray of coffee and a box of store-bought donuts. They weren't the lighter than air confections found at Angela's bakery back in Pine Haven, but they would have to do. The station was as quiet as she expected, with one lone officer on duty at the front desk. He recognized her from the previous day and ushered her through, after accepting two donuts but passing on the coffee.

She went back to the main work area to find Hardin standing at his desk with two other men. Sheriff Cormac and Kerry, the fireman she had met at the morgue. "Oh, hello, gentlemen." The sheriff gave her a cordial smile, but the fireman only glanced briefly her way, his eyes narrowing.

"So, anyway, we'll pick this up at a later date," the fireman said, his voice deep and gruff. He nodded at the sheriff and then gave Hardin a playful punch to the arm. "Remember what I said." He gave the deputy a nod and walked away.

"I'm sorry, am I interrupting?" Jessie asked, placing the coffee and donuts on Hardin's desk. The glance the two men shared was furtive, but she caught it, nonetheless.

"Oh, no, not at all," said Sheriff Cormac. "Kerry was just here filling me in on the call last night. It's a volunteer fire department so they always keep me in the loop. I know...probably not the way it's done where you're from."

Jessie gave a slight shrug. "I wasn't thinking that. I think it's pretty cool the way everyone keeps everyone in the loop. Must make doing your job that much easier. I brought some coffee and donuts." She smiled and pointed to the boxes.

Sheriff Cormac seemed confused. "Well, thank you. You didn't have to do that. We have plenty of coffee here. You shouldn't go wasting your hard-earned money on us."

"Oh, this is the least I can do. I feel like I'm taking up so much of your valuable time."

The sheriff hesitated, then gave in and scooped out two donuts. "Well...if you insist." He nodded his thanks and turned to walk out.

"Um, Sherrif Cormac...before you go, could I ask a favor?" Jessie said.

The older man circled back around to the desk. "Sure. What can I do for you?"

Jessie took a deep breath and let it out slowly. "I would like your permission to have the medical examiner from Pine Haven come take a look at Marley's body."

The silence was immediate, thickening the air in the department.

Jessie continued, not waiting for a response. "Look, just hear me out. I know you have your own way of doing things here, and I respect that. But I have an obligation to my client... and Marley's only remaining family. All she wants from me is to tell her what happened to her cousin. And honestly, right now I can't in good faith answer that. It's no slight on you or your people. I just need to connect some dots here and I need some of my resources to do that."

"It's been reported as an accident," the sheriff said. "If we go back on that, or report something that might scare the people around here..."

Jessie shot a look at Hardin, but he quickly dropped his eyes to avoid her gaze. At least now she knew what they had been talking about when she walked up. "Sir, what do we know about the man that attacked me and Deputy Hardin last night?"

The two men exchanged looks as the sheriff cleared his throat. "We are looking into that and treating it like any other breaking and entering. I'm certain it was just someone looking for drugs or something they could sell for drugs."

Jessie frowned. "That person didn't look like a druggie to me. And why would someone with a substance abuse problem bother to put on a white lab coat and have the clipboard with the information of the woman that you found dead? The woman that I've been asking questions about?" Her eyes shifted from the sheriff to Hardin. "And what about the receptionist, Peggy? Was she robbed or just rendered unconscious? I mean, if someone were looking for fast cash, wouldn't an older woman alone in a building have been an easy target?"

Hardin shuffled his feet. "She wasn't robbed. She had cash on her and a diamond wedding band." He gave the sheriff an apologetic look. "I mean, maybe Jessie has a point." His eyes fell to the floor, avoiding the sharp glance from Sheriff Cormac.

"Who can say what's in the mind of these junkies," he said. "We should just be grateful that Peggy wasn't hurt worse than she was."

"Is she awake yet?" Jessie asked. "When are you going to take her statement? I'd like to speak with her."

The sheriff held up both hands. "Whoa. Slow down there. She is awake and one of the deputies will be heading over soon to get her statement. You can review the statement, but I don't want you bothering Peggy. There's no need for that."

Jessie thought about his words and made a quick decision. It was time to push him on the subject. "Sheriff, let me help you. I have a lot of experience with cases like this, and what's the worst that could happen? I find out you are correct that this is nothing more than a series of accidents and coincidences. I have egg on my face, I'm out of here in a couple of days, and you get to say I told you so." Since setting foot in Bidonville, she had felt the sheriff didn't want her hanging around any longer than was necessary, so maybe this would get the man to relent.

When the man finally spoke, she knew her gambit had paid off. "Well, since our doc is out of town, I suppose it can't really hurt to have your big shot examiner come take a look. But the official report stands. Your guy can take a look, but his findings don't counteract or supersede our official documentation."

Jessie nodded. She was fairly certain what the sheriff was saying wasn't legal, but she wasn't about to rock the boat further. "Thank you. I promise that you will love Dr. Lindquist. He's no-nonsense, and you won't even know he was here."

The sheriff grunted, tossing her a nod as he walked away.

"Wow," said Hardin. "I thought for sure he would send you packing when you made that request.

Jessie turned on the deputy. "What were you talking about when I came in? And why was Kerry involved in the discussion?"

Hardin looked surprised and confused, his eyes widening. "Like I said, Kerry was here filling the sheriff in on the call last night. That's all."

"And the intruder? Why do I get the feeling that was a part of the conversation that you're leaving out?"

A blush crept up Hardin's cheeks. During her career in the military, Jessie had made it a point to know when someone was lying to her. It was a skill she had become widely known for. And now, in the second half of her life, it was a skill she relied on more heavily than she liked to admit. Hardin hadn't lied to her up until this point, and she hoped that his track record wasn't about to be tarnished.

"I was telling the chief pretty much what you said about it not adding up. There are plenty of places in town that would be easier to steal from if someone needed some quick cash. Also, Peggy is no threat to anyone. Why hurt her like that?"

A thought flashed through Jessie's mind. "Was it the sheriff's idea that this was a basic break in?"

Hardin hesitated for a moment, looking over his shoulder and dropping his tone. "Not exactly. Kerry told him that it was probably just some high school kids doing a senior prank. Or just someone looking for a quick drug score."

Jessie nodded. "Do you have a local clinic or well-visit site?"

"We do. It's on the other side of town. It's run by a nurse-practitioner that comes over from Fleetsville every other day. Why?"

"I was just wondering if you've had any recent spike in break-ins. Especially into the clinic."

He thought for a moment. "No. There haven't been."

"And yet the first one happens to be into a morgue? I don't buy it."

He didn't say anything, but she could tell from his countenance that he agreed.

"One other thing, who is this guy Kerry, and why does he seem to hate me?"

Hardin sat on the edge of his desk and poured himself a cup of coffee. "Kerry doesn't hate anyone. He's just not big on talking to people he doesn't know. You'll find that a lot with town folk who were born and raised here, ones that have never been outside Bidonville. They don't really trust strangers."

Jessie was about to ask another question when they were interrupted by a young man. He was tall and gangly, wearing an oversized sweatshirt and baggy jeans with holes in the knees. He nodded at Deputy Hardin. "Hey, have you seen my uncle?"

The deputy motioned for the boy to come closer. "He was here just a few minutes ago. Have you checked his office? Roger, this is Jessie Night. She's up visiting from Pine Haven."

The boy, whom Jessie guessed to be in his late teens, quickly moved to shake her hand. "Nice to meet you, ma'am.. I'm staying with my uncle, the sheriff, for a bit."

"Nice to meet you, Roger," Jessie said.

"Your uncle was just here," Hardin said. "He might have stepped outside to speak with Kerry for a moment, but he should be back in his office soon."

Jessie noticed the look that splashed over the young man's face at the mention of the fireman. It was one of annoyance and disgust. "Roger, is there something you need? Can we help?"

"No. He said he was only going to make a quick stop here on the way to dropping me off at school. I just hate being late; it makes me nervous." He clasped one hand in the other, squeezing slightly.

"Well, I actually drove over today to bring treats, so if you want, I can give you a ride. I'm done here..." Jessie looked towards Hardin for confirmation.

The boy looked around, his eyes darting around the

room. "Oh, I couldn't put you out like that...it wouldn't be right." He looked around, forlorn. "I'll find my uncle."

"I'd drop you off, but..." Hardin looked at Jessie, "I've got some paperwork to finish up from last night."

Jessie smiled and turned to Roger. "Well, that solves it. Deputy Hardin and your uncle have their hands full today. Let me drop you off." She turned to Hardin. "Plus, it will be my way of saying thank you to Sheriff Cormac for being so open minded about this case."

They left the station and made their way to her Jeep in the parking lot. Once situated, they pulled away from the curb, Roger silent in the passenger seat beside her. He fidgeted with the strap of his backpack; his gaze fixed on the passing scenery.

"So, Roger, how's it going? Adjusting to things here in Bidonville? I know you said you're just visiting, but I didn't catch where from," Jessie said, trying to break the ice.

He exhaled sharply but didn't turn to face her. "It's going okay. Not the senior year I was looking forward to, but what can you do? My mom will be back to get me soon. And I can go back home and finish out the year there."

Jessie could tell he was trying to convince himself this was the truth rather than her. She sensed there was more to his reticence than just teenage moodiness. Thinking of the scene at the police station, she remembered the way the boy had reacted to the mention of Kerry's name. "Your uncle seems like a good man," she said casually. "He must be pretty busy, being the sheriff and all."

Roger shrugged, his shoulders hunching up around his ears. "I guess," he said noncommittally.

Jessie hesitated, wondering how far she should push. She didn't want to spook the kid, but her instincts were telling her to press on.

"Well, I'm sure you're learning a lot from him. And you get the added benefit of having a firefighter to learn from as well. I only just met Kerry, but he seems like a nice guy."

Roger's head swiveled around slowly to face her. "I don't know which Kerry you met, but it couldn't be the one I know."

Jessie cut her eyes to him quickly before turning her attention back to the road. "Well, it was just my first impression. He seems a bit on the quiet side."

Roger let out a short laugh that was little more than a bark. "Yeah, well, wait till he gets a couple drinks in him. Then see what you think."

"You've seen that side of him?"

"Thankfully, no. But I've heard my uncle talking to my aunt about it." He turned his head and resumed gazing out the window. "Ask his wife about his temper. Well, if she ever shows back up that is."

They made the rest of the journey in silence.

"Oh, this is good," Roger said, looking up.

Jessie stopped the Jeep a bit shy of the turn off that led to the school. "You sure? I don't mind dropping you at the door."

He rolled his eyes. "I'm fine walking from here."

Jessie smiled. At least he didn't come right out and say he didn't want to be seen being dropped off by her. The boy climbed out, gave her an awkward wave of his hand and a mumbled thanks before slouching towards the turn off. Jessie pulled away, already thinking about the call she needed to make to Dr. Lindquist, and how she needed a way to find Kerry's address.

It was time to pay the fireman a visit.

13

Help from a Friend

Compared to the police station, the fire hall was practically a palace. Jessie pulled into the freshly paved parking lot and took in the building's aesthetics. The two-story building was constructed of warm, red brick, with large, curved windows along the front. A freshly painted sign proudly displayed "Bidonville Fire Department" in bold, gold letters above the main entrance.

Jessie parked her vehicle and took a moment to admire the pristine landscaping surrounding the station. Neatly trimmed hedges and colorful flowerbeds framed the walkway leading to the front doors, and a majestic flagpole stood at attention, the American flag gently fluttering in the breeze. As she approached the entrance, Jessie noticed a gleaming red fire truck parked in the expansive garage bay. Even though it wasn't, the vehicle looked brand new, with polished chrome and immaculate paintwork. It was clear that the fire department took great pride in their equipment and facilities.

Looking at the station, Jessie couldn't help but wonder about the disparity between the police station and the fire station. She knew that Bidonville's economy relied heavily on tourism, with outdoor enthusiasts flocking to the area for its pristine hiking trails and scenic beauty. A well-equipped fire department would be essential for handling any emergencies that might arise in the rugged wilderness, and the town likely prioritized funding for this critical service. After all, during the dry seasons, a misplaced cigarette or errant bolt of lightning could spell doom for many and set the economy back for seasons.

At the door, she reached down and fastened Blizzard's leash. She pushed open the door and stepped into the cool, air-conditioned interior of the fire station. Scanning the room, her eyes quickly settled on the large figure of Kerry, hunched over one of the dining tables set up picnic-style in the corner of the room. His red hair, disheveled and unkempt, stood out against the tidy surroundings. She cleared her throat loudly and waited for the man to look up.

His face lifted and a scowl darkened his features. His eyes flitted from side to side in the large space, and Jessie imagined he was cursing the fact that no one else was around to pawn her off on. He stood up but didn't step around the desk. "Can I help you?"

Jessie walked towards the man but stopped short when his eyes fell to the big shepherd at her side. "Oh, he won't bother you." To emphasize, she dropped the leash.

"Stay." Blizzard immediately dropped into a sitting position and froze in place. Jessie continued walking towards the man, her hand extended. "I'm Jessie Night. We met briefly at the morgue last night and again at the police station. But we didn't get a chance to speak."

Kerry regarded her outstretched hand like it was a venomous snake. Finally, he reached across the desk and gave her a quick shake. "I remember you. Is there something you need?" he asked bluntly, taking his seat again.

Jessie forced a smile, determined to keep the conversation civil. "I was hoping we could have a chat about Marley Shaffer's case."

Kerry leaned back in his chair, the cheap plastic creaking under his weight. "I don't know what more I can tell you. It was a terrible accident."

Jessie pulled up a chair and sat down, leaning forward to meet Kerry's gaze. "I understand that, but I just have a few questions about the first responders on the scene. Were you the first to arrive?"

Kerry's jaw clenched, and he looked away, his fingers tapping nervously on the desk. "I was the first to reach those two hikers that found the body. They hiked out until they got into cell range. The police showed up shortly thereafter and we all walked in together to the site where the body was found."

Jessie was nodding along as he spoke. "So, at no time did you enter the area alone?"

He narrowed his eyes, squinting in her direction. "Not once." A flash of anger passed over his features. "Are you implying something, Miss Night?"

Jessie held up her hands to diffuse the situation. "I'm

not implying anything, Kerry. I'm just trying to piece together the facts. Surely, you can understand that."

He leaned forward, the bulk of his stomach pushing at the tabletop. "What I understand is that people come up here trying to stick their noses in business that ain't theirs. Trying to change how we do things. Trying to tell us that we poor, unwashed mountain folk are too stupid to handle things and we need to start conforming to the society that you created." His eyes were practically smoldering at this point as he sat back against the chair.

Jessie forced herself to give him as warm a smile as possible. "Sir, I can assure you that is not my intention. Something happened to Marley Shaffer out there in the woods, and all I'm trying to do is figure out what. If it was an accident, then it will come out in the investigation, and I'll be on my way."

He cocked his head to one side. "And if it weren't? An accident, that is."

"Then...we deal with that too." She met his gaze with a hardened one of her own. "Look, we got off on the wrong foot. I really just came by for a formal greeting. You're a first responder, you know why I'm in town. At some point I figure we will need to work together. I was just hoping you would be open to that." She stood up, pushing away from the chair.

Kerry stood as well, keeping his eyes downcast as Jessie walked back towards the door. She stopped and changed direction, heading over to some pictures on one of the walls. They were framed black and white landscapes that were hauntingly beautiful. Stunning vistas of the mountains, as well as some old, abandoned buildings sitting back from what looked like well-worn hiking trails.

She pointed to the photographs. "These are really beautiful. Did you take them?"

He grumbled under his breath as he moved to stand near her. "Yeah. That was a long time ago."

"You've got a really great eye," Jessie said, studying the pictures.

Kerry shuffled in place a bit. "Not really. I just point and shoot. The trees, the rocks, the land...they do all the hard work. I just happen to be there at the right time."

She smiled at the big man and stepped back, looking around. "And my compliments to whoever maintains your station. This place is spotless."

He tried to hide the grin that almost broke out. "That would be me as well. We don't have a lot here in Bidonville. But I aim to take care of what little we do have. Everything here needs to last as long as I do. Who knows when we'll get funding for new gear."

Jessie eyed the man with appreciation. She knew what it was like to make do with what you had in a department. In the military, you got used to making things last well past their expiration date. "Your wife must be very proud of you and the job you're doing." Immediately, she felt a shift in his attitude as his body stiffened. "Oh, I'm sorry, I just assumed you were married and—"

He interrupted with a grunt. "If that's all the questions you have for me today, you should probably be heading on out. I have some work to catch up on."

Jessie was about to apologize again, but she knew it

wouldn't be received well. She simply nodded her head and made her way back to the patiently waiting Blizzard. She picked up his leash and headed out the door and back to her Jeep. She climbed behind the wheel and turned over the engine.

Before pulling away, she opened her phone's navigation. She stared at the screen, concentrating. "Now what was the name of that street...oh yeah...Bent Creek Way." She punched the name in and smiled at the results before turning her head to look at Blizzard. "He's hiding something. What do you say we go take a peek around our friendly neighborhood firefighter's house?"

She pulled out of the fire station parking lot and pointed her Jeep east. Her phone pinged and she pulled over just long enough to read the text from Dr. Lindquist aloud.

"I'm in. I'll be there by nightfall."

14

A Sheriff's Dilemma

The dimly lit room was thick with tension as the three men sat around a battered wooden table. The only sound was the occasional creaking of chairs and the tapping of restless fingers on the tabletop. Sheriff Cormac, worry etched in every line of his face, sat at the head of the table, his eyes darting between the two other men.

"She's getting too close," growled the first man, his voice even, yet menacing. "If she keeps snooping around, she's going to stumble onto something she won't like."

The second man leaned forward; his dark eyes boring into the sheriff. "You should have sent her away the moment she arrived, Cormac. Now we've got a real problem on our hands."

Sheriff Cormac wiped the sweat from his brow, his hands trembling slightly. "Look, if I had done that, it would have looked even more suspicious. She might have come back with reinforcements, and then we'd be in an even worse situation."

The first man slammed his fist on the table, making the sheriff jump. "That's a risk we can't afford to take! You need to get rid of her, Cormac. Now."

The sheriff held up his hands, his voice pleading. "I understand your concerns, but we need to be smart about this. I'm pretty sure she'll be leaving soon. We just have to wait it out and not draw any more attention to ourselves. Once the doc arrives—" He stopped mid-sentence.

The two men's eyes zeroed in on him.

"What doc?" said the first man. "Cos we all know it can't be Doc Miller, right?"

The sheriff faltered; his eyes darted from one to the other as he struggled to swallow the lump in his throat. "Well, see, she raised the fact that if she could get her doctor to just have a look at the body, it would speed things along. She said she'd be outta here that much faster..."

The first man gave him an incredulous look. "And you allowed it? Damnit, Cormac."

The second man growled deep in the back of his throat. "You should have let me handle it from the beginning. There should not have been a body to find."

Just then, the door creaked open, and Caroline stepped into the room, a tray of biscuits and a pot of coffee in her hands. "I thought you gentlemen might like some refreshments," she said, her voice wavering slightly as she took in the tense atmosphere.

The first man sneered at her, his lip curling in

disdain. "We're busy. We don't want none of your damn biscuits."

In an instant, the second man was on his feet, his chair clattering to the floor behind him. He slammed his hands down on the table with such force that the dishes rattled. "Speak to my wife like that again," he snarled, his voice dripping with venom, "and it will be the last thing to ever come out of your mouth." They locked eyes until the much smaller man finally looked away.

Caroline, her face pale and her eyes wide with fear, quickly set the tray down and backed out of the room, mumbling an apology as she went.

The men sat in silence for a moment, the weight of the confrontation hanging in the air. Finally, the first man spoke. "Forgive me. It was not my place to speak to your wife like that. But this situation... It has me vexed."

The second man settled back into his chair and turned to the sheriff. "Is there anything to be learned from the body?"

The sheriff raised his shoulder until they met his earlobes. "How should I know? I'm not a freaking doctor."

The second man balled a fist and started to rise but was stopped by a gesture from the smaller one. "Hold on. Maybe this could work out."

The sheriff didn't like the tone in the man's voice and looked at him wearily. "What do you mean?"

The smaller man smiled. "Well, we are in need of a new doctor, right? Now, granted, the chances are that whoever is coming to help Miss Night is not going to want to stay around town. But they could help us with our immediate need."

The sheriff felt a line of cold sweat break out along his spine, wetting his shirt. "Do you really think that's a good idea? I mean...that would mean letting this new doc in on certain aspects of our life here."

The man scowled. "What other choice do we have?" He gave a stern look to the larger man. "We need a physician. You've seen what happens when we try to handle things without one."

The bigger man huffed, his lip turning up in a sneer. "What was I supposed to do? He made fun of my wife's cooking."

"He criticized it. There's a difference," the smaller man said.

The sheriff raised a hand. "We don't need to rehash this. The thought of it leaves me...unwell. Let's just focus on getting through these next few days. But for the record, I am not in favor of involving another doctor in this."

The first man turned, fixing him with bright eyes. "Well, then it's a good thing what you are and are not in favor of have no impact on our decisions whatsoever. You just remember what your job is."

The sheriff gave him an angry look before quickly looking away. "I remember."

The smaller man gave him an evil smile. "Keep that in mind. Do your part, and she'll be just fine."

The sheriff bristled, but sank back in his chair, his eyes focused on the table before him.

The larger of his two friends stood up, his massive

body seemed to fill the room. When he spoke, his voice was low and threatening. "You better get this under control, Cormac. You know what will happen if you don't."

The sheriff nodded; his face ashen. "I understand. I'll take care of it."

15

X Marks the Spot

Jessie pulled her Jeep up to the curb, her eyes scanning the small, unassuming house before her. It was a simple, single-story structure with weathered, white siding and a bright red door that seemed strangely out of place. Atop the house, a large rooster weathervane creaked in the gentle breeze, a mixture of brightly colored metals with a tail that carefully matched the color of the door.

She stepped out of the vehicle, taking in the unkempt yard and the drawn curtains that obscured the windows. The house had an air of neglect about it, as if its occupant had little interest in maintaining appearances. It was the complete opposite of the fire station aesthetic. Whoever lived here didn't seem like the same person who maintained a meticulously clean work space.

Jessie approached the front porch, her footsteps muffled by the overgrown grass. There was a green seed-spreader, an old water hose attached to a spigot coming from the side of the house, and various pieces of untreated lumber strewn about the yard. Stepping up to the door, she peered through a small window to one side. Her eyes strained to make out the details of the dimly lit interior. The window was covered in a layer of grime and dried streaks that made seeing through it difficult.

But she could make out movement inside. A shadow detached itself and then ducked down behind what she assumed was a sofa.

There was someone skulking around inside Kerry's house.

Instinctively, Jessie reached for the door handle, but it was locked. She knocked on the door and called out. "Hello, is someone there? I'd like to talk to you, please." The sound of a back door slamming shut answered her. She ran around to the back of the house, her pounding heart driving her legs.

Rounding the corner, she caught a glimpse of a figure racing through the back yard. She could make out blue jeans, and a red tee shirt racing from the yard and heading for the tree line. "Hey! Stop!" Her voice carried across the yard as she set out after the fleeing figure.

The figure ignored her plea, running through the back gate and disappearing into the woods beyond. Jessie followed, her feet pounding against the soft earth of the narrow trail that led from the house.

She pushed low-hanging limbs and vines from in front of her face as she raced forward, only to find the figure a short distance ahead, standing frozen before two large trees standing on either side of the narrow trail. Jessie looked at the trees, each marked with a large, red 'X' painted on the trunks at eye level.

The figure turned as Jessie approached.

It was a young man, maybe in his early twenties. He was tall, his limbs long and gangly. While his clothing covered much of his skin, what Jessie could see was dark and smooth. His head was bald, and she noticed immediately that he had no eyebrows that were discernible. Large eyes set a little too close together stared at Jessie, wide with fear. They darted between her and the two trees, the man rubbing his hands together in agitation before dropping into a deep squat, wrapping both arms over his head to clasp at his ears as he rocked slowly back and forth, a deep, frightened whine emanating from him.

Jessie stopped where she was, stretching her arms forward to show him her empty hands. "Hey. It's okay. I'm not here to hurt you." She saw him flinch at the word hurt. "I just want to make sure you're okay. My name is Jessie."

The man didn't answer at first, only moaned low in his throat. His eyes were squeezed shut and he dropped his hands to wrap his arms around his torso as his rocking increased. "Please. Please don't take me. Don't hurt me."

Jessie watched him, saw the traumatic response to her presence he was experiencing. She thought briefly, then quickly dropped to the damp ground and sat cross-legged. She waited for him to look up at her, seeing that she had now made herself smaller than he was. "It's okay. No one is going to hurt you or take you anywhere. Why do you think that?"

He gave her a look of genuine confusion. "You were chasing me. You scared me."

Good job, Jessie.

She kept her tone soft. "I was only concerned. You ran away, so I thought maybe you were in trouble." That was only a half-truth, but she forgave herself considering that she was only just beginning to realize how deeply she had scared the boy.

He stopped his rocking, his dark eyes briefly meeting her own for the first time. "You weren't trying to get me?"

Jessie gave him a smile. "Not at all. Cross my heart."

He looked away, his breathing slowing. "I did what I was supposed to. Run. Hide. But I went the wrong way." He glanced back at the trees. "Can't go past there. Nope. X means stop."

Jessie looked over his shoulder at the trees before lowering her eyes to him. "I'm sorry I frightened you. Can you tell me your name?"

He looked up. "I'm George. G-E-O-R-G-E."

She smiled again. "Well, that's a great name. It's nice to meet you, George. I'm Jessie."

He didn't meet her eyes but nodded. "I know. You already said your name."

"That's true. I did, didn't I?" She waited for a second before slowly making her way to her feet. "Hey, why don't you let me walk you back to your house? Away from these woods."

George looked over his shoulder at the two trees and slowly nodded, drawing himself up to his full height. Slowly, he walked past Jessie, heading back the way they had come. She followed, not wanting to frighten him further.

"George, I really meant you no harm. I know the man who lives at this house. Kerry. I didn't think anyone else would be here when I dropped by. Do you know Kerry?"

George nodded his head sharply. "Yes. Kerry is my brother. He takes care of me all the time. He's the best big brother."

Jessie nodded, walking slowly behind the man. They entered the back yard and Jessie stopped, looking around. In her haste to pursue, she hadn't really noticed what filled the yard. There were sculptures and figurines everywhere, made from bits and pieces of scrap metal and wood. The majority of the shapes were windmills of some type. Some in the shape of giant flowers, or spinning balls, while others mimicked animals or small children. All formed from bits of polished metal and siding, all painted in the same bright red as the weathervane and the front door.

And the X's that marked the trees.

"George," she said, looking around in awe. "These are very beautiful. Did you make them?"

He shook his head, a smile breaking out on his face. "No, Kerry made them for me. He said this is my safe place."

"I see. And is red your favorite color?"

He nodded quickly. "It's my only color."

She frowned and was about to speak when she saw

the look on his face. His eyes grew wide with fear as he focused on something over her shoulder. Before she could react, she felt the cold steel of a gun barrel pressed to the back of her head.

"You so much as twitch, and I'll blow your goddamn head off."

16

Family Bonds

Jessie didn't move. Her spine was stiff as a rod as she focused her attention on George. The man's expression told her he was grappling with a mixture of fear and confusion. Her heart was trip hammering as she recognized the gruff voice that had spoken.

She very slowly raised both hands, fingers spread wide. "Kerry, I'm not a threat to anyone here."

George's eyes widened in terror; his gaze fixed on his big brother. Jessie didn't need to turn around to take the measure of the man. She knew from the look on George's face that Kerry meant every word of the threat he had just uttered.

"What are you doing here?" Kerry said, his tone laced with anger. "You're trespassing on my property. And that gives me the right to shoot you in these parts of the woods."

Jessie didn't move, showing the man she was not a threat. "Kerry, listen to me. I'm not here to cause any trouble."

"Then why the hell are you sneaking around my house and harassing my brother?" Kerry demanded, the gun still pressed firmly against Jessie's head.

George stepped forward, his voice trembling. "K-Kerry, she wasn't hurting me. I swear. She just scared me was all. And... and I did exactly what you always told me to do if a stranger comes to get me. Pull the alarm and run and hide. Only, I got more scared out back...and Jessie was nice enough to come get me and bring me back home. Back to my garden where I'm safe."

"George, I'm going to need you to go back into the house now, okay? And I want you to go to your room and put your headphones on."

Jessie felt a chill creep up her back.

"Kerry, I'm sorry. I shouldn't have got scared. But it was my fault...she was really nice to me."

"It's okay, George. Inside now. And put your head-phones on."

Jessie watched as the young man shuffled off towards the house, giving one last forlorn look over his shoulder before closing the back door behind him. She took a deep breath and closed her eyes, waiting for the inevitable. With the barrel of a gun pressed against her head, there was nothing she would be able to do to protect herself.

Kerry leaned in close. "Now. What are you really doing here?" Jessie breathed a sigh of relief when he withdrew the gun and she heard the click of the safety sliding back in place.

Jessie spoke calmly, trying to defuse the situation. "Kerry, please. I'm just here because I had more questions after our conversation at the firehouse. Your behavior made me think you might know more about Marley's case than you were letting on. I'm not accusing you of anything, I just get the feeling that you might know something that could help steer my investigation."

Kerry let out a bitter laugh. "So, you decided to break into my home and interrogate my brother? That's a funny way of asking questions, Jessie."

She shook her head, her voice steady. "I didn't break in. I also had no idea you have a brother. I saw someone inside and I knew it wasn't you. I followed them out here. I just wanted to make sure everything was on the up and up."

There was a tense moment of silence before Kerry slowly lowered the gun. Jessie turned to face him, her heart still pounding in her chest.

"Come inside," Kerry said, his tone still laced with suspicion. His eyes darted to the back of the lot where the tree line began. "We'll talk there."

Jessie followed Kerry through the same door George had just entered. The thought briefly struck her that she should ask to bring Blizzard inside with her just in case Kerry decided she was indeed trespassing. But she also didn't want to antagonize the big man any further than she already had.

The inside of the house was dim, the only light came from the windows that dotted the family room where they now stood. Inside, Jessie could see the meticulous touch that had graced the fire station. While the outside of the house may have left something to be desired, the inside was spotless. The furniture, while slightly worn, was clean. The carpet showed signs of being recently vacuumed, and the slight scent of lemon in the air told her that the wood surfaces were dusted and polished.

Everywhere she looked, there were pops of red color decorating the small space.

Turning to Kerry, Jessie gave him a nod. "Kerry, I apologized to your brother for scaring him, and now I want to apologize to you as well. I should never have come to your house, especially when I thought you would not be home."

Kerry motioned towards the worn couch. He made his way across the room towards the small hall that it emptied into and stood there, listening. Satisfied they were alone he moved over to the chair next to Jessie. "I don't have anything to offer you to drink." His tone told her that even if he did, he probably wouldn't have offered.

"Thank you, but I'm fine."

"My brother is all I have," Kerry said, his voice low and strained. "The truth is, I would do anything to keep George safe. I'll be damned if I let anyone hurt him."

Jessie frowned. There was that word again. Hurt. She leaned forward, her elbows resting on her knees. "I understand that, Kerry. But what does that have to do with Marley's case? Who would try and hurt your brother?"

Kerry ran a hand through his hair, his eyes filled with a mixture of frustration and fear. "You don't get it, do you?

In this town, people like George... they're not accepted. They're seen as different, as a burden. I've spent my whole life protecting him from that cruelty."

Jessie waited a second before speaking up. "Is that who you taught him to be wary of? The people from town? The people you spend your days protecting?"

He gave her a sharp look. "Not exactly. Most people, they're fine. But there are elements here that see someone like George as prey. And I won't have that. You mentioned my wife earlier. Well, she left me some years ago, when George was a teen. He acted out a lot more back then, and she couldn't take it anymore." He gave Jessie a hard look that she couldn't decipher.

"It's obvious that he loves you, and you love him. You've built him something special here. You made all those figurines out there?"

Kerry nodded. "He loves to watch the wind move things. It makes him happy. When he was younger, he would stare at things like that for hours."

"And the color red?"

Kerry sighed. "He was born color blind. Well, almost. He can only see shades of the color red. When he was a boy, he'd sometimes wander off and couldn't tell this house from any other. That was when I painted the door red and put up that weathervane. So, he can always find his way home, no matter where he is."

"And the trees? That's why they are marked with a red X? Boundaries that aren't to be crossed?"

Kerry stiffened, narrowing his eyes. "Look, I know you're looking for answers here. And I know you mean well. To that end, I'm sorry for the way I treated you." He leaned forward. "But you're not going to find anything here. The best thing you can do is leave town, tell your client it was an accident, and don't look back." He could read the question in her eyes. "And no. That wasn't a threat. It was advice."

Jessie stood to leave, running her hands down the front of her jeans. "Well, thank you for the advice. And I will be leaving. As soon as I have finished my job."

Kerry pursed his lips into a thin line and shook his head. "I'll show you out." He headed out of the room and towards the front door. Jessie slowed, some of the framed pictures on the wall caught her attention.

"These are more of those haunting buildings from the fire station, aren't they?" she asked.

"Yeah. A man needs hobbies and now you've seen all of mine."

Jessie moved along the wall stopping before one in particular. "Are these the two trees out back? Before you painted the Xs on them?"

Kerry bit his lip, staring at the pictures longingly. He didn't answer, just moved to the front door and held it open. She walked past and he cleared his throat as she stepped out onto the porch. "Have a good day. And, Jessie? Don't come back here uninvited again."

Jessie nodded, knowing she had pushed her luck far enough for one day. At least with him.

She made her way to the Jeep and climbed in, taking a moment to reassure Blizzard that she was just fine. Her mind was racing, deciphering all the information she had gleaned, as she put the car in gear. She knew she should go back to the bed and breakfast and wait for Dr.

Lindquist. But there was something else that pulled at the back of her mind.

An idea that was as crazy as it was dark. She shouldn't do it. But she needed to test a theory, and that meant following her instincts down a literal dark path.

17

Discovery in the Shed

Jessie pulled her Jeep to the side of the road. She drove far enough to make sure she could not be seen by anyone in Kerry's house. She eased onto a densely packed trail that would obscure her vehicle from casual view. She looked ahead at the dense forest looming before her. She glanced at Blizzard, who sat alert in the back seat, his ears perked and his eyes fixed on the tree line.

"Ready, boy?" Jessie asked, her voice barely above a whisper. Blizzard's tail thumped against the seat in response.

Jessie stepped out of the Jeep and moved around to the passenger side where she opened the glove box and took out a few items. She let out a deep sigh as she clipped the Ka-Bar TDI knife to her belt. The hard plastic sheath was strangely reassuring standing in the shadows of the large trees. She looked at the remaining items lying on the seat. There was a black telescopic baton, mace, and a small but powerful taser. She clipped the taser to her belt as well, before reaching back into the glove compartment to pull out a dark green fanny pack, which she shoved everything else into and fastened around her waist.

Blizzard looked at her, head cocked curiously to one side.

"Don't judge me," Jessie said, adjusting the pack so that it sat on the center of her waistline. "It might not be the height of fashion, but it comes in handy."

She motioned for the shepherd to exit the vehicle, and he was at her side in a single, graceful leap. Together, they headed into the woods, the underbrush scratching at their legs. They moved parallel to Kerry's property, making their way through heavy growth until Jessie spotted the barest hint of the trail she had traversed when following George from Kerry's house.

She followed it until they reached the two trees marked in red. She stopped and looked down at Blizzard. She clenched her hands into fists. "No turning back now."

She looked down at her watch and activated the Track-Back navigation feature. It was designed to lead the wearer back to the point it was originally activated in the event they were to become lost. She had no idea what the terrain might become as they headed into the forest, but with the navigation on her watch, they'd be able to find their way back to the marked trees no matter where they ended up.

A half-mile into the trek and Jessie felt the woods begin to change. The air was thick with the scent of decay and the eerie silence that only a forest can possess. But the silence was too great. No skittering of animals, no crackling of branches under hoof. Even the insects didn't buzz. She watched Blizzard closely, his nose quivering in the air, ears perked. He was alert but didn't show any signs of possible danger.

They forged ahead and Jessie found that deeper into the forest, the path began to slowly widen, until it began to resemble the basis of a dirt road. The trees and canopy grew denser, but the trek was easier. She grew comfortable with the silence. The only sounds were the rustle of the leaves overhead and Blizzard's soft panting at her side.

She was beginning to question whether it had been worth her time venturing out, if they would find anything of use, when a weathered structure emerged from the foliage. It was a ramshackle structure, its wood gray and rotting, nearly consumed by the encroaching vegetation. Vines snaked up the walls, and the roof sagged under the weight of years of neglect.

Jessie approached cautiously, trying to make out just what it had been at one time. It had the barest, rudimentary details of a house. A door that had long ago fallen in, flanked by a single, glassless window. With Blizzard on her heels, she stepped closer and peered inside. It was a single room, wooden walls and no other entrance or exit to be seen. In one corner of the room was a hole cut into the rotting flooring. There were no signs of life, and she knew the structure was nowhere near sound enough to support her weight.

She kept walking and noticed that the dirt path she was on forked in a couple of directions. She followed one and almost immediately noticed another structure off the trail in the distance. This one looked even more like a house. The entire structure was leaning to one side, but there was definitely a tin roof sitting atop it.

The farther she walked, the more dilapidated buildings she came across. All set back from the trail, barely visible through the dense undergrowth and the vegetation that fought to reclaim it. She came to a small clearing and saw a tiny shed, with no visible windows, sitting near the edge of the trampled vines and weeds. Pausing, she bent down to examine the clearing and could make out definite patterns along the grass and vines leading to the shed. Unlike the other structures, this one looked like someone—or something—had recently visited.

She walked the short distance to the entrance of the shed and paused. Blizzard stuck close to her, his body tense and his hackles slightly raised. Jessie stood still, taking in everything about the building. It was as old as the others, but unlike the rest, had been kept up to some degree. Some of the wood siding looked newer in places, and the roof line seemed more intact. There were also two sturdy, iron, U-shaped bars bolted to either side of the door. Lying on the ground was a thick, wooden beam.

One that could fit perfectly into the U-bars, effectively preventing anyone opening the door from the inside.

Jessie hesitated a split-second before she extended her hand and pulled the door open.

Fetid air hit her immediately and she couldn't help but cover her face with a hand as she coughed. The pungent odor of old sweat and unwashed bodies hung in the air. The tang of urine and feces mingled with the mustiness of mildew and decay. Jessie turned her head to one side, the odor making her stomach churn. She fought herself, trying to stop her mind from racing back to her previous life.

She had smelled this before. In unregulated prison sites that had been liberated by soldiers. Places where humans faced the slow erosion of their dignity. This place had been used as a cell. But how long ago, she couldn't tell.

She forced herself to take a few steps inside, waiting for her eyes to adjust to the darkness. No light leaked into the space except for that from the doorway. She reached behind her and pushed it open as far as she could, letting in more daylight and fresh air. Her eyes took in the decrepit structure and she could see that it was as barren inside as out.

The only exception was something in the far corner that squatted in the near-dark. She made her way over to something that came up to her waist. It was covered in a black tarp and she pulled it away to reveal a stack of pallets. On top of it was a thin, threadbare mat, stained in ways she could not have imagined.

She took out her phone and turned on the flashlight feature to examine the stains. There were a multitude, but she zeroed in on the darker, rusty ones, trying to ignore the other patterns and smears that painted a grue-some picture of suffering. Taking out her knife, she pried splinters of the stained portion of the pallet away and shoved them into her fanny pack before turning to Bliz-zard. "I don't know about you, but I've had enough of this place."

The dog leaned in, pressing his weight against her leg, trying to support and comfort his human. Jessie turned and led them out of the hellish shed, pushing the door shut after exiting.

She stopped, whirling around to stare at the distant tree line at the same time that Blizzard's muscles stiff-ened. Something shuffled in the foliage. A shadow moved. Blizzard released a low growl from his chest. Jessie held out her arm, palm down, indicating that he was not to leave her side.

They both stood frozen. Jessie trained all her senses on the surrounding area until her instincts told her they were once again alone. She felt a cramping in her right hand and looked down. Without realizing it, she had been holding the hilt of her knife in a death grip. She released the blade and worked the numbness out of her fingers, before ushering Blizzard back onto the road the way they had come.

Before it was out of sight, she turned and took some pictures of the shed, and then snapped a few more of the ramshackle houses she passed on the way back to town. Questions swirled in her mind, each more disturbing than the last, as they hiked out of the woods. Her ears were attuned to the forest around her, and she kept a watchful eye on Blizzard's body language.

There were indeed dangerous animals in these woods. But these were animals that walked on two legs. As she reached the two trees just outside of Kerry's property, she had more questions than answers.

Something terrible had happened in that shed. And if it was the last thing she did, she was going to find out what.

18

Happy to See an Old Friend

Jessie's heart leaped when she pulled back into the bed and breakfast and saw the black sedan with medical coroner plates. The Jeep came to a stop next to it and she ushered Blizzard out, the two of them rushing up the stairs to the front door.

Inside, she paused as she passed Caroline. The older woman seemed distracted, her eyes red and unfocused. Jessie was used to the woman's affable greetings and happy demeanor. But now, she seemed lost in a world of melancholy.

"Caroline? Are you alright?"

The woman's eyes drifted over Jessie without really seeing her. Finally, recognition flowed over her features, and she gave Jessie a warm smile. "What? Oh, Jessie. Why yes, I'm just fine. Just been a long day for me. I'm a bit worn out and will probably turn in early tonight. Do you want me to fix you a plate?"

Jessie shook her head. "Maybe you should let me make something for you instead, so you can just relax."

The woman looked horrified. "Absolutely not. You are a guest here. You will not be doing any work, understand?"

Jessie smiled and nodded. "Well, can't blame me for trying."

"Oh, before I forget. Your friend arrived and I put him in the Jaybird room just down the hall from you." She turned and began shuffling towards the back of the house.

"Thank you, Caroline. Are you sure everything is okay?"

The woman half turned, her eyes dropping to the floor. "Oh yes, I'm just not as young as I like to think I am. Goodnight, Jessie."

She was lying, and Jessie knew it. But it wasn't her place to grill the woman. Everyone was entitled to a bad day every now and then.

She hurried up the stairs and headed down the hall away from her room. She found the suite with the Jaybird on it but hesitated to knock. A voice drifted through the thin wood door. If Dr. Lindquist was on the phone, she didn't want to disturb him. Turning, she headed back to her room and began pulling her shoes off. The bed elicited a sigh of relief as she sat down, thinking about how great a hot soak would feel for her aching muscles.

Her feet ached as she rubbed at the soles and forced her ankles to rotate in circles to try and relax the muscles. A soft tapping on the door caused her to look up at Dr. Lindquist. The smile that broke out on her face was radiant. "You have no idea how happy I am to see you," she said, standing to shake his hand.

He tried to act annoyed, but Jessie could see that he wasn't really in a bad mood. "Well, what can I say? Your case intrigued me once I started going through your notes and that atrocious autopsy report. Have you spoken to the doctor about his findings?"

She ushered him into the room and had him take a seat next to her. "No. He's on vacation. And I haven't been able to find out where or get a number for him from the sheriff."

"Well, that's a shame. I would have liked to speak with him as well. And what's your take on the sheriff?"

"Overall...he's a good man. I can tell he cares deeply about this community. But at the same time, there's something going on that I can't quite put my finger on." She proceeded to tell him everything that she had experienced up to that point, from her run-ins with Kerry and the mysterious stranger that attacked them in the morgue, to her most recent findings when she ventured deeper into the woods.

The medical examiner shook his head when she finished explaining everything. "Well, I don't know about you, but it doesn't sound like everything is on the up and up here. And I know you want to think the sheriff is a standup kinda guy, but in my experience, they always know what's going on in their town. Now what they choose to do with that info might vary; but they always know. And this business with the shed? Terrible. You're sure it was used to keep someone prisoner?"

She nodded gravely. "Trust me. I've seen this before. It's not something one forgets."

"What are you going to do next?"

She pursed her lips, a small crease forming in her forehead. "I've been thinking about that. I'm going to pay the receptionist that was attacked at the morgue a visit. See if she can provide me a description of who did that to her. Then, I need to get back out to those structures where I found that shed. My gut tells me there is more going on out there, and I need to figure out what. Oh yeah—" She reached for the fanny pack lying in the middle of the bed and opened it. "I took a splinter of wood from the pallet in that shed. Pretty sure this is blood, so maybe you can run a test on it."

The doctor arched an eyebrow at the piece of wood she held in her hand. "Well, I will head over to the morgue in the morning and take a look at the body and see if I can analyze...this, as well." He carefully took the wood from her. "Again, I can't guarantee you how much I'll be able to tell without being able to do a full autopsy, but I'll do my best. As far as you visiting that abandoned town, I'm not sure you should go alone. That isn't something I can help you with, but luckily, I brought along a friend who can." He nodded toward the doorway.

Jessie turned her head to see Alex standing there, smiling.

She was on her feet, wrapping her arms around him before she pulled quickly away.

"Oh, he gets that, and I get a handshake? I see how it is," Dr. Lindquist said, playfully.

Jessie felt a blush rising as she stepped back from the officer. "What are you doing here?"

Alex shrugged. "I have a ton of personal days that I need to either use or lose. So, I figured why not take a couple to check out this beautiful mountainside community I've heard so much about."

Jessie rolled her eyes. "Beautiful on the outside maybe. But something tells me the core may be a bit dirtier than it seems."

Alex sighed. "It always is. I understand we're visiting an abandoned town tomorrow?"

"It's the craziest thing. I've never seen anything like that place."

Dr. Lindquist stood up, looking from one to the other. "Well, you guys map out your fun. I'm going to go visit the kitchen. See if I can find a baggie or something to put this in." He waved the piece of darkened wood before giving the two of them a nod and excusing himself.

"It's good to see you. I'm glad you're here...even though I'm sure you could have found a hundred other uses for your days off," Jessie said.

"Something told me when you called the doc for help, that you could probably use more than just a medical examiner on your side."

She nodded. "You're not wrong. There's something off about this place. The people are nice enough...but so closed off and guarded. And before you say anything, it's not in a don't-trust-newcomers way. There's something not quite right. I just can't put my finger on it. Like, this town relies so heavily on tourism, but I've yet to see a single backpacker in town. And why does everything close so early here? And don't get me started on the animals in the woods that everyone seems to be so wary of...so having a second set of eyes is certainly appreciated."

"Well, my eyes are yours to use. I overheard most of what you told the doc, but is there anything you need to fill me in on that you didn't see fit to tell him?"

She walked over to the door and pushed it closed slightly. "Did you tell Caroline that you're with Pine Haven police?"

He shook his head. "No. I didn't see the need."

"Good. Let's keep that under wraps. Anyone asks, you're just a friend who came along for the ride with the doc."

"Got it. Have you found any allies here that you trust so far?"

Jessie knew what he was getting at. She hadn't planned on being in Bidonville this long. She had thought it would be an open and shut case. The deeper she dug, the more she was finding. The longer this case went on, the more likely it would be that she would need a local in her corner. "Not sure yet. I'm working with a Deputy Hardin. He seems genuine, doesn't seem to have an agenda. But the jury's still out."

"And the kid?"

"You mean the sheriff's nephew? He seems like any other kid I've ever met from a potentially broken home. Sullen. Withdrawn. Why?"

"A lot of time, kids see and hear a lot more than adults realize. Because a lot of time they may seem withdrawn and in their own little world, adults stop seeing and often say things around them they might not around other adults. And kids are like sponges. They absorb everything."

Jessie nodded thoughtfully. "Excellent idea. Maybe we can find time to meet with him after visiting the hospital tomorrow."

Silence crept into the room followed by the awkward tension that sometimes follows.

"Alright. I'm going to hit the sheets," Alex said. "I have to share a bed with the doc, and he already warned me he's a snorer."

"I'll see you in the morning. Oh, and Caroline puts out a good spread. So, we can at least fuel up before heading out."

Alex smiled as he stepped out of the room. "Sounds good. Sleep tight, Jess."

"You too." She closed the door after him, reflexively locking it, and plopped down on the bed. She felt lighter than she had since setting foot in Bidonville. She didn't realize how soothing it was to her nerves to have Alex at her side. She glanced down at the shepherd, his eyes slowly closing as he drifted off. Tomorrow was going to be a long day. But it would also be a day that might bring her one step closer to wrapping up this case. And that meant one day closer to going home.

She showered, then retrieved the knife she had taken into the woods with her and placed it under her pillow.

Just in case.

The thought barely registered and she was deep asleep.

19

Everything by the Book

The next morning Jessie, Alex, and Dr. Lindquist met in the kitchen just after the sun had cast its first lights through the mountain mist. They were greeted by a robust pot of freshly brewed coffee, as well as a complement of scrambled eggs, bacon, waffle strips and breaded chicken tenders, all lined up along the counter in silver warming trays.

"Wow," said Alex. "You weren't kidding. This lady knows what she's doing."

"Well, I've been cooking all my life, so I would hope so."

They turned to see Caroline walking into the kitchen with a mischievous smile spreading across her face.

"Good morning, Caroline. You've gone above and beyond with this," Jessie said, indicating the breakfast laid out before them.

The older woman waved her hand dismissively in the

air. "Nonsense. I like to cook and having guests in the house just gives me even more of a reason. And before I forget, in that pot on the stove is some warm maple syrup, maybe with just a hint of brandy." She put her hand over her mouth to suppress a schoolgirl's giggle. "But don't tell anyone."

Alex gave her a conspiratorial laugh. "Oh, I'm not saying a word about it. Just means that much more for me."

Caroline's eyes went big as she gave his arm a playful tug.

"Will your husband be joining us?" Jessie asked.

The woman's mirth melted away, and Jessie saw the same pained look she had given her the night before. She blinked her eyes rapidly and looked away, turning to the cabinets over the counter. "No, not this morning. He leaves the house early during the week. But maybe tomorrow." She pointed at the cabinets she had just opened. "Dishes and cups are there. Silverware is in the first drawer to your left. I'll leave you to it." Her shoulders slumped as she turned to leave them.

Jessie's eyes lit up as a thought crossed her mind. "Caroline, would it be okay if I left Blizzard with you today? I'm going to be out with my friends, working on this case, and it would be very helpful if I could leave him behind. If that's alright, I mean."

She half turned, the sparkle returning to her eyes. "Oh, that would be lovely, dear. It would be no problem at all."

"Thank you," Jessie said. "He likes you. And he's very protective of the people he likes."

Caroline considered her words and nodded. "I suppose he is. But yes. Just let me know when you're leaving, and he can join me in the study. I've some needle point that I've been neglecting." She left the kitchen and Jessie listened as her feather-light shuffle disappeared down the hall.

Alex gave her a curious glance, but she waved him off and pointed to the food laid out before him. "Eat up, gentleman. It's going to be a long day."

THE MORGUE WAS JUST as quiet and cold as it had been the night Jessie and Deputy Hardin had surprised the intruder. Hardin hadn't sounded too happy to get her call, but he agreed to meet with her at the gray and brick building. He was waiting in the parking lot, leaning against the driver's side door of his squad car, when they arrived.

Jessie nodded at the officer and introduced her companions. "Deputy Hardin, this is Dr. Lindquist. He's the medical examiner for Pine Haven and will be examining Marley's body."

The deputy nodded and gave the doctor's hand a reluctant shake. "Yeah, Sheriff Cormac said it was okay to let you in, but that I'm to stay with you the whole time."

Jessie nodded. "After what happened last time we were here, I'm all in favor of that. I'm going to go over to the hospital and see if Peggy might remember anything about who attacked her."

Deputy Hardin gave her a questioning look. "What

are you doing that for? I'm sure Peggy needs her rest. Plus, her attack is a police matter, and does not pertain to what you are here for. Did Sheriff Cormac sign off on this?"

Jessie looked around. "I haven't seen him. But feel free to run it by him. But that intruder we interrupted was caught with Marley's medical record in his hands, so that may or may not connect them to my case. I really won't know until I ask her a few questions." She started to leave but didn't want to leave things with the deputy like that. Especially given the fact that he would be responsible for watching after Dr. Lindquist. "I'm sorry. Don't worry, I'll be very respectful. I'll share everything she tells me. It will help you bring the monster who hurt her to justice."

Deputy Hardin thought for a second and then gave her a stern nod. "Keep me informed."

She gave him a smile then motioned with her head for Alex to follow her out. She saw Hardin's eyes track Alex across the room. The deputy was astute, and undoubtedly something about the way Alex carried himself had given him away. But no questions were asked, and Jessie wasn't about to volunteer anything that might rock that boat.

Outside of the morgue, they climbed into Jessie's Jeep.

"Your friend Hardin knows. That I'm a cop, I mean," Alex said as he clicked his seatbelt.

"Maybe. But if we can get this case closed soon it won't matter. Hardin is a stickler for doing everything by the book. He won't make a move without the sheriff giving him permission. And the sheriff is missing in action this morning. Chances are, we can get a lot accomplished before Hardin has a chance to run anything up the chain."

She pulled out of the station and pointed the Jeep north towards the town's community hospital. They pulled into the small parking lot of the two story, brick structure, and both marveled at the tiny footprint of the hospital.

"I thought Pine Haven was a tiny town," said Alex as he climbed out of the Jeep. "But it's practically a metropolitan compared to this place."

Jessie led them into the building and to the front desk reception area. She greeted the older woman sitting behind the desk with the biggest smile she could muster. "Hello—" she glanced down at the name printed on the woman's badge, "—Ms. O'Brien. We are here to visit a friend of ours named Peggy Sawyer. Could you tell me what room she's in?"

Ms. O'Brien lowered her head, staring first at Jessie and then Alex over the top of her glasses. "The two of you are friends of Peggy's? Cos I am a friend of Peggy and I've never seen you around before."

Jessie refused to let the woman see her frustration and instead just gave her another warm smile. "Oh, that's strange. Well, I was the person who found her at the morgue and called for help. I just wanted to make sure she was okay. Such terrible business you know."

The woman narrowed her eyes at her, letting out a sigh. "It really was awful. Who could do such a thing?"

"That's actually what I hope to find out. I just have a couple of questions for her that might help catch the person that did this."

Ms. O'Brien leaned forward and took two tags with the word VISITOR printed on them. "Wear these. She's on the second floor. Room 203."

Jessie and Alex made their way to the elevators that took them up one flight, the doors opening to a small nursing station. Neither of the two women at the station looked up from what they were doing as Jessie and Alex followed the signage to Peggy's room.

The small, rural hospital seemed to be operating at a sluggish pace. As they passed room after room, they didn't see any other patients or staff members on the floor. A short walk placed them outside of a small, dark room. The only light flowing in was from a tiny window near the ceiling against the outer wall. Opposite the window was a single bed with an elderly woman lying propped up against two pillows. Her hands were crossed peacefully over her chest and if it weren't for the rhythmic beeping of her monitor, Jessie would have sworn the woman was dead.

Jessie approached her bedside, her footfall soft on the linoleum flooring. She gently placed a hand on Peggy's arm, careful not to startle the woman. "Ms. Sawyer? Peggy? Can you hear me?"

Peggy's eyes fluttered open, confusion clouding her features as she took in faces she didn't recognize. She blinked a few times, her gaze sharpening as she studied Jessie and Alex. "Who are you?" Her voice was hoarse, a mixture of fear and suspicion.

Alex stepped forward, his arms raised in a non-threatening manner. "My name is Alex Thomas, and this is

Jessie Night. She's a private investigator working on a case here in Bidonville and I'm helping her out."

Jessie continued, speaking in the same soft tones Alex had started. "We'd like to ask you a few questions about what happened to you. Do you remember how you came to be here in the hospital?"

The woman's eyes narrowed to slits. "I already told the police everything I know. Why are you here?" She struggled to sit up, wincing with the effort.

Jessie felt a tug in her heart at the woman's distress, but they needed answers. "Someone from the police was already here to speak with you?"

The woman pursed her lips tightly but nodded. "A man. Young thing, about your age. I told him what I knew."

Jessie's eyes trailed over to Alex before she returned her attention to Peggy. "Well, we aren't with Bidonville Police. But I think the person that put you in this bed might be tied to a death I'm investigating. Would you mind telling me what you told the police officer?"

"If you're after the person that did this, then you would be working with the police. Wouldn't they share my statement with you?"

Jessie gave her a stiff smile. "At some point, yes. But the longer we take to get on the same page, the greater the chance that whoever did this to you might slip away."

Peggy huffed, rolling her eyes as she turned her head to one side. "Pssh. He ain't going nowhere."

Alex looked confused. "You say that like you know who attacked you. Do you know them?"

She swiveled her head around, leveling her gaze at

Alex. "Now why the hell would someone hit me in the back of the head if we knew each other?"

Jessie took a breath, steadying herself. "Peggy. Anything you can tell us, no matter how small it might seem, could help. Just start from the beginning."

Peggy's fingers twisted the thin hospital blanket as she drew it up around her. "I was working late, trying to catch up on paperwork. I like to take advantage of Doc Miller being out of town to do that, and I heard a noise coming from the back of the morgue. I went to investigate and that's when the man attacked me. That's all I remember."

Jessie leaned forward. "But I thought you were found in the break room."

Peggy shrugged. "Maybe that's where I was. I'm old and get confused a lot."

Jessie regarded her, weighing her words. Peggy was definitely old, but she didn't really seem confused. Contrary. But not confused. "Can you describe the man? Did you see his face? Any identifying features you might recall?"

Peggy's eyes shifted away from Jessie. "Identifying features? Like what?" She began fidgeting with the blanket again. "I don't remember anything other than he was bigger than me."

Jessie took in the woman's diminutive frame. She took up practically no room in the single bed. Bigger than her was most of the town. "Did he seem at all familiar? Like, maybe he reminded you of someone you've seen around town?"

The woman crossed her arms, clearly becoming more and more annoyed at the line of questioning. "No, I'm sure I've never seen him before in my life. I don't know anyone who would do something like this."

Alex stepped forward, but the look Peggy shot him stopped him in his tracks.

The woman grunted as she wrestled her body back against the mattress. "I'm tired. Y'all are wearing me out down to the bones. I've told you all I know. Now leave an old woman to get a bit of peace." She rested her head back and closed her eyes, slamming the door on any more discussions.

"Thank you for your time, ma'am," Jessie said.

They made their way to the door and Alex took his phone out, frowning at the screen. "Well, as fun as that was, we need to get over to the morgue. Apparently, Doc Lindquist has already found something we need to see."

20

A More Thorough Exam

Jessie white-knuckled the steering wheel as she guided the Jeep towards the morgue. "She was lying."

Alex looked over her, perturbed. "What?"

"Peggy. She was lying to us. She knows more about who did this to her than she's letting on."

"How can you be so sure?"

"Her whole vibe was off. She seemed more annoyed than anything at the fact we were there. Why wouldn't you want to do all you could to help catch the bastard that put you in the hospital? Plus, she mixed up where the attack occurred. First it was in the morgue proper and then the break room. Also, she was parroting me."

Alex's eyes grew wide. "Like when you asked about details regarding the attacker's physical description and she repeated that back to you. I learned about that in the detective's training."

Jessie nodded. "It usually happens when they are stalling, trying to think of the most plausible lie."

"But don't you think some of this can be attributed to her age? I mean, taking a hit to the back of the head at any age can be rough. I can't imagine how she must feel."

Jessie chewed her inner cheek in consideration. "Possibly. But speaking of that, did you notice there was no bandage of any kind on her head? She didn't act like it hurt either. Something is off. I feel like she's covering for someone. But why?"

They pulled into the morgue parking and Jessie eased the Jeep to a stop next to Dr. Lindquist's black sedan.

"Hopefully, the doc will be able to provide some clues," Alex said.

It was a short walk to the small refrigerator room where Jessie had surprised the intruder and that was where they found Deputy Hardin and Dr. Lindquist standing over the body of Marley Shaffer. She had been placed on a rolling stretcher that was acting as a makeshift examination table.

Marley's naked body was covered by a thin sheet. Only her shoulders and head were exposed, and even that was enough to make Jessie avert her eyes. Even though the dead always had a serene look on their face, there was an indignity about a body lying in such a sterile setting, being gawked at by strangers. That never sat right with her. "That was fast. What did you find?"

He lowered his chin, staring at her over the top of his glasses. "It's more like what I didn't find." He walked around to Marley's side. "As you can imagine, I was not permitted to open the body. Because again, I'm not here in any official capacity. But I was able to look inside another way."

On the table next to the stretcher, Jessie saw a coiled, black, snake-like hose with what looked like a camera attached to one end. "What's that?"

"It's a bronchoscope. When you told me the victim had drowned, I brought it with me thinking it might come in handy. There's a high-definition camera lens at the tip that I can snake through the nose and down into the lungs. The hose is attached to a camera at one end that allows me to take photographs of what I see." He turned to indicate his laptop which sat next to the bronchoscope. He pressed a button and it flared to life. On the screen were images in varying shades of pink and white.

"What are we looking at, Doc?" Alex asked.

The medical examiner began flipping through images. "These are images of the airways and lungs from inside Marley's body. I was able to fly through the trachea, bronchi, smaller airways...everything. Even her alveolar sacs—in the deeper part of the lungs where gas exchange occurs—" he pointed to small, rounded structures that resembled bunches of grapes, "—and everything is perfectly clear. This young woman was in exceptionally good health."

Jessie pinched her chin between thumb and forefinger as she stared at the images. "So, no sign of water in the lungs?"

Dr. Lindquist shook his head. "Not even a hint. This woman was dead long before she was dumped in the water."

Jessie lifted her head and stared at Deputy Hardin. The man was standing back from them, the muscles of his jaw clenching and unclenching. "Looks like this wasn't an accident after all."

The doctor looked up from the laptop and removed his glasses. "That's not all. With this finding, I convinced the deputy here to let me draw some tissue samples and do a further, deeper evaluation of the body. Again, there were no signs of struggle that indicate she may have been thrashing about in water. Fast-moving rivers are filled with rocks and vegetation. Someone trying to save themself from drowning would have flailed about, grabbing at anything they could...it's human nature. But there are no signs of broken nails, no bruising from being slammed against anything. Nothing." He lifted one of the woman's arms. "And then there's this. There are signs of muscular atrophy in her limbs and face. For someone with such a healthy respiratory system, her body was fairly emaciated."

"She was starved," Jessie said, her voice little more than a whisper.

The doctor was nodding. He took a deep breath. "There are also signs of...deep bruises along the inner thighs and pelvis. A further physical exam also shows that her vagina was enlarged at the time of her death. I was able to palpate her pelvis, and the symphysis pubis— the joint located at the front of the pelvis—is separated. Normally, I would need an x-ray to see this, but with her emaciated state, it was pretty obvious." He looked up at Jessie.

Alex's voice trembled. "What are you saying?"

Jessie swallowed the lump that had been forming in her throat. "He's saying she was pregnant. That she just gave birth."

There was a silence in the room that threatened to smother them. Finally, Dr. Lindquist cleared his throat. "We need to do a more invasive examination. I need to collect deep blood and tissue samples from her. If I can collect them from the pelvis and uterus, I can tell more about the baby...find out what exactly may have been going on." His head turned in the direction of Deputy Hardin.

The officer nodded. "Do it. Use whatever equipment you need here in the medical facility. I'll let Sheriff Cormac know."

"Do we need to wait for his blessing?" Jessie asked.

Hardin shook his head, his eyes hardening. "No. The sheriff hasn't been responding to my calls today, so just go ahead. I'll take the heat on this when I reach him." He started to leave the room and stopped, turning to face the medical examiner. "Can you tell... I mean, is the baby still alive?"

Dr. Lindquist shrugged. "I can't tell if it was a live birth. Yet. But hopefully the tissue samples can help with that."

Hardin didn't speak, just turned and left the room.

"Christ," said Alex. "What the hell is happening in this town?"

Jessie ground her teeth until her jaw ached. "There's someone out there doing horrible things." She looked at the body lying on the gurney. "And something tells me Marley wasn't the first victim." She drew in a sharp breath and looked at the medical examiner. "Thank you. For moving so quickly. Were you able to get the analysis on that blood sample I gave you earlier?"

"Still running," he replied. "This isn't exactly state-of-the-art equipment up here. But I should have that answer for you shortly."

She nodded, then turned, leaving the room with Alex trailing behind her. In the parking lot, they found Hardin pacing in circles, speaking into his phone. His voice was harsh, his words fast and clipped. He saw them approaching and finished his call.

"Just left a message for the sheriff. I'm heading over to his place to fill him in," he said.

"Is this normal?" Jessie asked. "That your boss just goes incommunicado while you're working a case?" Her tone was harsher than she intended but she didn't care.

He didn't answer, but something in his features told her what she needed to know.

"Hardin, if there is something more I need to know..."

He didn't answer right away. "You know what I know."

She glared at him before taking her phone out. "What about this? Do you know anything about these?" She called up the photos of the ramshackle buildings she had taken in the woods.

Hardin's face went noticeably pale as he studied the photos. "Where did you get these?"

Jessie placed her phone back in her pocket. "I took them. A couple of miles hike through the woods."

His face went dark. "Are you crazy? You can't just go wandering through the woods around here like that."

Jessie snapped. "And why not? And don't give me that shit about dangerous animals."

The look on his face was one of exasperation mixed with genuine concern. "I told you. The woods aren't safe. They are easy to get lost in and there are sheer drops in places that you can't see until it's too late. If you don't know they're there then you can take a fall that will break your neck. We don't have the resources that big cities might have if something happens."

Jessie placed her hands on her hips. "Oh, I'm calling bullshit. This town is supposed to be dependent on tourism but I've yet to see a single backpacker coming through here. And if it's so dangerous to go into the woods, why would you even promote this place?"

The officer opened his mouth to answer but was interrupted by his phone buzzing. He looked at the screen before raising it to his ear. After a couple of nods, he spoke. "I'll be right there." He turned to Jessie. "That was the sheriff. He's back at the station and needs to see me right away. I'll fill him in on everything that's happening." He turned to face Alex. "I assume you're carrying? If not, you might want to reconsider."

And with that, he climbed into his squad car and pulled away.

"What now?" Alex asked.

Jessie turned to her friend. "We find the only other person in this town who seems willing to talk. The sheriff's nephew." She hesitated before voicing her next question. "Do you have another gun with you?"

He arched his eyebrow. "I do. Back at the room."

She let out a breath. "Good. Because after we speak to the kid, I'm going back out into the woods. Hardin knows something about those buildings I showed him. And now I want to know what it is."

21

Nasty Bruises

When they turned onto the road leading to the school, Jessie thought maybe Roger hadn't been embarrassed about the school seeing her, but the other way around. She pulled into the parking lot and killed the engine. The building itself reminded her of an old warehouse someone had slapped a coat of rust-colored paint on and added a few rounded windows to the front. It was surrounded by a small plot of land, with a patch of grass serving as a makeshift playing field and a handful of picnic tables scattered about for outdoor lunches. To one side a rusted metal swing set and a couple of tetherball poles stood, making Jessie wonder what age range the school serviced.

The parking lot was small, but fairly full, and parked end to end were two small yellow school buses to one side. Off to one side of the building were two smaller structures that resembled raised trailers. Jessie frowned at the outbuildings. The town barely seemed large enough to support one school, let alone have a need for overflow classrooms.

No one stopped or greeted them as they walked into the building, the double doors opening to a gleaming, high polished hallway with blue and gray metal lockers along either side. Alex pointed to a door to the left marked 'Principal's Office'.

Jessie drew in a breath as they headed for it. "I know I said not to, but this might end up being a good time to flash your badge if it comes to it."

Alex nodded his agreement as she pushed the door open and stepped into the office. There was no counter or bell to announce their arrival. They literally stepped into a small, cramped room. Jessie took in the cluttered space with a quick glance. There was a single, tiny window that looked out over the playground cut into a wall that was lined with filing cabinets and bookshelves. In the center of the room sat a large wooden desk, its surface barely visible beneath stacks of paperwork and half-empty coffee mugs.

The too-small desk combined with the poor lighting gave the room the overall feel of something that was an afterthought; not part of the general design of the school. Behind the desk, a severe-looking woman in her late fifties peered at Jessie over the rims of her glasses, her expression one of barely concealed annoyance.

When she spoke, her tone was clipped and impatient. "May I help you?"

Jessie extended a hand in greeting as she looked at the name plate sitting on the woman's desk. "Principal

Hawking, my name is Jessie Night. This is Alex Thomas. I'm a private investigator from Pine Haven and I was wondering if I could have a moment of your time?"

The principal pursed her lips and stared. "You can have exactly one minute. That's all I can give you today. What can I help you with?"

"We were wondering if we could speak with a student that goes here. His name is Roger. I'm not sure about his last name. He's the nephew of Sheriff Cormac, and while I know it's not standard protocol to speak with a minor without their guardian present—"

Principal Hawking held up a hand. "Let me stop you right there, Ms. Night. No, you may not speak to this child because you are correct in that it would be against our school policy. But also, you may not speak with them because there is no child by that name enrolled in this school."

Her words startled Jessie for a moment. "Roger would be new. I believe he just transferred in not long ago. He's only staying with his uncle temporarily."

The principal dropped her chin to her chest, leveling Jessie and Alex with a fixed gaze. "I don't care how temporary they are supposed to be. I know every child that enrolls in this school be it for a day or a year, and I'm telling you that one does not exist. And you say they are Sheriff Cormac's nephew? Well, that can't be."

"Why not?" asked Alex.

"Because in order for him to have a nephew he would have to have a sibling. And he doesn't have one. And before you say anything, neither does his wife. I've known both of them since they were no taller than ants and they are both only children." She looked from one to the other. "Now. If you'll excuse me, I have real work to do by the end of the day." She didn't wait for a response but lowered her eyes back to the stack of papers she had been entrenched in, leaving Jessie and Alex to make their way back out the door.

They stopped in the parking lot, Jessie staring at the cracked pavement. "Alex, what the hell is going on here?"

The officer shook his head. "And you're sure this kid was enrolled here? That he wasn't just staying with the sheriff until his mother returned?"

She thought for a moment before giving him an imploring look. "Alex, I dropped him off here myself. Hardin told me about the boy's mother—the sheriff's sister—so, yes, I know he is going here."

"Did you see him actually walk in?"

She frowned. "No. I didn't. Come on." She led Alex around the side of the building to the back where it opened to reveal a dirt running track with a few rows of aluminum bleachers to one side. There, sitting on one of the metal seats, was Roger. His head was lowered, resting on folded arms balanced on knobby knees.

"Roger?" Jessie asked as they approached.

He looked up startled, grabbing for his backpack. When his eyes landed on Alex, he looked like he might bolt but stopped at the sound of Jessie's voice.

"Wait. We aren't here to cause any problems for you," she said. She drew closer and got a look at his face. "What the—Roger, who did this to you?"

The teen's face was bruised badly under one eye and his nose was bleeding. He dropped a crimson tissue he had been unsuccessfully trying to use to staunch the bleeding. He turned away, trying to hide his features.

"Nothing. Nobody did anything. I just...I fell. I'm clumsy like that," he replied, bending to retrieve his tissue. He nodded in Alex's direction. "Who's this?"

"He's a friend of mine," Jessie said. "He was passing through and stopped for a visit."

Roger narrowed his eyes. "Passing through? Yeah, right. Because so many roads lead through Bidonville on the way to better destinations."

Alex gave the boy a look. "You're right. I'm not just passing through. I'm here to help Jessie with her case. You gonna tell us who hit you?"

The boy turned but winced deeply, grabbing at his midsection.

Jessie reached to help steady him and eased him back down to the bleachers. "How bad is it?" She nodded towards his chest.

Roger let out a rattled cough. "Just the wind knocked out of me...or so I thought. Might have cracked a rib."

Jessie shook her head. "Okay, we're taking you to see a friend of ours—"

Roger gave her a panicked look. "No. It will just make it worse."

Jessie glanced Alex's way before responding. "Our friend's a doctor. Not one affiliated with the town, so you don't have to worry about who he might say something to. Just let him have a look and then you can be on your way."

The boy looked around reluctantly, his eyes settling on the school. "And no one will know?"

Jessie shook her head as they walked back towards the parking lot. "No one." Once he was settled in the back of the Jeep, she climbed behind the wheel, waiting for him and Alex to buckle up. "I apologize in advance for the bumpy ride. But I'll try and miss the really big potholes." She eased the vehicle out of the lot and onto the main road, looking up occasionally at the boy in the back seat. "Roger. Why haven't you been going to school?"

There was no answer forthcoming and Jessie was tempted to let it drop. But there was a reason she had wanted to talk to the teen in the first place and that meant getting him to open up. "I'm sure it's a shock being here, compared to what you're used to. I bet the culture here is very different." His answer was a huff of air that told her a lot without saying anything. "As an adult, it's been hard for me to relate to a lot of what I'm seeing here in Bidonville. I can't imagine what it must be like for you. Does your uncle know what you're going through with school? That you're not even enrolled here?"

He turned to look into the rearview mirror, locking eyes briefly with her. "I don't go to school because I don't belong there. I don't really belong anywhere. I'm just waiting to go back to my real home."

Jessie didn't speak, letting his words hang in the air.

"Did the other kids do that to you?" Alex asked.

Roger's tone was sharp when he answered. "No."

Jessie thought back to what the principal had told them. "Roger, I didn't catch your mother's name. What was it again? And is she Sheriff Cormac's sibling or his wife's?"

This time the teen squirmed in his seat. "Why are you asking?"

Jessie cut her eyes to the road in front of her. "Just curious about the sheriff is all. I know he's been under a lot of stress with the job and the death of Marley Shaffer. I was just making sure that you're getting the support you need at a time like this in your life. That's all." She gave a quick glance to Alex. "Do you ever hear him talking about work? Or that horrible accident?"

Roger shrugged. "He talks about it every now and then. Not often. But I'm pretty sure he doesn't think it's an accident."

Jessie sensed the sudden tension in Alex as he turned in his seat. "What makes you say that?"

"Just the few times it's come up, I've heard the way he says accident to Aunt Irma. He doesn't make the quotes in the air with his fingers when he says it; but his voice does."

Jessie gripped the wheel harder. "Do you know if he has any suspects?"

"No idea. They shut up around me a lot. Once, when I walked in on them talking, I heard Aunt Irma say she wouldn't put it past him. But I don't know who they were talking about."

They arrived at the morgue and Jessie threw the car in park, before hopping out to help Roger.

Roger looked around frowning. "The morgue? What kind of doctor is this friend of yours? Does he even know how a live body works?"

Jessie was about to deliver a smart retort when Deputy Hardin exited the building in a hurry, rushing towards his car. Behind him, Dr. Lindquist hurried, trying his best to keep up with the deputy.

"What's going on, doc?" Alex asked, just as Hardin jumped into his cruiser and sped off. "I thought Hardin was with the sheriff?"

Dr. Lindquist was out of breath as he approached. "He was. He came back to tell me the sheriff was fine with me doing what I needed to. Then he got a call. Apparently, there's been a death in town."

Jessie's eyes widened. "Who?"

The medical examiner frowned in concentration. "Someone named...Carry. Or...Kerry. Yes. Someone named Kerry."

Jessie turned to the doctor. "This is Roger. He's got a black eye, bloody nose, and can you check his ribs? We'll be back in a bit." Before the confused examiner could answer, she was behind the wheel, Alex at her side, pulling out of the parking lot.

22

_____

No More Happy Memories

The commotion at the little house with the red door started before Jessie had even reached the house. The street was lined with cars, many of whom seemed to be neighbors who had heard about the fireman's death. But there was also an ambulance and a couple of police cruisers, including the sheriff's SUV. Jessie came to a stop on the side of the road and made her way towards the house, followed closely by Alex.

A police officer dressed in gray jeans and a flannel top stopped her at the door. "Ma'am, you can't come in here. This is an active crime scene." His hand slid closer to the gun on his waist.

"It's okay. She can come in." Sheriff Cormac's voice floated from somewhere just over the officer's shoulder. The policeman stepped aside, allowing Jessie and Alex to push past.

"Sheriff Cormac," Jessie said, stepping up to the man. "What happened?"

The sheriff looked tired, his shoulders sagging as he eyed Alex suspiciously.

"This is Alex Thomas. We work together down in Pine Haven. He caught a ride up with the medical examiner," Jessie said.

The sheriff nodded at Alex then turned his attention to Jessie. "It's Kerry. Looks like he took his own life."

Jessie's mouth dropped in shock. "What? Why...I mean, that doesn't make sense. I just saw him. He seemed fine." Her eyes grew wide with concern. "George. What about George?"

The sheriff pointed down the hallway. "He's in his bedroom. He was the one who found the body."

Jessie's hand covered her mouth. "Oh no. Can I see him?"

The sheriff hesitated then nodded. "He hasn't spoken since we got here."

Jessie took a deep breath and turned to head down the hall. Alex stopped her with a hand on her arm. "Jessie, if it's alright with the sheriff, I'd like to stay out here...see the crime site." He turned to the sheriff. "I won't get in the way. Promise."

Sheriff Cormac eyed him up and down. "No civilians allowed, I'm afraid."

Alex looked questioningly at Jessie, and she nodded. He fished in his jacket and found his detective's badge, showing it to the older man.

The sheriff gave Jessie a hard stare before letting out a

weary sigh. "This way." Jessie turned back to the hallway as Alex and Sheriff Cormac moved away.

At the end of the hall, she found a door half open. She knocked gently. "George? It's Jessie. Are you here?" There wasn't an answer, so she pushed the door slowly open, peering inside. George was sitting on the foot of the bed, not moving, his shoulders hunched and his eyes fixed on the carpet.

Jessie approached him slowly, her footsteps soft on the carpeted floor. She lowered herself onto the bed beside him, careful to maintain enough space between them that he wouldn't feel threatened. "George?" Her voice was soothing and gentle. "I heard about your brother. I can't begin to imagine what you must be feeling right now."

George didn't answer but Jessie thought she saw his lower lip tremble.

"Would it be okay if I just sit here with you for a minute? We don't have to speak."

Again, no answer. Jessie turned her body to focus on the floor in front of her, mimicking George's body position. They sat like that in silence. Jessie was acutely aware of the sounds going on both inside the house and out. Voices called out, sirens blared, doors opened and closed.

And still they sat in silence. She had no idea how much time passed before George finally spoke.

His voice was low, trembling with emotions. "He's gone," he whispered. "I tried to get him down...but I couldn't."

The rawness in his voice cut through Jessie like a knife. She reached out to place a hand on his arm, but he flinched away from her touch. "I know, George. I'm sorry you had to go through that. No one should ever have to experience that."

He remained motionless as tears began to run down his face. "What did I do? I can't figure out what I did that made him want to leave me."

Jessie felt a lump forming in her throat. Her own voice sounded weak when she spoke. "George, I don't think there is anything that you could have done to make this happen. If...if Kerry hurt himself, it wasn't because of you."

"Then why? I thought he loved me. He always said he did. Is this what people do to someone they love?"

Jessie exhaled softly as she wrestled with her own emotions. She wanted to tell him no...but experience had taught her that you never know why someone might hurt themself. "George, I am sorry to ask this, but can you tell me what happened? What you remember?"

He lifted his head slightly, his eyes focusing on something in the distance. "We had just finished lunch. Kerry made me fish sticks because he knows I like those. We were talking about our fishing trip this weekend and I told him I was going to catch the biggest fish. Then, he told me to clean up the kitchen while he went out and finished painting one of the new metal spinners he made me in the back yard. I did the dishes and put them away just like he taught me and was starting to sweep the floor. That was when Kerry came back in and told me to go to my room and put on my headphones. I did that, like always. I was waiting for him to come tell me it was okay to take them off, but he never came back. He always came back to tell me when it was okay to take them off. I got tired of waiting and took them off myself...even though I know I'm not supposed to. I went outside to see what he was doing and..." His voice trailed off and his body tensed.

"It's okay. You don't have to go back to that memory," Jessie whispered.

He was quiet again. Not moving. Barely breathing. "What do I do now?" For the first time, he turned his face to Jessie. "I don't know what to do. Kerry took care of me. He said he always would. Who will do that now?"

Jessie felt the fear underneath the man's questions, and it was all she could do not to break down. "You are going to be okay, George. I know it might not seem like it right now, in this moment, but I am certain you are going to be taken care of."

"I don't want to go back. Kerry said I would never have to go back."

Jessie frowned to herself. "Back where, George?"

He didn't answer, just resumed staring off into space.

Jessie had a thought and turned to the man. "George, you said Kerry told you to put your headphones on and go to your room. He does that when he doesn't want you to hear something, right? Was anyone in the house when he told you to do that?"

George shook his head. "No. They didn't come in."

"So, someone was here visiting with Kerry? Do you know who it was?"

"No. I didn't see anyone. I was in the kitchen when the car pulled up. But I only heard it. Didn't see it."

Jessie placed a tentative hand on his shoulder. This

time he didn't pull away. "George, I'm going to find someone for you to talk to about all of this. They are going to help you, okay. Are you alright staying here until someone comes for you?"

He only nodded, more silent tears starting to stream down his face. Jessie gave his shoulder a squeeze and stepped out of the room, pulling the door behind her. She hurried back to the main living area and then braced herself as she stepped into the backyard.

The metal sculptures that filled the space cast long, ominous shadows as Jessie made her way to Alex. He stood staring at the tall, metal sunflower from which Kerry's body had swung. Alex was scribbling furiously in his notebook when she walked up. Off to one side, Sheriff Cormac and Deputy Hardin were conversing, their faces long with sorrow and resignation. Jessie's eyes were drawn to the plastic tarp that had been used to cover the body of the fireman.

"So, what do we have?" Jessie asked.

Alex pointed at the metal sculpture with the eraser of his pencil. "The body was hanging from one of the petals of this structure. The sheriff was already here when Hardin arrived. Kerry was found by his brother, who called 9-1-1. The call was picked up by Sheriff Cormac who headed right over."

"Who cut him down?" Jessie asked.

Alex jutted his chin in the sheriff's direction. "Those two."

"Did you happen to get a look at the body before they covered it?"

He shook his head. "No. Everything was just as it is

now when I came out. There's no medical examiner to call on. I seriously doubt they'd allow Doc Lindquist to examine the body."

"Never," answered Jessie. She walked slowly over to the body. The tarp covered most of it, but Kerry's arm was visible. Jessie bent down close for a look. "Can I borrow your pencil for a second?" She used the tip to lift the edge of the tarp further. "Look here." She indicated the knuckles of his hand and potential bruising on his forearm. "These could be defensive."

Alex nodded. "Also, how did he manage this? There's no sign of a chair or step ladder. The petal he hung from is a good eight feet off the ground and just out about three feet from the trunk of the sculpture." He scratched at his cheek in thought. "I mean, I guess he could have climbed up and out onto it somehow..."

"What about the rope?" Jessie said, looking around. "What kind of knot did—"

"Hey! What are you doing?" It was Sheriff Cormac. He stormed over to where Alex and Jessie were, Deputy Hardin in tow.

Jessie stood, handing Alex his pencil. "Sheriff, did you notice the marks on his hand and arm? Do you think they could be defensive in nature?"

The sheriff waved his hand in the air and rolled his eyes. "Okay, enough, Miss Night. This is a simple, cut and dried case of suicide. It's a sad day made all the sadder because this was such a beloved member of our community. People are going to be grieving at his loss. There is nothing here for you to be questioning."

Jessie fought down the anger that was rising in her

spine. "With all due respect, Sheriff, you said the same thing about Marley Shaffer. And it turns out that her death was anything but an accident."

Dark red splotches spread from the sheriff's neck to his face. "You know, I can admit when I am wrong, and I'm sorry about what happened to your client's cousin. But this we didn't get wrong." A look came across his face that Jessie hadn't seen before. A cross between intense dislike and a thinly veiled smirk. "But you should be happy. Wrapping this up also wraps up your case here in Bidonville as well."

Jessie frowned. "How so?"

"Because like most suicides, Kerry left a note. And in it, he confessed to killing Marley Shaffer."

23

All Wrapped Up

"The note was in his pants pocket," Deputy Hardin said.

Jessie looked at the man. Compared to the sheriff, he at least looked remorseful. "Can we see it? Or am I just supposed to take your word for the contents?"

Hardin snuck a look over at the sheriff, who was supervising the removal of the body. "Fine. But only to put your mind at rest."

Yeah. Good luck with that.

The deputy had a black, police-issued duffle bag emblazoned with the words 'EVIDENCE' printed in yellow lettering, slung obliquely across his shoulder. Opening it, he produced a sealed Ziploc bag with a piece of yellow legal pad paper sealed inside.

Alex moved to stand next to Jessie, reading the hand-written note over her shoulder.

I'm sorry. I'm so deeply sorry for what I've done and for the pain I know my actions will cause. I can no longer live with the guilt and the weight of my sins. It's a burden too heavy to bear, and I fear it will crush me if I continue on.

First, George, please know that none of this is your fault. You have been the one pure thing I've ever known. I'm sorry I won't be there to protect you anymore, to be the brother you deserve. But I hope, in time, you'll come to understand why I had to do this.

I need to confess my crime. One that has haunted my every waking moment since that fateful day. I killed Marley Shaffer. I didn't mean for it to happen. She meant everything to me and if she had given me the chance, I could have made her the happiest woman in the world. But when she told me she didn't, and could never feel the same way about me, I broke. The darkness rushed in and I snapped. It was over before I even realized what I had done. I took her life. And in doing so, damned my own.

There is no atonement for what I've done. No number of good deeds can wash the blood from my hands.

Tell Marley's family I am sorry for what I did. I hope they can find some measure of peace in knowing that her killer has been brought to justice. Even if that justice was delivered by my own hand.

And George. I need you to be strong. I'm sorry I couldn't be the brother you needed me to be.

The letter was signed in a scrawl that Jessie assumed was Kerry's signature. She read over the note twice more before handing it back to Deputy Hardin.

Sheriff Cormac walked up just as she finished reading. "You see, in his own words, Kerry admitted to the horrific act he committed."

Jessie chose her next words carefully. "And you're sure that's his signature on it? Interesting how this just wraps everything up in a neat little package and puts a bow on top." She felt the heat radiate from the sheriff as he drew in breath.

"Miss, I don't know how you do things in your neck of the woods and, honestly, I don't much care. But here, we give just as much respect to those that have departed us —no matter the circumstances—as we do those left behind. Kerry was a pillar of the community and will be mourned by many." He grasped his belt and hitched his pants higher on his waist. "What happened here has been explained in the man's own handwriting. I don't pretend to know what was in his head, but I will not let you besmirch what is left of his name. Now, if you'll excuse me, I have to see this through. And I suspect your business in our town is done."

He turned to walk away but Jessie's next words caused him to hesitate. "What about George? What will happen to him?" When he didn't answer and continued on his way, she turned her attention to Hardin.

The deputy had a hard time keeping eye contact. "We've already discussed that. There is a group home a couple of counties over that will take him in. They are sending over a social worker to speak with him."

Jessie frowned. Group homes weren't the best, and she could only hope that this was being done as a last resort. "George said something about not wanting to go back. Do you know what or where he was referring to?"

A look passed across the deputy's features that Jessie couldn't decipher. "No. I'm surprised he spoke to you at all. I've never really known him to speak to anyone other than Kerry."

"I suppose you're going to verify that signature?" Jessie gestured towards the letter.

Hardin nodded. "There are plenty of examples of Kerry's writing on file at the fire department. Won't be hard to verify. But I can tell you from a glance...that's his."

Jessie could feel her temper and exasperation rising. "Hardin...Deputy...don't you find this a little too convenient? I mean, why now? Why kill yourself when you've practically gotten away with murder?"

He stared hard at her. "You changed things. Kerry was always keen on what happened with Marley. Even more-so once you showed up. He was keeping tabs. My guess is he knew you were closing in on the fact that it was a murder and not an accident."

"A guess? That's your guess when it comes to solving a murder? See, that's where we differ. I would not guess, but look at the note itself. Why is it so impersonal? He was dedicated to George, and yet he hardly mentions him? This note is overly detailed in confession. Most suicide notes I've seen are often more vague or focus on the emotional state of the person writing it." She looked around, opening arms at the space where they stood. "And why here? Look at this place. This was his art. He built it as a safe haven for his brother. I saw how much

George loved this yard. Why would Kerry spoil it like this for him?"

The deputy looked around, taking in a few deep breaths, but he didn't respond.

"Tell me this doesn't feel off to you," Jessie said.

"How has Kerry's mood been lately?" Alex asked. "Since the discovery of Marley's body."

Deputy Hardin scratched his head. "No different. He's always the same."

Alex was nodding as the deputy spoke. "So, no noticeable change in behavior, but suddenly his guilt overcomes him to the point that he kills himself?"

Before Hardin could answer, the sheriff walked up again. "Found this in a search of Kerry's bedroom." He held up a cell phone. "Looks to belong to one Marley Shaffer."

"May I?" said Jessie, holding out her hand. She frowned. "I thought you found Marley's phone with the body? The one you have back at the department."

He shrugged and handed it over. "Guess that was a burner. That would explain why there was nothing on it. Looks like Kerry kept a trophy." It was unlocked and Jessie was able to bring it to life with the press of a button. She immediately called up the messaging app and looked through them with a frown. There were messages back and forth to Aura. He had been talking to Marley's cousin, pretending to be Marley. That explained why Aura had not thought anything suspicious might be going on with her cousin.

Still, Jessie wasn't convinced. She handed the phone back to the sheriff. "What about the pregnancy?

Marley's body showed she had very recently given birth."

The sheriff nodded, grimly. "For all we know they had an affair and that was the result. Kerry obviously had a thing for the woman. We don't know just how far things went between them."

Jessie frowned. Nothing was adding up in her mind. "And what about the shed I found? The one a few miles out of town that looked like someone had been staying there. Or kept prisoner."

A cloud passed over the sheriff's face. Not one of anger or annoyance, but fear. But as quickly as it descended, it vanished. "What shed?"

Jessie pulled out her phone and showed him the pictures. Not only of the shed, but the abandoned buildings as well. "Do you know what these are?"

The sheriff batted his eyes. "No idea."

It was a lie, and he knew that Jessie saw it on his face. He opened his mouth to elaborate but was cut short by the buzzing of his own phone. Deputy Hardin took the phone in Jessie's hand from her and added it to the evidence bag along with the note Kerry had left behind.

The sheriff turned, shoving the phone back into his pocket. His face was red and his breath came in huffs as he approached Jessie. "You left my nephew alone at the morgue with some doctor I've never heard of?" His voice was low and menacing, a vein along the side of his forehead throbbing to the point Jessie feared it might rupture.

"Your nephew was the victim of bullies at school. A school that he doesn't technically attend, I might add. I just thought he should have his ribs checked, that's all. I was going to call you, but that's when the call came through about Kerry."

He glowered at her, his lips drawing up in a sneer. "First, you had no right going to that school and questioning him. Second—" He stopped, taking a deep breath to try and calm himself. "You know what...never mind. I'm having the body of Marley Shaffer released so you can have it transported back to her loved ones in Pine Haven. Then you, your doctor, and whoever this is—" he jabbed a finger in Alex's direction, "—can be out of town by morning. Your case here is officially closed."

Jessie drew in breath to argue with the man, but he turned on his heels and stormed off, heading for the doors leading into the house.

Deputy Hardin swallowed hard, staring at Jessie and Alex. "He's very protective of his nephew. You really should not have involved him in any of this." He zipped the evidence bag closed and hurried after the chief, leaving Jessie and Alex in the backyard, staring at one another.

"What the hell?" Jessie said.

Alex exhaled sharply. "There is something going on here, and I feel like everyone knows it but is reluctant to talk about it out loud."

Jessie took out her phone. "I'm giving Lindquist a heads up. I've a feeling the sheriff is headed his way and he's not going to be in the best of moods when he gets there." Her phone dinged instantly after sending the message. She looked up at Alex. "Looks like the good doctor wants to meet with us tonight back at the bed and breakfast. He said he's found something interesting in the blood work I gave him."

Alex frowned. "Did he say what it was?"

Concern washed across her features as she scrolled further down the message. "Just that it's too complicated to text and it's something worse than he could have ever imagined."

24

Forgiveness for the Wicked

Sheriff Cormac paced back and forth in the tiny room before finally dropping down onto a rough, wooden crate that acted as a chair. "All I'm saying is, did you have to kill him?"

The bigger man laughed cruelly. "Nobody killed him. He did it himself. Didn't you read his sad little note?"

The sheriff bristled and fought to control his anger. "There had to be another way."

The big man crossed the space separating them in two monstrous strides, his boots crunching on the debris littering the floor. "Well, there wasn't. You made sure of that by letting that investigator keep digging deeper and deeper. You weren't doing shit, Cormac. Someone had to step up. For fuck's sake, she questioned Roger. Who knows what the fuck that kid said to her?" Spittle flew from his mouth as he turned on the sheriff.

"Yeah, well now thanks to your rash actions, she's more suspicious than ever."

The man glowered at the sheriff, his massive hands balling into fists at his side.

"And how did you respond to her suspicions?" The voice came from the woman leaning against a dirty table behind the giant man. Her voice was calm and steady. It relaxed the larger man, yet made the sheriff's sphincter draw tight.

Sheriff Cormac swallowed what felt like a throat full of sawdust. "I've officially closed the case. Told her we had all we needed and that her friend's killer had met justice. She's set to leave town tomorrow."

The big man growled at the sheriff. "She better, Cormac. Otherwise, we take care of her our own way."

"Don't be a fool. That would—" He didn't finish the sentence as the man was suddenly leaning over him, his face so close the sheriff could feel the heat of his sour breath.

"What'd you just call me?"

The sheriff fought to control his bladder, but the woman started cackling behind them. "He called you a fool. Which is probably not far from the truth. Now get off him."

The man stepped back, but the sheriff continued to squirm on the uncomfortable crate. He could still smell the man's foul breath coating his skin.

"Now, Sheriff, there is still one more matter we will need your help with," the woman said. Her tone made the hair on Sheriff Cormac's arms come to attention.

"I'm listening," he answered, sweat forming on his palms.

The woman leaned forward, baring rotted teeth and thick, pronounced gums. Her misshapen face gave him a crooked smile. "The doctor. We want him."

Sheriff Cormac swallowed hard. "That's really not a good idea. He's a personal friend of hers. He'll be leaving tomorrow along with Jessie and her friend."

The woman didn't answer right away. Her milky eye locked him into a stare. "Well then you better think fast. We can't be without a doctor. It would have prevented what happened with that poor Marley girl." She stopped, running her tongue over nearly non-existent lips. "I mean, surely you don't want what happened to her to happen to..." Her voice trailed off and she held a finger in the air, twirling it slowly around the knots in her unbrushed hair.

Tears threatened to burn the sheriff's face, and he felt a pain in his chest. "No. Don't. I'll do what I need to in order to get the doc to stay."

The big man moved over to stand by the woman's side. "You do that, Sheriff. Make him an offer he can't refuse. Or I will."

Sheriff Cormac met the man's gaze, a knot forming in his stomach. There was only so much he would be able to do at this point. Slowly, a thought formed in the back of his mind. One that would almost certainly mean his death. But after the life he had led, the darkness he had been complicit with...maybe that would be a good thing. He looked up, focusing on the woman's disfigured face. "Can I...Can I see her?"

The woman tilted her head to one side before looking at the large man. A grin was spreading from one ear to the other. "What do you think? Should we let him?"

The man made a show of considering the request, before shaking his head. "Nah. Not yet. Not till we get what we need first."

Anger and fear flooded the sheriff. "But we had a—"

The large man bellowed at him, his voice thunder in the small space. "You know the deal. You know what happens if you fail us again. Ask that question again, and she might be beyond the doc's help by the time you get to her."

Sheriff Cormac blinked away tears. He knew not to push. The big man never made threats.

He made promises.

The sheriff stood, taking a deep, steadying breath, before he nodded and headed out the makeshift door. Outside, he tilted his head back to the heavens.

Please forgive me for what I'm about to do.

25

Terrible Revelations

Inside the house, the fireplace roared even though it wasn't a particularly cold evening. Jessie sat in the living room, waiting for Alex and Dr. Lindquist to join her. She replayed the memories of the day over and over in her mind. Everything felt surreal. The trip to the school, the discovery of Kerry's body, the note that he had left, the sheriff's actions...all of it weighed on her. But the part she kept coming back to was what the school principal had said to her.

Not about Roger not being registered to attend classes —though that was something she wished she had pressed the teen on more. No. It was the part about Sheriff Cormac or his wife not having any siblings. The way the principal said it...it was a statement of fact.

Something about it made Jessie want to look into the man further. But she had seen what happened when she paid a visit to Kerry unannounced. He had threatened to shoot her. Instincts told her the sheriff might actually follow through on that.

Voices trailed into the room followed by Alex and Dr. Lindquist. Alex began pacing back and forth, mumbling aloud as his hands moved animatedly in the air. "It's almost too much to wrap my head around."

Jessie sat up straight, staring from one to the other. "What is?"

Dr. Lindquist had a tablet in his hands and was flicking rapidly at the screen before landing on an image and showing it to Jessie. It was a table of lab results arranged in columns by color.

She shook her head. "Okay, you might as well have handed me something in ancient Greek. What am I looking at?"

Alex jabbed a hand in the air, stopping the doctor from speaking. "Wait." He made his way over to the living room door and stuck his head out, looking around, and then softly pulled the door shut before nodding for the physician to continue.

Dr. Lindquist dropped down on the coffee table across from Jessie and pointed to the tablet. "That is a cursory breakdown of the blood I was able to draw from Marley. With Deputy Hardin's permission, I was also able to do a quick, basic autopsy. First, can I say that whoever the physician was that did her first assessment was terrible at their job?"

Jessie was nodding quickly, trying to keep him on track. "That's because it was ruled an accident and an official autopsy was never performed."

Dr. Lindquist grumbled. "Any physician worth their

weight in piss could have seen she needed a post-mortem. Accidental drowning my ass."

Jessie arched an eyebrow. She had never seen the medical examiner like this. "What did you find?"

"She had what is known as a retained placenta. Marley passed away during childbirth. She never delivered the placenta."

The words stung Jessie. She tried to imagine anyone dealing with what Marley must have endured. Her mind drifted back to the dirty, fetid shed. "So, she was held captive, with no medical attention, and forced to give birth?"

"How do you know she didn't have medical attention?" Alex asked.

"The condition she was in. She was practically skeletal. She wasn't eating enough for a pregnant woman," she answered.

"I would concur with that," said Dr. Lindquist. "And, judging from other physical findings, I'd say she was also assaulted multiple times."

Jessie swallowed. The more he spoke, the worse it was getting "Why do I get the feeling that the worst is yet to come?"

Alex looked at the coroner and nodded. "Tell her."

Dr. Lindquist let out a slow breath. "The placenta can tell us a lot about not only the health of the baby, but that of the mother as well. Now, mind you, I am working with only the most rudimentary of medical equipment here, but I did extract some blood and tissue samples and prepare some slides for examination." He pointed to the tablet Jessie held and took a deep breath before continuing. "When I looked at the blood samples under the scope, I couldn't believe what I was seeing. I thought there had to be some kind of contamination, or something like that. So, I drew another sample, making sure there was no chance of something being off this time. The results were the same. There is a shocking number of abnormalities that I was able to detect. The shape and size of the red blood cells were considerably out of range for anything even approaching normal. The same with the white blood cell counts. The size of the platelets was off the scale and when I ran a hemoglobin electrophoresis test...there were all kinds of abnormalities that showed up. I ran a comparison against the blood I drew from Marley. Her sample was fine. But everything in red on that report belongs to the baby. And it shows blood tests that are way outside of the normal range. I mean *way* outside."

Jessie stared at the report with entire columns of red. "So, what does all of this mean?"

He had been talking very fast and was slightly out of breath. He leaned in, dropping his voice to little more than a whisper. "Since Marley's blood work was completely normal, the only explanation for a variant like this is that it came from the father of the baby. And for his genetic material to completely override that of the mother to this degree...there is only one thing I can think of that could cause such an abnormality. The father is the product of a long line of incestuous reproduction." He sat back, looking from Jessie to Alex. "I've never seen anything like this. Chances are, if the child survived birth, it passed away within hours of delivery." He saw the sadness pass across Jessie's features. "Trust me. It would have been for the better. No child should suffer the way this one would have, even for that brief timeframe."

Jessie squirmed in her seat, thinking back to the abandoned dwellings she had found near the shed. "What about the blood sample I gave you? Were you able to get anything from that?"

The medical examiner held up a finger. "Ah, you beat me to it. Using sterile saline I was able to rehydrate a sample of the dried blood. Then I performed a quick type and match. And what do you know? It is a perfect match for one Marley Shaffer."

Jessie took in a deep breath and held it. Everything told her that the shed was being used to hold someone. And while she had hoped it wasn't the case, something squirming around in the back of her mind told her it was Marley. She looked up at Alex. "So, we now know that Marley was assaulted and murdered, and we have a crime scene."

"technically, the sheriff knows this as well, because of that suicide note." Alex resumed pacing. "Do you trust this sheriff if we bring him in on this?"

Jessie thought for a moment. "I want to. But I just get the feeling he's hiding something. He's too hellbent on making this all just go away."

Alex asked the question they were all thinking. "Do you think he's part of this?"

"I've been wondering that myself. Do I think he's a murderer? No. But he definitely knows more than he wants getting out."

"Maybe he's trying to protect his family," Dr.

Lindquist said. "I mean, Roger wanted me to call his Aunt Irma after I finished examining him at the morgue. She showed up and had the sheriff on the phone. I could hear him on the other end. He seemed genuinely worried about the boy. She handed me the phone and I assured him the kid was going to be just fine. There was no faking the worry and the fear in his voice."

Jessie frowned. "I suppose that could be part of it. But if that's the case, then he at least knows what there is to be afraid of."

"What about your friend in the FBI?" Alex asked.

She shook her head. "This isn't a case they could take on. As far we know it doesn't involve trafficking from state to state, or a serial killer. They would have no jurisdiction."

Alex's eyes lit up. "That we know of...a serial killer, I mean. From what you described in that shed, how can we be certain that Marley was the first woman to be held there against her will?"

His words struck Jessie, and she was on her feet, a chill racing up her spine. What he said made her remember something. "In the shed, there was something missing. Restraints of any kind. Other than the beam that kept the door shut from the outside, there was nothing to stop Marley from leaving."

Alex scratched the side of his head. "Fear. That can be just as strong as any chain. You said yourself that this place was incredibly remote. What if screaming got her nothing but...punishment, of some type. After a while, maybe she realized the futility of it."

Jessie was shaking her head. Not in disagreement, but

at the horror of the images her mind was creating. "I can't imagine the sense of helplessness. And to be in the condition she was...the terror not only for yourself but your unborn child as well."

"So, if we can't bring in the FBI, we can't trust the sheriff and his people here, and we can't utilize any of Pine Haven's police department, where does that leave us?" Alex asked.

Now it was Jessie's turn to pace. "Deputy Hardin. He's all we might have going for us."

Alex was shaking his head before the words had finished leaving her mouth. "We know nothing about him. From what little I've seen he's pretty far up the sheriff's ass."

"But that doesn't mean he agrees with everything that might be going on," Dr. Lindquist interjected. "He was quick to take the lead on letting me do what I needed with Marley. He seemed genuinely mortified at what had happened to her. He did that knowing he would probably take heat from the sheriff. There has to be something decent in there you can tap into."

Alex didn't say anything, but Jessie could see the muscles in his jaw clenching and unclenching. Another thought struck her. "The sheriff knew Marley had given birth before she died. I mentioned it myself when we were on site at Kerry's house. He never said anything about starting a manhunt for the baby. Neither did Hardin. They had no way of knowing the child wouldn't have survived."

"Unless they did know," Alex said.

"Ultimately, that would have been the sheriff's call to

make," Jessie added. "Hardin stepping up at the morgue could have been because he was the only law enforcement on site. He would not have felt that way with the sheriff standing right next to him. So while it's more damning evidence against Sheriff Cormac, it doesn't mean Hardin was involved as well." She resumed pacing the floor, deep in thought. "We need help. He may be our only solution. I'll talk with him in the morning."

"We're supposed to be gone in the morning," Alex reminded her.

Jessie thought for a moment. "Well, as far as he is concerned, the case is closed. But, seeing as how this is such a scenic, naturist spot, he can't begrudge us staying on a bit to do some sightseeing. Maybe a bit of hiking even..."

Alex stared at her, a thin smile starting to spread. "And let me guess where we will be hiking to."

Dr. Lindquist looked at them, his head snapping from one to the other. "Are you crazy? You're going back out into those woods to that shed, aren't you? Jessie, there is something dangerous out there." He glanced down at the tablet lying on the coffee table. "More dangerous than you can imagine." They didn't speak, but he saw the resolve in their eyes. "Well, you can count me out when it comes to traipsing through the woods. My knees aren't built for that anymore. Besides, I called for a messenger and sent some samples of blood and tissue to the CSI lab down in Pine Haven. They have some equipment that can do a much deeper dive into the analysis and maybe tell us exactly what we are dealing with. I'm hoping they'll email me the results sometime tomorrow."

"Perfect," said Jessie. "You wait here for that, while we do some digging. Before we head out, I'd like to look into any possible missing persons reports for the surrounding area going back a couple decades. Especially anyone matching Marley's description. This place doesn't seem to be very adept at hiding things. We might get lucky."

"Maybe we should talk to the sheriff's wife as well," said Alex. "She might be easier to rattle than Cormac."

"I doubt we would have any luck with that," Jessie said. "Cormac warned me to stay well clear of his family." She half turned in the doctor's direction. "But maybe she would speak with someone else...someone who maybe dropped by her place to check on her nephew? Especially if that someone swung by after the sheriff would have left for work..."

Lindquist looked from one to the other before sighing in resignation. "Fine. But I'm telling you, one of these days, the two of you are going to get me killed."

26

A Shadow of a Thought

Caroline sat at the foot of the bed in the small bedroom at the back of the house. She hated the space. It was cramped, with barely enough room for the full-size bed and a single cramped nightstand. The single closet was barely big enough to hold her few dresses and the bathroom was an addition that contained a water closet and sink only. The lack of a window made the room dark and even more restrictive than it was. While she agreed in principle that the larger rooms were best suited for the guests, she secretly wished for something that she looked forward to at the end of a long day of cleaning and preparing meals for people who typically didn't want to eat anyway.

She sat perfectly still, her back ramrod straight, staring at the peeling, dull wallpaper that mirrored her own existence. Had she always been like this? Surely not. There had to be a time when she was...alive. Her thoughts drifted to the choices that had led to this moment in her life. But she was fooling herself. There were no choices. At least not for her. She thought back to that night so long ago, when she was fourteen and given to her husband of twenty-six. She had one purpose in the clan's eyes. And she fulfilled that purpose as often as she could, almost yearly, until her body told her it was time to stop.

Some of the little ones lived, but many didn't. They cried for a few moments, some lasted an hour, but most were discarded not too long after they came into the world. Their poor deformed bodies taken away by her gran, never to be spoken of again. It wasn't until more and more babies were delivered stillborn that the clan realized there was a problem. It wasn't a problem they could see a fix for...all they could do was make it a numbers game. The more babies that were born, the more chances the clan had of continuing to exist.

Every now and then something miraculous would happen. A baby would be born that didn't look and act like the majority of the clan. It would be born with normal features and bright, attentive eyes.

These were children that could *pass*.

But even though they could sit in the schools of the townsfolk, and shop in their grocery stores, and attend their churches and meetings, something was still off about them. They were like shiny new apples with worm-filled, rotted centers.

At their heart, they were still clan. They might smile and mimic the customs of those they looked like, but it wasn't who they were deep down in that part of themselves they kept hidden. At least hidden from anyone but the rest of the clan.

Still, they were able to get an education and that helped when it came to taking care of some of the worst members of the clan. The ones who would never pass for anything resembling a human being.

And then one day, the boy was born. And so much changed with his coming. He was smart. Smarter than all the others. And crueler in his core. He grew from a cruel boy to an even crueler man. Still, he was the one who figured out the problem they were having with their dwindling numbers was because of the poison that came from everyone breeding with their kin folk.

New blood. New DNA was what he called it. It was time for the clan to restock their genetic pool, which was becoming more and more shallow with each birth.

Despite his brilliance, the boy was flawed in ways the clan could never see. He came up with plans they set in motion. Plans with holes and gaps in it that would require acts of great violence to fill.

And that violence was the path that led Caroline to the life she had now. Taking over a bed and breakfast that she never wanted. Learning to bake. Making a home that was nicer and cleaner than any she had ever known as a child.

Doing all of that to end up living in a room barely big enough to turn around in and married to a relative who only visited her a couple nights out of the month. Actually, that was a blessing. She had long grown tired of these trysts and part of her was hoping he would get tired of them soon as well. She knew when that happened, he'd have no reason to keep her around.

She could only hope he'd make it quick when the time came.

It was times like this she wished she could cry. But the almost unspeakable deeds she had survived over the years hadn't been able to elicit a drop of wetness from her eyes. Why should she think longing for a life that had never been would be any different?

The single, hard knock at the door caught her attention. She stood, straightening her dress and running a hand through her hair. She had taken a risk calling him to her, but she knew what would happen if he found out later she knew something and held back telling him.

She took a deep breath and reached for the doorknob. Her husband's hulking frame filled the doorway, and she nearly recoiled at the foul wave that rolled from his mouth.

He stepped inside, nearly having to duck his head to fit through the opening. "What?"

She immediately dropped her head, averting her eyes from his. "I overheard them talking about something tonight. Something I thought you should know."

His upper lip pulled upward in a contemptuous sneer as he stormed into the room, closing the door behind him. The tiny space became claustrophobic in his presence. Out of habit, Caroline's eyes cut to the bed and she had to fight the urge to lie down on her back. She felt like a dog that had been conditioned to roll over in fear when its master entered the room.

"Well, spit it out."

The annoyance in her husband's voice made her flinch. "The doctor. He found some stuff out from Marley's body. And Jessie was at the shed." She repeated as much of the conversation that she understood, ending with what their plans were for the next day.

The big man scowled, scratching mindlessly at his cheek. Truthfully, he didn't understand some of what Caroline had said, but he had the gist. "This is good."

Caroline felt ice grip her spine. She had thought he would be upset. Maybe even afraid. The fact that he liked what she said meant that they had already planned something awful. She moved back to the foot of the bed, head lowered, waiting to see what her husband might do next.

He lurched towards the door and disappeared into the hall, the floorboards creaking under his mass as he left the house through the back door.

Caroline breathed a heavy sigh of relief. A shiver passed over her and she reached for the threadbare blanket piled next to her. She liked Jessie and from what little interaction she had with the investigator's friends, they seemed like good people as well. She shook her head, clearing it of emotions. There was no use in feeling sorry for them.

What's done is done. They were already dead; they just didn't know it yet.

Caroline frowned; a shadow of a thought darkened her mind. But she could save one of them. Yes...it was dangerous. But she was tired of being alone. Her husband wouldn't like it at all. But the clan had been benefiting off her for years. Maybe it was time she did something for herself. And if it got her killed, then so be it.

Before she was hauled off and never heard from again, one of Caroline's previous guests had once told her that bad things sometimes happen to good people for no reason. If that was true, then surely even worse things happen to bad people. Caroline wasn't a good person, and she knew that when her time came, she would deserve the fate she met.

The shadow in her mind began to shift into a plan.

Yes. She would keep one of them.

27

An Unannounced Visit

Jefferson Lindquist followed the directions Caroline had given him that would take him to Sheriff Cormac's house. The freshly baked morning glory muffin she had just taken out of the oven sat in a napkin on the passenger side seat. Despite the tempting aroma, his stomach was not settled enough to eat. He didn't like the idea of trying to pry information from Irma Cormac under the guise of checking in on a loved one. Still, his thoughts drifted back to what he had learned from examining Marley Shaffer's body. If there was a chance he might be able to learn something that would help Jessie and Alex catch the monster who did that to her...well, then a little nausea and cramping was a small price to pay.

His mind was racing as he tried to decide what to say to the woman. Should he start with small talk, or just jump right in? How much time to spend on the boy? If he brushed the kid off too quickly, would that give away his true intentions to Irma? He shook his head. No. It wasn't like he was up to anything nefarious. He was genuinely curious about how Roger was doing, and the rest would just be conversational.

Which he wasn't very good at. There was a reason he was more comfortable working with the dead than the living. The intricacies of human interaction often eluded him, and the thought of extracting information from the sheriff's wife made his palms sweat. But he also realized that the truth was more important than his current discomfort.

The sheriff's house came into view, a modest two-story structure with a well-manicured lawn. It was almost story-book perfect. There was even a partial white picket fence stretching across the front of the yard and down one side of the house while a gravel driveway bordered the other. Dr. Lindquist eased the car to a stop, crunching the rocks beneath his tires.

He walked up the path to the front door, his footsteps heavy. Before he could knock, the door swung open, revealing a woman with tired eyes wearing a forced smile. The doctor couldn't help but flinch at the suddenness of the action. "Oh, hello," the woman said. "I saw you car pull up. I didn't mean to startle you."

He gave her his most genuine of smiles, hoping it didn't put her off. "Mrs. Cormac. I'm sorry to not call, but I don't have your number. My name is Dr. Lindquist. I was the physician that saw your nephew and I wanted to check in and see how he was doing. Those rib bruises he had can be tricky." A change came over her face. He could see the concern flood her features.

She stepped aside. "Please, come in." She moved ahead of him, leading him into the comfortable living room, picking up a couple of newspapers and magazines to stack on a small console table behind the couch. "I'm sorry the place is such a mess. I wasn't expecting company, as I said."

The doctor held up a hand. "Your home is beautiful. Please, don't make a fuss on my account."

Irma gestured for him to have a seat on the couch. "Can I get you something to drink? Some water or coffee?"

"No but thank you. I feel bad enough just dropping in unannounced. I really just needed to know how Roger is doing. How's his breathing?"

"Oh, he seems fine. A little sore and tender around that bruise on his side, but he's alright. Looks like he's getting a bit of a shiner under his eye though."

Dr. Lindquist nodded. "Yes, I told him that might set in. A pack of frozen peas applied for five-minute stretches a couple of times a day will help. Is he here? Would you like me to give him a quick check?"

"No, my husband dropped him off at school. But I can call and have him bring him back for you..."

Dr. Lindquist waved her off with his hand. "If you think he is fine I'm okay with that. I just wasn't sure if you have a regular doctor in town that you see."

Irma hesitated for a moment before answering. "No. I mean, we did, but he's on vacation. I'll have him check on Roger when he gets back in town."

Dr. Lindquist forced a smile on his face and then leaned forward slightly. "Pardon me for asking, and feel free to tell me it is none of my business, but is everything okay with Roger? He seemed a little...I don't know... distracted when I examined him. I asked what happened to him—meaning the bruises and bloody nose—and he just kind of shut down. In my experience, when a teen responds like that, they're usually under some kind of stress or something is off somewhere in their personal life."

Irma's eye twitched and she began picking at invisible lint on her pants-leg. "I can't imagine what would be bothering that kid. He's got it made here."

Dr. Lindquist frowned. There was something in her tone that caught his attention. There was an underlying current of annoyance. "Oh, I meant, maybe what he's going through with his mother. I guess there is still no word as to when she will be returning for him?"

It was quick, lasting barely a heartbeat, but the coroner saw it. A flicker of confusion crossed Irma's face, but was quickly replaced with the tired stoicism she had greeted him with. "Yes. Well, we still don't know how that will play out. I mean...the hope is, um, she will be back soon."

Dr. Lindquist nodded. "Recovering from a broken hip like that will take time."

Irma nodded slowly. "Well, she's a tough one. I'm sure she'll be back on her feet before we know it."

The coroner looked at her, his mouth twisted to one side as he considered his next words. "And that would be the case if it were true. See, I was told she was a repeated drug offender and had disappeared on a bender."

Irma gave him a sharp look, her gray eyes narrowing. "What that poor woman is going through is a private, family matter. We didn't feel like Roger needed to know the truth."

"Maybe. Or maybe you weren't let in on what the sheriff was telling everyone else. Which makes me wonder what else is he keeping from you, Irma? Did he tell you about Marley Shaffer?"

Her gaze faltered and she looked away. "A shame what happened. Terrible accident."

The doctor watched her but couldn't tell if she was lying or truly didn't know what had happened. He leaned in, dropping his voice. "It wasn't an accident. She was killed, Irma." The woman resumed her fidgeting and again let her eyes drop to her lap. "Irma, did the sheriff tell you Marley was pregnant? That she was being held somewhere and forced to give birth? Her baby most likely did not survive, but can you imagine what that poor girl went through? Something bad is going on around here, Irma, and if you know anything, anything at all that could help me figure out who really hurt Marley..."

Her head snapped up, her eyes bright and pleading. "You need to leave. And I don't just mean my house. Your presence here just makes it worse for everyone."

"Irma, what is going on? Is your husband involved in the death of Marley Shaffer?"

Her eyes grew wide. "What? Are you crazy? Of course not. Everything he's done has been for—" Her words choked off, her eyes focused over Dr. Lindquist's shoulder.

When she dropped them to the floor, he turned to look behind him and saw the largest man he had ever seen in his life. The last thing the doctor remembered was seeing a fist splitting the air as it rocketed towards his face.

28

Late Night Beckoning

Jessie waited in the kitchen for Alex. Blizzard sat at her feet hoping to catch a bit of the muffin his human was so clearly enjoying. She was just pouring a cup of coffee when the detective joined her. He was dressed in a long-sleeve thermal shirt with a red and gray flannel vest zipped over it. Jeans and hiking boots completed his wardrobe.

"Something tells me you packed knowing where we might be headed," Jessie said, offering him a cup.

He took it from her and sipped at the brew. "As the boy scouts used to say, always be prepared."

She frowned. "I didn't know you were a boy scout."

He gave her a crooked grin. "I wasn't. I just liked their motto."

"So, I think we need to do a little research before we head out back to those abandoned structures you found," Alex said after taking a couple more sips.

"Yes. We need to find out if there are any other reports of women going missing in this area."

Alex sat his cup down in the sink. "It would also be a good idea to look at any topography surveys of the area. See what we can find out about any previous settlements in the area. Those structures you found could be left over from an early colony. Maybe gold miners."

A rustling caught their attention as Caroline made her way into the kitchen. "Gold miners? There's no gold in these mountains." She smiled as she crossed over to the dishwasher and began loading it. "Forgive my intrusion. I just heard you mention the mines and didn't want you wasting your time looking for any, in case that's what you had in mind."

Alex smiled at the older woman. "Oh no, no intrusion at all." He glanced over at Jessie. "We were just talking about doing some sightseeing now that the case Jessie was working on has been closed."

Caroline's eyebrows shot up. "Oh, you found out everything you needed? That's great news."

"Yes, it is. And I can't thank you enough for your hospitality while I've been here. We were planning on leaving today, but it's so beautiful around here, I wanted to get in another day of hiking. Maybe take some pictures." A spark flashed through her eyes and she took out her phone. "Speaking of pictures...I was doing a little exploring around the area and came upon these. Do you recognize these old buildings?" She pulled up the photos she had taken and handed her phone over to Caroline.

The woman reached into her apron pocket and pulled out a set of reading glasses before staring at the screen. She nodded once and handed the phone back to Jessie. "That's Lost Cove."

Jessie took the phone back, unable to hide her surprise. "You know this place?"

Caroline lifted her shoulders, letting them drop as she spoke. "Well, most everybody that was born and raised in these parts knows about it. It's an old settlement a few miles up the mountain. Hard to get to unless you know what you're looking for."

Alex moved closer. "What can you tell us about it?"

She scrunched her face up in concentration, as if trying to call up distant memories. "From what I remember it was first settled just before the Civil War. It was a hub for logging, moon shine running, and farming. Moon shine and a few other illegal activities was its main business though, whether people wanted to admit that back then or not. One of the reasons those activities flourished is because of its location. It sits almost right on the border of Tennessee and North Carolina in a little gray area that neither state really wanted to claim. Neither state's judicial system could make a move on the occupants there because it was in a legal no-man's land, so to speak. Of course, while that was great for a time, it also became part of the reason the town eventually became abandoned.

"When the railroads started being built, and town became connected to county utilities, Lost Cove was cut off. Not being claimed by either state meant it also wasn't part of expansion plans. After a while, the town pretty much died off, because the families living there started moving out. From what I recall, the last family left in 1957."

Jessie digested the woman's words. "And there's been no one there since? Just the structures left as they were?"

Caroline thought for a minute. "There was a fire swept through the area in the early 2000s. Burned a lot of buildings from what I was told. That was the last time anyone went up there. Occasionally, a hiker will have heard about it and show up wanting to go gawk and explore. But otherwise, it stays the same as it was that day the last family came down from there."

"Do you know where those original settlers landed?" Alex asked.

Caroline gave him a confused look. "Well, here of course. Bidonville welcomed them with open arms."

Somewhere, in the back of Jessie's mind, a tiny alarm sounded. "Caroline, you mentioned there was a fire up there. By any chance, do you know who might have responded?"

She scratched her head for a moment. "Well, it wasn't really a response that was mounted. There was nothing to save, so from what I remember it was just a few of the fire fighters that went up there to make sure it burned itself out completely so there wouldn't be a chance of it burning down the whole forest."

"By any chance, would Kerry have been one of the respondents?"

She nodded slowly. "Now that you mention it, yes. He wouldn't have been fire chief back then, but yeah, he would have been one of the few to hike up there and check on things."

"Thank you, Caroline. You've been extremely helpful," Jessie added.

The woman turned, moving some dishes from the sink to the dishwasher. "If you're going up there, be sure and take in the views from the Poplar Gorge overlook. You can see the entire mountain vista as well as the valleys below from there. Beautiful place, especially at sunset. But certainly, take plenty of water and some food with you. I can pack you something to nibble on. Just let me know."

Jessie smiled warmly. "Thank you, Caroline. But that won't be necessary. As lovely as the overlook sounds, I don't think we want to be up there after dark. We might just go take a couple pics and then head back." She looked down at the white shepherd sitting at her side, his bright eyes focused on her. "What do you say, big guy? You ready for an adventure?"

Caroline turned to face them. "Oh, you don't want to take him up there. That part of the mountain is crawling with rattlers and baby copperheads this time of year. Your hiking boots will pretty much protect you, but if he gets bit, you'd be hard pressed to carry him out of there in time..."

Jessie frowned, looking down at the dog. She had been all through the woods with him before and never thought about something being able to hurt him. "Well... I mean, I feel so guilty leaving him with you yet again."

Caroline bent down and scratched Blizzard's head. "Don't even think about it. I'll keep him safe and sound and cozy." She looked up at Jessie, a twinkle in her eyes. "I'll treat him just like he belongs to me."

"WHAT DO YOU THINK?" Jessie asked. They were standing outside on Caroline's small porch.

Alex rocked back and forth, shifting his weight from one leg to the other. "Was it just me or did something feel off about what she was saying? It didn't feel like a lie...but something else."

Jessie thought for a moment. "Not a lie. But a truth volunteered too easily can still have a hidden meaning behind it."

"She wants us to go up there."

Jessie was nodding. "And I don't see that we have a choice."

"We could call in the State Police."

"And tell them what?" Jessie answered. "Would they override the sheriff and his mountain of evidence—and I use that word loosely—pointing to the fact that everything has been taken care of?" A thought flashed across Alex's face, lighting his eyes up. "What is it?"

"What you just said about evidence reminded me that maybe there is more out there that we've missed. You found that blood sample in the shed that was a match for Marley Shaffer. You also saw other buildings, or old houses up there as well. What if there is more evidence in them? What if the shed wasn't the only place someone was being held?"

She nodded, remembering the way the door was constructed at the shed. "Maybe Lost Cove isn't as deserted as this town likes to think."

"Is there a library around here?"

Jessie pulled out her phone and tapped at the screen. "There is. Not far from here either."

Alex smiled. "Then we should go there. Even if the sheriff is covering something up, there will be old newspapers there that could shed light on disappearances in the area. And they should also have some topography maps of the area. I'd like to get a look at this Lost Cove before we go wandering up there."

Jessie nodded in agreement. "Good plan. Let's go do a little digging and see what pops up."

Together, they stepped off the porch and headed for town.

FROM INSIDE THE HOUSE, Caroline watched the two of them leave her porch. Sadness clouded her eyes as she whispered her goodbyes. A nudge at her leg snapped her out of her reverie and she looked down at the shepherd. "Oh, are you hungry? Let's see if we can't find you something better than those dry dog treats your mama left you."

She led him back into the kitchen and began rummaging around in the refrigerator. There was some cold bacon left over from the night before. Normally she would keep it for her husband's late-night snack. But if everything worked out the way she hoped, she'd never again have to get out of bed at his beckoning and make him a BLT.

She slipped a piece to Blizzard and ruffled his white fur.

"That's right, boy. You eat up. Soon, it's just going to be me and you."

She smiled to herself, her previous melancholy already slipping free of her conscious mind as she stared at the dog, a single thought repeating in her mind.

I get to keep one of them.

29

Accidents Aplenty

The library was a quaint, single-story structure that had once been a modest ranch home. The building was set back from the main street, nestled behind a few winding roads, another afterthought thrown up in what Jessie was quickly realizing was a poorly designed town. Its weathered wooden exterior and faded red roof whispered neglect. A gravel parking lot, barely large enough to accommodate six cars, stretched out in front of the library, its loose stones crunching beneath Jessie and Alex's feet as they approached the entrance.

"I take it reading isn't a big part of the pastime here," Alex remarked, his eyes scanning the deserted lot.

"I'm starting to think there isn't much of a pastime here at all," Jessie replied, a wry smile playing across her lips.

They pushed on the front door and the hinges

protested with a creak. The musty smell of old carpets and even older books filled their nostrils as they stepped inside. The interior was dimly lit. Narrow beams of sunlight filtered through the partially drawn curtains.

They made their way past rows of shoulder-high bookshelves, their footsteps muffled by the threadbare carpet. Other than the rustling of their clothing, the only other sound came from the ticking of an unseen clock somewhere in the building. As they reached the back of the building, Jessie couldn't shake the feeling that the library was laid out backwards. Why put the front desk at the back of the building? But that was where they found the librarian. A woman who appeared to be in her late sixties with graying hair that rested on her shoulders.

She looked up from her desk, her eyes widening slightly behind her thick-rimmed glasses. "Welcome to the library," she said, her voice soft and hesitant. "I'm Mrs. Abernathy. How may I assist you?"

Jessie stepped forward, offering a friendly smile. "Hello, ma'am. My name is Jessie Night and this is my friend Alex Thomas. We're visiting from out of town and are looking to do some sightseeing. We heard about an old abandoned town near here called Lost Cove, and we were thinking about hiking up for the day to take some pictures."

The librarian narrowed her eyes. "Where'd you hear about Lost Cove?"

Jessie shrugged. "Mostly the internet. A site that curates interesting, forgotten places."

Mrs. Abernathy gave her a grunt. "Most places like

that are forgotten for a reason. But, if it's what you want to do, have at it. How can I be of assistance?"

Alex cleared his throat and moved forward. "Well, we'd like to get a look at what we might be walking into. It would be great if you had any old topography maps that might show the town. I understand there was a fire a few years back, so anything we could see of the terrain might help us navigate a little better."

Mrs. Abernathy gave him a frown, her eyes sweeping up and down his frame. "That fire was decades ago. And it devastated—" She hesitated, catching herself. "The area. But I'll see what I can find prior to that."

"Also, I'm a bit of a history buff when it comes to stuff like this. Any chance I could see the newspaper archives from here and the surrounding counties?" Jessie added.

The librarian sighed. "How far back you interested?"

Jessie made a show of pretending to consider the woman's words. "Oh...maybe the last thirty-five years if possible."

Mrs. Abernathy's eyebrows shot up higher than the rim of her glasses.

"I mean...if that's not possible, I understand," Jessie stammered.

"Didn't say it wasn't possible. But for that far back you're going to need to use a combination of online archives and microfiche."

Jessie shuddered on the inside as her mind flashed back to the last time she was in a library and was told she would be using microfiche. She shook the unpleasant memory and gave the woman a tight smile. "That will be fine."

The woman rose to her feet and turned her back on them, heading away from the desk. "The computer lab is this way. I'll bring you everything else you need." She stopped, looking over her shoulder. "I'm afraid there won't be any maps available after the fire. You'll be on your own for that."

The computer lab was small and cramped, with a single dusty window that let in a sliver of light. Surprisingly, there was a late-model computer sitting at one of two cubicles, a large flat-screen monitor dominated the small desk space. Next to it, in the second cubicle, the microfiche reader emitted a low hum. The smell of old ink and paper permeated the air.

"The computer is linked to our digital archives," Mrs. Abernathy said. "I'll be back with the old maps and the microfiche files of newspapers prior to our digital records."

Jessie and Alex made their way to the computer as she left the room. Alex took a seat and fired up the monitor.

"People really don't like talking about Lost Cove around here," Alex said.

"So I've noticed. I'm starting to think it might not be as abandoned as claimed. See what you can find out about it and I'll start going through the older newspaper articles looking for any mentions of missing women as soon as she comes back."

Alex turned to face the screen, his fingers already playing across the keyboard. Mrs. Abernathy returned, pushing a plastic trolley. Sitting atop it were a couple of file boxes and some long rolls of paper.

She placed the boxes next to the microfiche reader. "You know how to use one of these?"

"I do," Jessie answered.

The librarian nodded and gestured to the rolls of paper. "These were site survey maps of Lost Cove. They're old, but it's all we got. Be careful handling them."

Before either could reply to her, she turned on her heels and made her way out of the room, leaving them with only the gentle hum of overhead fluorescent lights.

Jessie looked at the boxes, opening them to reveal a row of small, flat plastic sheets, each about the size of a standard index card. Each film had a slightly glossy appearance, its surfaces reflecting the dim light of the room. They were arranged by date and she gently picked up one of the microfiche sheets, holding it delicately between her fingers.

She carefully placed the first microfilm into the reader and stared at the magnified image on the screen. It was from the Yancy Gazette, the newspaper that apparently serviced the overall county where Bidonville was located. Since the microfilms weren't searchable like modern digital documents, she had to resort to manually sliding the film in the reader, moving from one tiny image to the next. Each image was a page from the paper. She sighed, glancing at the two boxes containing rows of microfilm. This might take longer than she thought.

Next to her, she could hear Alex playing the keyboard followed by the fast clicking accompanying the scroll of a mouse's wheel. Occasionally, she would hear him pause as he scratched out notes on his ever-present notebook, or the click of his phone's camera as he took pictures of something. She returned her attention to the task at hand, her eyes taking in headlines of articles at a glance as page after page of the newspaper appeared and disappeared before her.

After an hour, she stood, stretching her legs. Alex did the same.

"Any luck?" Jessie asked.

"There aren't a lot of references to the town. Not much more than what Caroline told us. But I did manage to find some pictures of the houses and even some of the residents." He pulled up the photos of the computer screen he had taken and showed them to Jessie.

She flipped through grainy, black and white photographs of hastily erected dwellings, some with people standing in the doorways or on crooked porches. She swallowed hard. Something about the look of the people in the photographs, the hard lines etched on their faces, their slumped shoulders, the dark, soulless look in their eyes. She had seen this before. During her time in the military, she had investigated many cases in areas of the world where the people had given up. Whatever light they might have once possessed had been snuffed out by horrors that she could never imagine. War had a way of dimming even the brightest of souls.

The look of complete loss of hope was what she saw in these pictures. Whoever these people were, they had lived a very hard life.

"They look like they've lived through hell," she whispered.

Alex exhaled deeply. "What about you? Anything yet?"

She shook her head. "Nope. But the good news is I'm almost to the mid-seventies."

Alex laughed. "Well, I don't think I'll find anything more about Lost Cove. So, why don't I start looking through the recent news archives on this while you continue working through...whatever that is. We can save the topography maps for last."

Jessie raised an eyebrow at him. "What do you mean whatever that is? Alex Thomas, do you not know how to use a microfiche reader?"

A sly grin spread across his features. "I've never even seen one of these before. Maybe once we are back in Pine Haven you can teach me how to use one. And after that, maybe you can teach me how to hook up a VCR player."

She rolled her eyes at the man before sitting back down at the reader. A half-hour later, a headline jumped out at her. "Alex, look at this." The detective stood to look over her shoulder. "It's an article referencing the disappearance of a seventeen-year-old girl who was hiking through Poplar Cove. Says it was the second disappearance of a young woman in three weeks."

Alex stared at the article, his eyes skimming through the words. "It says her backpack along with torn remnants of her clothing were found at the bottom of one of the cliffs. The thinking is she fell and her body was taken by animals."

Jessie thought back to all the warnings she had constantly received about dangerous wildlife in the mountains around Bidonville.

She skimmed quickly through a few more pages and it wasn't long before a third account appeared that read almost exactly like what had befallen the first two women.

She switched out the films, excitedly placing a new sheet in the reader. It wasn't long before she came across another story of a disappearance. This time it was a couple that had hiked into the surrounding forests. There were photos of a campsite in disarray, alongside a tent that had been ripped to shreds. The boyfriend's body had been found mutilated on site, but the body of his girlfriend had never been found. Again, the death was attributed to a fatal bear mauling.

"Looks like we found the source of all the dangerous animal warnings for the area," she mused. "Three disappearances and a killing, all within two years."

Alex returned to his computer and quickly began a search. Twenty minutes later, he leaned back in the chair to address Jessie. "I've found a handful of similar attacks in the late nineties through the mid two thousands. After that, they appeared to have stopped."

"What about accidental deaths?"

A few clicks later and he spoke up. "Yes. There have been a rash of bodies found at the base of cliffs. Accidental falls where a broken neck was the cause of death. A couple of bodies found during spelunking accidents."

Jessie stared at him. "Let me guess. All these were accidents."

He stared at her, slowly nodding.

"Goddamnit. Sounds like a serial killer has been haunting this place for decades."

Their shocked silence was interrupted by Alex's phone buzzing. He pulled it out and stared at the screen, frowning. "Hello? What...? No, I haven't." There was silence as he listened. "Thank you. We'll check it out and I'll get back to you."

"What is it?" Jessie asked.

"That was the crime lab back home. They said they had some results on the bloodwork Dr. Lindquist sent them. Said it was urgent that he see them, but they haven't been able to reach him by phone."

Jessie looked at her watch. They had been at the library for almost three hours.

She felt a chill race up her spine. "Shouldn't he be back at the bed and breakfast by now?"

"Definitely."

Jessie stood, Alex at her side as they hurried out of the computer lab. They quickened their pace as they left the building and headed back into town. She didn't like the feeling that had suddenly gripped her gut.

30

Swimming Through Mud

Dr. Jefferson Lindquist felt like he was swimming through mud as he fought his way to consciousness. The first sensation he registered was cold—a deep chill that penetrated him to the bones. His eyelids felt heavy, fighting his attempts to open them. When he finally managed to pry them apart, he was greeted with darkness, broken by thin slivers of light that made their way through cracks between the wooden slats of the walls around him.

Damp earth and rotting wood clawed at his nostrils. The smells were accompanied by the metallic tang of blood.

His own blood.

Panic rushed through him as he began to remember what had happened. He had been hit by something. No. Not something. *Someone.* While he was visiting with the sheriff's wife.

Someone had come up from behind and punched him in the face.

Medical training took over, pushing through the fog of confusion and the din of hammers pounding at the inside of his skull. He flexed his fingers and toes, relief washing over him as they responded appropriately. Next, he focused on one of the thin cracks of light, tracing it with his eyes. His vision seemed intact, though his head throbbed mercilessly.

"Name...date...location," he mumbled to himself, his voice raspy and unfamiliar. "Jefferson Lindquist. It's ... Tuesday? No. Wednesday. I'm in..." He faltered. The sudden realization that he didn't know where he was sent a fresh wave of panic rippling through him.

Gingerly, he probed at the back of his head, wincing at the lump he found there. He must have fallen backwards from the hit, striking his head on the floor. The nausea that struck him told him it was most likely a concussion. He ran his fingers over his face. He could tell from the deviation that his nose had been broken by the punch, but thankfully there didn't seem to be any real damage done to his cheekbones or orbital rims.

He tested his memory, calling up the conversation he had with Irma Cormac. He made sure there were no gaps in his memory leading up to the attack. He remembered their conversation and all the details of Irma's house, both inside and out. He remembered the morning glory muffin waiting for him in his car. That was all present.

Good.

He had never been in a fight before. Never been physically assaulted. The thought of striking another human being with his fists had always made him uneasy. He had, of course, seen the after-effects of great violence visited on the human body. It was something he was all too familiar with. But it was always at a distance. Always laid out on a cold table before him.

Never in a million years did he think he would be on the receiving end.

He tried to sit up, but his muscles immediately protested. The world began to swim and he closed his eyes against a fresh wave of nausea. The cold of the bare, earthen floor he lay on became an asset, helping to calm his mind and ease the throbbing pain in the back of his head.

Helplessness washed over him. The likes of which he had never known. Tears welled and though he tried to fight it, his thoughts went to worst-case scenarios. 'What ifs' started to rapid-fire through his brain. Each triggered an increase in his heart rate and breathing. He could feel the panic attack swelling within, the muscles in his throat tensing to release his fear and tension.

"Don't scream."

Everything stopped with the doctor. His breathing, heartbeat...the world stilled at the sound of the small voice that seemed inches away. He turned his head in the direction of the sound and saw darkness. But then, movement—the subtlest of shifts in the black—stood out. There was a figure crouched in the corner, and Jefferson didn't know whether to be relieved or terrified.

"Hello? Who's there?" His voice was strained and pitched.

"Shh. Keep your voice down."

This time he could make out that it was the voice of a young woman. Her whisper was filled with fear and carried a warning. He swallowed, the sudden rush of adrenaline making his head throb. "Where...where are we?"

It seemed like hours before the girl answered.

"Hell. We're in Hell. We must have done something really bad and now we've been sent to Hell."

The finality in her voice chilled the doctor far more than the earthen floor ever could. She had given up all hope, and he knew that despair that deep was contagious. "What's your name? I'm Jefferson."

After a moment, she whispered her name. And when he heard it, his fear only deepened.

31

A Scent of Pine-Sol

T he tires on the Jeep bit into the pavement as Jessie slammed on the brakes, bringing it to an abrupt halt in front of the bed and breakfast.

"Still no answer," Alex muttered, his phone pressed to his ear. The worry lines on his forehead deepened as Dr. Lindquist's voicemail picked up for the fifth time.

Jessie killed the engine. "This isn't like him. He always answers, even if it's just to say he's busy."

They burst through the front door, the usually warm and welcoming atmosphere now heavy and worrisome. Their footsteps echoed on the hardwood floors as they bounded up the stairs, taking them two at a time.

"Dr. Lindquist?" Jessie called out. She wrapped her knuckles against his door, the sound sharp in the silent hallway. She glanced at her watch. "He should definitely be back by now."

Alex reached forward, trying the handle. It turned easily, revealing an empty room. The bed was still made, untouched since morning. "Damnit," he hissed, running a hand through his hair. "Where the hell is he?"

Jessie didn't answer as she turned to survey the small second floor. There were only a handful of rooms, the hallway, and an extra half bath that comprised the floor. To her knowledge there was no one else staying at the house so she didn't see a problem with trying the two other rooms. Once that was done, they moved to the main floor, methodically checking every room.

The only space left was the small corridor that ran behind the kitchen, ending at a closed door. Jessie had seen Caroline make her way to that room many times and assumed it was the owner's suite. She was about to head for the door when it opened and Caroline entered the hallway, Blizzard at her side.

The woman was clearly surprised to see them, her shuffling gait slowing as Blizzard rushed past her to greet Jessie. She bent down to briefly scratch the dog's back before nodding at Caroline.

"Jessie," the woman said. "I wasn't expecting to see you back. So soon, I mean. I figured you'd be halfway through the woods to Lost Cove by now."

"Um, yeah...we hit a slight delay."

Caroline frowned, her eyes darting between Jessie and Alex's tense faces. "Is everything okay?"

"We were looking for Dr. Lindquist," Alex said, his voice strained. "Have you seen him?"

Caroline shook her head. "Not since he left this

morning. He mentioned something about visiting the sheriff's house, I think."

"Did he say anything else?" Jessie pressed, leaning forward. "Anything at all about where he might go after that?"

"No, I'm sorry," Caroline replied, worry etched into her face. "Is something wrong?"

Jessie tried to give her as reassuring a smile as she could muster. "No. I'm sure it's nothing. Do me a favor, if you see him before we get back, could you tell him to call me right away? And can you give us the sheriff's address?"

"Of course," the older woman said. She took Alex's notebook and scribbled on the paper before handing it back. Reaching down she rubbed Blizzard, her eyes following Jessie and Alex as they headed for the door. "And don't worry, I'll let him know to reach out to you the minute I see him."

Neither of them spoke as they climbed into the Jeep and Jessie peeled away from the curb, heading for Sheriff Cormac's house. She gripped the wheel tightly, gritting her teeth.

"I know what you're thinking," Alex said. "And I'd advise you not to go there."

She didn't look his way but shifted her weight against the seat slightly. "I'm not going anywhere."

Alex held his breath for a moment before speaking. "You're thinking if something has happened, it's your fault for sending the doc over there." He turned his head for a moment, looking out the window. "And I know that's what you're thinking, because it crossed my mind as well. Don't forget, it was both our idea for him to do this."

Jessie's grip became white-knuckled as she considered his words. "I refuse to let my mind go there, because nothing has happened. For all we know he's still chatting it up with Cormac's wife." She almost believed her own words.

The Jeep eased to a stop in front of the sheriff's house. Alex looked down at the crumpled piece of paper he held tightly in his fist. "This is it. I don't see the doc's car in the driveway."

Jessie studied the house before climbing out. There was no sign of movement inside. The front blinds hung open and by all accounts nothing seemed to be amiss. It was almost too still. Too perfect. She took a deep breath and pushed open the car door. Alex joined her as they headed up the drive that led to a short, stone sidewalk to the front door. Jessie could just make out the impression of a set of tires in the gravel as they stepped onto the walk.

Pressing the doorbell, Jessie leaned forward, listening for any sounds that might come from within. She was about to ring a second time when the door swung open. The sheriff's wife stood framed in the doorway, her face a mask of politeness.

"Can I help you?" Irma asked, her voice steady as her eyes darted between Jessie and Alex.

Jessie forced a smile. "Mrs. Cormac? I'm Jessie Night and this is my colleague, Alex Thomas. We are friends of Dr. Jefferson Lindquist and were wondering if we could speak with you for a moment?" She forced her voice to remain calm, tamping down any hint of tension and fear that was threatening to grip her.

Irma hesitated for a fraction of a second before stepping back. "Of course, come in."

Stepping into the house, Jessie noticed how immaculate it was. The small entryway table was adorned with pictures and knick-knacks and beside that stood an antique coat rack with a green, vinyl jacket hanging from one of the hooks. There was a patch on one sleeve with an emblem of the mountain range and the words Bidonville PD emblazoned around it.

Irma led them into a comfortable living room where she perched on the edge of a leather recliner. "What can I do for you?"

Jessie kept the same casual tone, but her gaze burrowed into the woman. "As I said, we're friends of Dr. Lindquist—do you remember him?"

Irma scrunched her face up and then widened her eyes. "Oh yes, that nice man who took care of Roger yesterday."

Jessie nodded. "Yes. That's right. Well, he was supposed to come by here this morning to check on Roger. Have you seen him?"

A flicker of something passed across Irma's face, so quick Jessie almost missed it. Fear? Guilt? "No, I'm afraid not. I was out most of the morning. To my knowledge, no one came by."

Jessie's instincts screamed that Irma was lying, but she kept her expression neutral. "I see. Is Roger home? Could he have spoken with Dr. Lindquist?" She knew the answer but needed to see the woman's reactions.

Irma shook her head, her fingers twisting in her lap.

"Roger's at school. No one was home all morning. I'm afraid if the doctor did come by, we would have missed him."

Jessie could feel Alex's discomfort as he shifted behind her. "That's strange," Jessie pressed, her voice hardening slightly. "Dr. Lindquist was quite certain about his plans to visit. You're sure you didn't see him at all?"

More twisting of her fingers and this time Irma looked away, her eyes drifting upward and to the right. Her smile wavered ever so slightly. "I'm positive. Is something wrong? Has something happened to that doctor?"

Jessie didn't take her gaze off the woman, her eyes hardening just a bit. "Well, we certainly hope not. He's just not answering his phone and he's not back at the bed and breakfast. I was concerned."

Irma offered a nervous smile. "Oh, honey, maybe he went to the coffee shop or somewhere. I mean, if he came by and we weren't at home, maybe he's killing time somewhere and is planning to stop by again later."

Jessie hated to admit that she might be right. It was something that hadn't occurred to her. Except that didn't explain not answering his calls.

Irma must have read her thoughts. "And as for the phone, there are so many dead spots in this town for reception. That's why almost nobody around here relies solely on their cell phones."

Jessie forced a smile and nodded. "You're probably right. For all we know he's already back at the bed and breakfast feasting on Caroline's famous cookies or something."

Irma's laugh came out more like a cough. "You're probably right. If he does happen to stop by after you leave, I'll be sure to tell him to call you."

"You do that," Jessie said. She turned to leave but stopped short, staring at the small side table near the door that led out of the sitting area. It was askew ever so slightly and one of the small figurines sitting atop it was facing the wall instead of outward. She squinted and could just make out a spot of a dried, dark substance near the corner.

Irma tracked Jessie's eyes and was on her feet immediately. "Oh, you caught me just as I was cleaning. Doing some dusting you know."

Jessie cut her eyes to Alex before turning back to Irma. "Yes. I know how that is. Well, we won't take up anymore of your time. Thank you for all your help."

"My pleasure," Irma said, ushering the two of them to the front door. "Say hi to Caroline for me," she called after them as they walked down the sidewalk.

Once inside the car, Jessie snapped her seatbelt in place and turned to face Alex.

"What do you think?" he asked.

"That bitch was lying. She had definitely seen Lindquist this morning. And for everything to be exactly in its place except for that side table and the figurine on it…something happened in that living room. Also, I think I spotted blood on the corner of the table."

Alex narrowed his eyes as he stared at the house. "That tracks with the smell of Pine-Sol. Granted maybe she was cleaning. But now I'm wondering what it was she was wiping down."

Jessie eased the Jeep away from the house.

"Where to now?" Alex asked.

Her voice was like steel when she answered. "To the police station. It's time I had a heart to heart with the sheriff. And God help anyone that steps between us."

32

Twisted

Heavy, plodding footsteps outside the shed door caused Dr. Lindquist and the girl to cease their whispers. His spine went stiff as he tilted his head in the direction of the door. The girl scurried backwards, the darkness swallowing all trace of her. The footsteps stopped just outside the shed walls and Dr. Lindquist could hear someone grunting in effort, followed by the thud of something heavy hitting the ground.

The door swung open, the bottom of it scraping across uneven terrain. The evening light was soft but still burned the doctor's eyes. He squinted, holding up a hand to block the glare. A figure stepped in the doorway, so big that it filled the opening and stopped the light from pouring in. Dr. Lindquist felt his stomach roll. Memories flashed through his mind. Memories of a very large man striding toward him in Irma Cormac's house.

The man took one step and was inside the room, his girth smothering down on the occupants. Dr. Lindquist felt his blood freeze as a massive paw reached out and latched onto his upper arm, dragging him to his feet. The doctor tried to fight back. It felt like he was swatting at an oak tree for all the good it did. He found his voice and attempted to scream in protest. His reward was a hard shaking; like an angry child might do to a rag doll.

Two more steps and Dr. Lindquist felt himself swept out of the shed into the open air. An unceremonious shove sent him sprawling to the ground. The hulking figure turned and lifted a massive wooden beam, dropping it effortlessly into the brackets bolted to either side of the door. Adrenaline pushed through the pain in the doctor's head, and he began to scramble away from the monster on hands and knees. The vice-like grip once again latched onto his arm and pulled him upright.

A shove that nearly decapitated him sent the doctor flying forward. He stumbled, regained his footing and then struggled to keep pace with the giant. "Where are you taking me?"

No answer. Not even a grunt in reply.

"You won't get away with this. People will know I am missing. And they will definitely be looking for that young woman you're holding captive."

The large man stopped abruptly, his head swiveling to face Dr. Lindquist. The look in the giant's eyes nearly caused the doctor to lose control of his bladder. He didn't speak but drew close enough that his breath was like a foul mist coating the doctor's face. Then, he turned and continued walking. His pace picked up to the point that the physician nearly had to break into a jog to match it.

Dr. Lindquist was marched a quarter mile down a winding dirt path that wasn't quite wide enough to be called a road. His head was throbbing, and his face felt like one big toothache. But if he stumbled or slowed, he was treated to another shove or yank of his arm. The man took a sudden right, charging through undergrowth and thickets. Breaking through, Dr. Lindquist saw a dilapidated shack squatting before them.

It stood alone in a clearing barely larger than its footprint. Graying wood created unsteady exterior walls that were swarmed with weeds and wild vines. Above a front door that hung askew was a small window, its glass long broken out. Water damage had stained the framework a rusty red. It reminded the doctor of a hollowed-out eye socket.

They stepped up onto the shallow porch and Dr. Lindquist was amazed that it did not collapse under the weight of his captor. The man brushed open the rickety door and ushered Dr. Lindquist through with a shove to the back. Thick, stagnant air choked the doctor, and he raised an arm to shield his nose. The place smelled of mold...and something far worse.

The room was lit by a kerosene lantern that sat on an overturned box crate in the corner. A stained, mildewy mattress had been placed on the floor. Next to it was a plastic bucket that buzzed with flies. Large patches of dark mold spread across the wall and parts of the ceiling like an unchecked disease.

A cough came from the wall behind him, and he

turned to see another figure squatting on what looked like an old wooden chair with a thin plastic back and seat cover. The figure stood and moved closer, leaning heavily on a cane, until they were close enough that Dr. Lindquist could make out the mangled features of a woman.

No. Not mangled. Misshapen. Twisted. He swallowed a lump as he recognized the end product of years of genetics gone wrong. Her face was asymmetrical with one side drooping lower than the other. Her eyes were uneven and a crooked nose only enhanced the unevenness of her jaw. The skin on her face was rough, marked with an unusual assortment of moles and warts. Dr. Lindquist could tell that she needed the aid of a cane because one of her legs was shorter and malformed compared to the other.

But the most unsettling aspect of her appearance was the smile she offered him as she hobbled closer. Her teeth were crowded into her mouth so tightly that some of them appeared to be sideways. Fetid breath, hotter than the trapped air around him, struck Dr. Lindquist as she spoke.

"You a doctor, I hear." Her voice was deep and rattled with trapped phlegm.

He nodded, unsure if it was a question or a statement.

She blinked rapidly, and he noticed the dryness to the orbits as her gaze took him in from head to toe. Despite the deformities that crippled her features, he could see a spark of intelligence in the woman.

Her throat crackled as she cleared it. "I have one use for you, and one only. If you don't fulfill that use, I'm going to have Clint over there pull your head off with his hands—" She gestured at the giant who had ushered Dr. Lindquist into the shack. "I've seen him do it before and I assure you it looks like a most painful way to die." Her tone was short and matter of fact. "So, it would behoove you to do what I need of you."

Dr. Lindquist swallowed hard, his heart pounding relentlessly in his hears. He tried to find his voice, but it had abandoned him.

The woman continued. "I'll take your silence as a yes." She turned away and dropped back down in her chair. She raised the tip of her cane and swept it around the dirty space. "This here is going to be where you live. I'll make sure you're fed and get water every day. Someone will also come by and empty the shitter once a day—" She pointed at the bucket. "Clint here will let you go out on the porch for a bit every couple of days."

The doctor's mind was racing. Vertigo threatened to send him to the floor. His voice was small and trembled when it finally came to him. "What... how long will I be here?"

She cocked her head to one side, her face a mask of confusion. "Why, as long as I need you. Or until you're dead. Which is what will happen when I have no more use for you."

He could only stare. His eyes roving the room, trying to understand the situation he had found himself in. "I... I can't be here. I have a life and a job and people who will miss me."

She frowned, clearly confused by his words. "Well, that was your old life. Your new one is here. And if you're thinking your friends will come looking, well I can only hope they do." Her crooked smile carried the promise of great violence and chilled the doctor to the core of his being.

He needed time. Time to think and plan. "What is it that you think I can help you with?"

She studied him with those crooked eyes again before speaking. "Think? I don't think. I know. We are in need of a new doctor. Our community is hurting right now. We're dying off. That girl you were locked in the shed with? I need you to take a look at her and make sure she can carry a baby. And then, once she's with child, you'll make sure it's healthy and breathing when it comes into the world."

The doctor's mouth dropped open as he stared incredulously. "I...I'm not a gynecologist. I can't do what you're asking."

Her frown returned as she shifted uncomfortably. "I thought you said he was a doctor?" She addressed Clint's massive form.

The man shrugged. "He said he was. Want me to kill him?"

Dr. Lindquist spoke quickly. "I am a doctor. Just not the kind that you need."

"What kind are you?" asked the old woman.

He cleared his throat. "I'm a medical examiner. I perform autopsies. I examine the bodies of the dead to determine why they died."

She seemed to lose herself in thought for a moment. "Seems to me a doctor's a doctor. If you know your way around a body, then what does it matter if it's dead or alive? You'll stay here for the night and Clint will be outside to kill you if you step foot out of the house." She struggled to rise. "The girl will be brought over in the morning so you can take a look at her and make sure everything works."

She made it clear there was nothing more to discuss as she shuffled to the door. Clint followed, letting the door slam behind them.

Dr. Lindquist looked around at the prison he now found himself in. Shock gave way as the realization of his situation hit him. He was a dead man. That much was certain. The only thing he had left to consider was how he wanted to go out. He looked around, the dim light of the lantern illuminating the filthy space around him.

And the light gave him an idea. A terrible, reckless idea.

33

Wait Till Daylight

Sheriff Cormac stared at the woman standing before him. Red splotches moved from his neck to his face as he struggled to control his anger. "Ms. Night, you are dangerously out of line." His lip quivered in barely contained anger.

Jessie stood before him, both fists planted firmly on his desk. "Sir, I don't mean to be out of line, but you have to see how all of this looks to me." She locked eyes with him, refusing to look away. This wasn't the first man in a position of authority she had confronted, and she needed him to know that.

His lips were white he had pressed them so tightly together. "What makes you think I give a rat's ass how something looks to you? This is my county, my police station, and my investigation. I won't be told by someone who has no connection to the people of this community how something needs to be handled. Now, I'm sorry you think your friend is missing—"

Jessie cut in. "I don't *think* anything. I *know* he's missing."

The sheriff glowered. "Just because you don't know where he is, that means he's missing? For all I know he hustled it back to Pine Haven to get away from you. Where's his car?" Jessie hesitated and the sheriff took it as an invitation to continue. "So, he's missing...but so is his car?"

Jessie felt her back stiffen. It took all her willpower not to punch his smug face. "Sheriff, he wouldn't have gone back to Pine Haven without telling us. He would not have left his clothes in his room. He would most certainly answer our calls. Something is very wrong here. And not just with Jefferson Lindquist." She gave him a knowing look, one eyebrow raised.

He narrowed his eyes in return. "Why don't you just say what it is that's on your mind, missy?."

Tension built in the air. Alex stiffened next to Jessie and Deputy Hardin began to fidget in place. He took a step forward, but she started speaking before he could reach her. "I think someone in this town killed Marley Shaffer, and it wasn't Kerry. I think that same someone is responsible for the disappearance of my friend. I also think that this person is connected with Lost Cove and whatever is going on up there. And finally, I think that you not only know what's going on but you're complicit in it as well."

The sheriff slammed his meaty hand down onto the desk so fast that it sounded like someone had fired a gun inside the department. Jessie expected the outburst and didn't flinch. He pushed off the desk with his hand, drawing himself to his full height. "I think that maybe I'm going to have Deputy Hardin escort you out of here before I throw you in jail."

Jessie smiled. "On what charges? Which ones will you make up to try and keep me here?"

His eye twitched and his cheek trembled. "If you know what's good for you, you'll leave. Right now. And not just my office. When you get back to Pine Haven, call me if your friend isn't there waiting on you. Then we can start the clock ticking to fill out a missing person's report."

Jessie ground her teeth, her hand clenching into a fist. "Maybe, I'll just call the state police. Report to them what's going on and see if they can't come have a look around your home. Because when I was there this morning, it certainly looked like there had been a disturbance. And you know what?" She turned to Alex. "Didn't Lindquist leave his medical examiner kit back at the bed and breakfast? Doesn't he have some luminol in there?" Out the corner of her eye she saw the sheriff twitch. "And how long after a scene is cleaned can it still show traces of blood?"

Alex rocked back on his heels. "Yeah, I'm pretty sure he keeps some in his kit. And as far as I know, it can detect blood for a couple of months usually; depending on what was used to clean it up, of course."

Jessie turned back to the sheriff. "I'm willing to bet that even you can't stop a search warrant, sheriff."

Together, she and Alex stormed out of the police

department, stopping on the landing just before the sidewalk.

"What do you think?" Alex whispered.

"I think we circle around back and see how long it takes him to rush back to his house, bleach in tow."

They started for the side of the building but were stopped by a figure stepping out of the shadows. Jessie dropped into a defense stance, fist at the ready, only to recognize the form standing before them. "Roger? What are you doing out here?"

The boy's eyes were wide and he looked around frantically. "You shouldn't have done that. You shouldn't have threatened him. He'll take it out on Irma now for letting you in the house earlier."

Jessie shared an angry look with Alex before turning back to the boy. He had his arms around his chest, clutching them to his body. "Roger...are you saying the sheriff hurts your aunt?"

His face contorted in pain. "No. I mean...not really. He doesn't mean it. He just works so hard and is under so much stress right now." He dropped his gaze when she tried to search his eyes.

"Roger. Look at me. Was the sheriff the one who gave you that black eye and hurt your ribs?"

The boy bit his lip to keep it from trembling. "Is what you said true? Is Dr. Lindquist really missing? I liked him. He was good to me."

Jessie glanced at Alex knowingly. In her experience, when someone didn't answer a direct question that made them uncomfortable, it usually meant the answer was yes. She returned her focus on Roger. "We don't know exactly what happened. But we're going to find out."

Roger nodded nervously, looking around.

"Roger, do you know something?" Alex asked. "Anything that could help us find Dr. Lindquist?"

The boy pursed his lips as if trying to decide what he should and shouldn't say. "I...Dr. Lindquist was at the house this morning. I didn't see him personally, but I was headed out the back to cut through the woods to town when his car pulled up. I figured he was there to talk to my uncle or Aunt Irma."

"Was the sheriff there?" Alex asked.

"My uncle wasn't there then," Roger answered, shaking his head. "But he usually comes home just before lunch."

"And do you know if he did that today?" Alex asked.

A blush crept up the boy's neck and he cast his eyes down. "I don't know. I was in school."

Jessie took a deep breath. "Roger. I think we both know that isn't true. I don't know what the deal is with you and school, but you haven't been going. I know that because I spoke to your principal." The boy looked up at her, his eyes wide with surprise. "Don't worry. That isn't something I'm here to deal with. I'm sure you have your reasons just as I'm sure your aunt and uncle have theirs for letting you skip." She sensed it wasn't the time to bring up her suspicions about the sheriff and his wife being the boy's relatives. "But all I need to know is where my friend might be. You said he was good to you. Well, he's good to a lot of people. He's important to a lot of people. And if you can help us find him..."

Roger again looked around, biting the inside of his cheek. "He came home before lunch. Dr. Lindquist's car was still there."

Jessie exhaled sharply and looked at Alex.

"Were you in the house with them?" Alex asked.

Roger shook his head emphatically. "No. And I swear that's the truth. I stay out of the house as much as possible when my uncle is there. I was out back, so I couldn't hear anything. I heard another car pull up in front of the house, but I have no idea who it might have been. After a bit, I saw my uncle get in his car—he had pulled in behind the doctor's car—and he drove away. I stayed where I was until I was sure he was gone. Then I went into the house, but the doctor wasn't there. Aunt Irma seemed upset and was cleaning the living room. She told me to get a sandwich and go up to my room. That's what I did." He looked at the two of them sheepishly. "I was up there when you came visiting. I wanted to say something, but I was scared."

"It's alright," Alex said. "And you never saw who was in the other car or what happened to Dr. Lindquist's car?"

"No, sir, I didn't. Honest to God."

Jessie gave a questioning look to Alex. "What now?"

"I think I can help."

They wheeled around to see Deputy Hardin step around the corner of the building.

"Were you eavesdropping?" Jessie asked.

He nodded. "Yes, ma'am, I was. The sheriff sent me to follow you. See where you were heading. That crack about the luminol rattled him something fierce. I wasn't sure why..." He glanced over at Roger as he stepped closer to them. Alex took a half-step back, his eyes locked on the deputy. "You don't trust me. I can appreciate that," Hardin said. "But I am just as in the dark as the two of you on this."

Jessie turned to face him. "Then help us."

Hardin stared hard at her before shifting his gaze to Roger. "Go home. And don't talk about any of this with your aunt."

Roger swallowed hard before nodding and running off down the sidewalk.

Jessie turned sharply on Hardin. "Alright. Talk."

The deputy tensed at her tone, and his jaw clenched. "Something is going on with the sheriff. I don't know what it is, but it's definitely had an impact on his behavior. And what I'm seeing now is only making it even clearer in my mind. He's not a bad person. He's a good man...and a good sheriff. But that's not what I'm seeing."

"When did this change occur?" Jessie asked. "Was it when I arrived and started asking questions about Marley Shaffer's case?"

The deputy shook his head. "No. Well...that has certainly amplified it, but if I'm being honest, I noticed it before."

"Look, I know a thing or two about working under a sheriff who might operate in the gray areas a little too much," Alex said, glancing at Jessie. "In your opinion, is Sheriff Cormac dirty?"

The deputy flinched like he had been struck. But the hurt look in his eyes told them this was most likely something he had asked himself. "He is not. The sheriff is one of the most upstanding, law-abiding citizens of this town."

"How long have you known him?" Jessie asked.

"Well, I grew up here, but didn't really know him until I started on the force. And even then, he's not the type you get to know. Keeps everything pretty buttoned up about his life."

"In other words, you don't know him at all," Alex ventured.

Jessie held up a hand before the deputy could respond. She could sense his temper flaring. "What did he say to you just now? What about our exchange is causing you to be concerned enough that you followed us out here?"

"I'm just doing what the sheriff ordered me to do. He said if the two of you showed up and set foot on his property, I was to arrest you. And if you resisted in any way, I was authorized to use...extreme force." He didn't clarify what that force was.

He didn't have to.

Jessie moved closer until her face was only inches from his. "Do you know where Jefferson Lindquist is?"

His answer was immediate. "I do not." His eyes flitted away briefly.

Jessie's breath caught. "But you have an idea?"

"Maybe. I mean...I have no rationale behind this other than a hunch. But you mentioned Lost Cove. And it's not the first time that place has come up in the last couple of days when the sheriff has been around. I heard him mention it the day Kerry was found dead."

Jessie's brow wrinkled in thought. "Do you know who he was speaking with when it came up?"

Hardin drew in a breath and held it for a split second. "He was arguing with Kerry about something. But I swear I don't know what it was."

"Did he have anything to do with Lindquist's disappearance?" Alex asked.

Deputy Hardin didn't answer but swallowed hard and looked away.

"Okay, well this solves it," Jessie said. "I'm going back up to those abandoned buildings in Lost Cove to see if that's where Jefferson is."

She and Alex turned away, but the deputy stopped them. "Don't. At least, don't go at night. That place is a lot more dangerous than you can imagine. And it's not abandoned. Wait till first light. I'll take you."

Jessie tensed. "How do we know you won't be leading us into a trap of some kind?"

He sighed. "It's a trap alright. But not one I or the sheriff could have set. If your friend is up there, more likely than not, all we'll find are his bones."

"Then we're not waiting until daylight," Alex said, turning away.

"You go now and you'll both die. There's no way you can enter that place at night and live. You want a chance at all of saving your friend, then wait."

Jessie chewed on his words. "Seems like night would give us the element of surprise."

The deputy shook his head vehemently. "What's up there is vulnerable in the daylight. Half of them are blind and don't like to come out until it's dark."

Alex dropped his arms loudly to his side in exasperation. "Half of what, Hardin?"

He gave them a solemn look. "Monsters. That's what took your friend. And if you go up there now, they'll take you, and by the time the sun comes up you'll pray for them to finish you off."

_____

34

Too Late

"Monsters," Alex said. "What do you think he meant?"

Jessie's tone hardened. "Doesn't matter. I've killed monsters before."

They were sitting on Jessie's bed back at the bed and breakfast. Night had fallen, and Deputy Hardin had convinced them not to make an attempt at trekking into Lost Cove without him. He mentioned the treacherous terrain and the fact that they could easily fall off the side of the mountain or into a gorge in the dark of night. Even with the light of the moon, the forest would be pitch black. Reluctantly, Jessie had agreed. She had seen the landscape for herself and if she were being honest, she doubted she could find her way back to Lost Cove under the cover of darkness.

Hardin told them he would go to the sheriff's house to wait on his arrival. That way he could let the man know

that Jessie and Alex had not ventured near the home-
stead. He'd agreed to meet Jessie and Alex at the bed and
breakfast just before first light. Dawn would just be
breaking by the time he led them into the woods and up
the mountain to Lost Cove.

"The question is," Alex continued, "how much do you
trust Hardin?"

"More than Sheriff Cormac at the moment."

Alex nodded. He had his revolver out and was carefully cleaning it. "You think the kid was telling the truth?
That the sheriff hurts him and the wife?"

Jessie sighed deeply. "I don't know. I've known men
who were prone to physical violence with their loved
ones. He just doesn't give off that vibe. But if there's one
thing the military taught me, it's that people wear two
faces. One the world sees, and one that only a very
unlucky few get to witness. So, anything is possible."

At her feet, Blizzard huffed a great sigh as he
stretched out lengthwise on his back, his stomach
exposed for scratches. Alex nodded with his chin towards
the shepherd. "He accompanying us in the morning?"

Jessie thought for a moment as she rubbed his soft
fur. "No. I don't think so. We don't know what we're
heading into. I'd rather not put him in harm's way. Plus,
Caroline seems very attached to him. If anything were to
happen tomorrow...well, at least I know he'll be taken
care of."

Alex didn't respond to the morbid statement but
exhaled sharply and held up his revolver. "Done. And
tomorrow is not up for debate. You're going to be carrying
too."

She didn't disagree. She had grown up with guns and knew there were situations where they were called for. But she also knew they could sometimes give you a false sense of security. And her gut told her that tomorrow would be one of those situations where they could not afford that.

"Alright. I'm going to try and get a few hours of sleep, and I suggest you do the same. We'll be heading out of here before we know it," Alex said. He got up, nodded goodnight to Jessie, and made his way to his room.

Jessie lay back on the bed, staring at the ceiling. Alex was right. She should get some sleep. She'd need all the energy she could muster in a few hours.

But she also knew sleep wasn't going to happen. She lay there for an hour, waiting for the stillness that hits a house when its inhabitants had dropped off into dreamland. When she was certain there was no chance of disturbing anyone, she got out of bed, slipped on her boots, gave Blizzard a kiss on top of his head, and slipped out.

THROUGH THE WINDOW, Jessie watched the sheriff pacing back and forth in front of the couch. She couldn't make out what he was saying but, judging from the animated gestures and the angry way he stabbed at the air with his hand, she doubted he was in a very good place. Irma sat on the couch, her head down, hands clasped in her lap.

The woman wasn't speaking and when Jessie looked closer at the sheriff's body language, she could tell from the angle of his body that he was speaking with someone else just outside of her line of sight. He was waving something around in his hand, and Jessie strained to see what it was. He raised it higher, jabbing a finger at it. She squinted, trying to make out the shape.

A cellphone. Sheriff Cormac shook it and seemed to speak harshly to whomever was in the room with them.

A hunch flashed through Jessie's mind, and she whipped out her own phone. She thumbed through her contacts until she found the one marked 'DOC'. A quick press of the screen and she waited.

A split second later and the phone in the sheriff's hand lit up. He ceased his rant and looked down at it before stabbing a finger at the screen. Jessie heard Dr. Lindquist's voicemail pick up as she dropped the call.

Her heart pounded as she scrolled through the contacts to find Alex. She had just pressed the call button when she realized her mistake. She was too preoccupied with the phone and didn't hear the footsteps behind her until it was too late. She spun, looking up, just in time to see the butt of a rifle coming towards her face.

35

Make Them Family

The gentle buzzing of his watch's timer pulled Alex from a light slumber. His pillow being on the opposite side of the bed and the twisted sheets attested to the fitful night's sleep. Swinging his legs over the side of the bed, he reached for his phone and checked messages. There was one from Deputy Hardin that had come through a half-hour before he woke. It was to both he and Jessie and it stated that he would meet them on the street in front of the bed and breakfast.

A quick shower and change of clothing later and Alex exited the bedroom. He saw the door to Jessie's room was still closed and briefly thought about knocking. His fist was raised, but he stopped last minute, and instead made his way to the kitchen. He turned on the light and grabbed one of the granola bars sitting in a wicker basket on the table. It wasn't a homemade muffin, but it would have to do.

Out front, he saw a tan sedan and headed for it, nodding at Deputy Hardin. He looked around for Jessie before moving around to the passenger side and opening the door.

"Huh," he said, slipping in, "I expected Jessie would have beat me out here."

Hardin shook his head, glancing at his watch. "Nope. I've been here for the last ten minutes and you're the first person I've seen."

"Guess that means I get shotgun," Alex said, settling back against the seat. He looked around at the inside of the spacious vehicle. "Decided against an official cruiser?"

"That wouldn't have been a good idea. First, we're not going up there under any official business, and second, even though it's a fair hike to get to the Cove, there's no need taking the chance someone might see us coming. We need every element of surprise we can get."

Alex weighed his words thoughtfully. "So. Care to tell me about these monsters you were talking about?"

Hardin shifted uncomfortably in his seat. "Well, first off, you don't have to say it like I'm off my rocker or something. I didn't mean literal monsters." Alex didn't speak, just waited for the deputy to continue at his own pace. "I'm sure you and Jessie have probably realized that the abandoned ghost town of Lost Cove isn't so abandoned. It's also not filled with ghosts either. There are still remnants of the earliest settlers in those mountains where Lost Cove was founded. As the families that called Lost Cove home moved out...well, the mountain folk around the settlement moved in. I mean, there were shacks already in place, and a few of them even had early plumbing. But those mountaineers were not like the people of Lost Cove. They were...untamed. Years of keeping only to themselves had made them...more feral than human, let's say. There were rumors that they had been having relationships with members of Lost Cove for years before the settlers packed up and moved away. Some even said that was the real driving force behind them leaving the mountain. To get away from being picked off by those savages that preyed on them. Talk of constant raping and cannibalism in the winters drove the Lost Cove residents out. Many of them ended up here. Some were descendants of Lost Cove, and some were reputedly offspring of the others that lived up there." He stopped talking, his eyes locked in the distance.

"So, no one really knows who could be...?" Alex's voice trailed off.

"Old Doc Anderson knew. At least I think he did. But it was decided long ago that it didn't matter. Bidonville accepted everyone. Made them family. As for Lost Cove, we don't venture up there and they don't come down here." He swallowed, blinking rapidly. "At least that's how it was."

Alex stared hard at the man. "What about all the women who go missing or turn up dead in this area? Are they related to what's happening up in Lost Cove now?"

Again, Deputy Hardin swallowed, reaching up to scratch at his cheek. "I don't know. The sheriff always said the mountains were dangerous. Lots of accidents happen to campers up there."

Alex squinted. "Yeah. Accidents." A thought struck

him and he looked at his watch. They had been talking for a while. "Where is Jessie? This isn't like her to be late." He took out his phone, swiped at it, and held it to his ear. "Voicemail. She isn't picking up." A few flicks of his fingers and he froze, looking at the screen. "I've got a missed call from her a few hours ago. But no message." Unease gripped his spine. Alex was on his heels as he rushed from the car to the door of the bed and breakfast.

He took the stairs two at a time as he sprinted for Jessie's door. He knocked hard, leaning close. "Jessie? You in there?" A pause. "I'm coming in." He pushed the door open to find Blizzard looking up at him from the bed. He called her name again as he stuck his head in the bathroom.

"Is she here?" Hardin asked from the doorway.

Alex stood in the middle of the room, his hands on his hips. "No. I can't imagine where she might be." He walked over to the large armoire near the bed and opened it. "Her coat and boots are gone."

Blizzard and Deputy Hardin followed him down the stairs to the kitchen where they found Caroline turning the oven on.

The old woman looked up, startled. "Oh, Alex. I wasn't expecting anyone to be up and about so early. I'll have breakfast ready in a bit." She looked at the other young man at his side. "Officer Hardin. What brings you to my establishment?" A look passed between them that raised a tiny flag in the back of Alex's mind, but he wasn't sure why.

"I was meeting Jessie and Alex," the deputy said. :do a little sight-seeing."

Caroline frowned slightly. "Well, I was under the impression they had seen all there was to see."

Hardin nodded sheepishly. "Well, yes, ma'am, I'm sure they have. We were just going to wander about a bit further up the trails. Jessie was interested in taking some pics further up the ridge."

Caroline's eyes widened. "I see. Well, you better get going then. Get a jump on the sun."

"Actually, we were waiting on Jessie," Alex said. He heard his voice skip when he said her name. "Have you seen her this morning? She isn't in her room."

Caroline smoothed her apron. "I have not. But I only just got up a bit ago myself. Maybe she went for a run. She seemed fond of doing that."

The thought rattled around Alex's mind. "No...I don't think she would have gone without letting me know. And she certainly wouldn't have gone without taking Blizzard."

At the mention of the dog's name, Caroline's eyes lit up. "Yes, he seems rather attached to her. Crept out of my room just as soon as he heard her back in the house." She glanced at Hardin again.

And again, the flag popped up just a bit more. Alex cursed himself for not having Jessie's ability to decode body language. He shook the feeling off. Subtlety had never been his strong point. "You don't think she would have headed off without us, do you?"

Hardin flinched next to him, his mouth dropping open. "What makes you think that?"

"Call it a hunch." He placed at Caroline, clearly not wanting to say too much in front of her.

"She wouldn't go by herself," Hardin said. "Would she?"

Alex had to admit it didn't feel like something Jessie would do. "No, I guess not." His thoughts were racing as he tried to imagine himself in her shoes. "But I'm betting there's one place she might have gone."

Hardin read the man's eyes. "The sheriff's place. No harm in checking."

Together, they started to leave the kitchen, but Alex turned and motioned to Blizzard.

"Oh, you can leave him with me," Caroline said. "I'll watch over him."

Alex shook his head. "Not this time. If Jessie's not at the sheriff's, and decided to head up into the mountain on her own, then Blizzard might be our best bet for tracking her."

Caroline looked forlorn, her eyes darting from man to dog and back again. "But...those mountains, if you have to go up there, are no place for a dog." She stared hard at the deputy. "They might not see Blizzard as being any different from any other kind of animal up there..."

Alex frowned at the look that passed between the two of them. "Well, let's hope it doesn't come to us having to go up there and look for her. My number is on your registry where I signed in. Please call me if you hear from Jessie before we get back."

UNEASE BEGAN to turn to fear as it gripped Alex's spine. Deputy Hardin eased his sedan to a stop behind the Jeep off to the side of the road. Together, they got out and examined the vehicle.

"It's Jessie's," Alex said, staring at the Jeep. He stuck his head inside, looking around. "Keys are in the ignition, so she was planning on coming back." He walked around the Jeep, head down. "No other footprints except for the ones leading away from the driver side door. She was alone."

Hardin looked down the road and nodded. "Sheriff Cormac lives about a quarter mile just down this road. Looks like your hunch was right as to where she might have gone."

They hurried back into the car, and Hardin pushed the engine hard. He came to a stop in front of the house. Other than a single outside light mounted above the garage, the place was dark and eerily silent. Alex studied the house before climbing out. "Maybe no one's up yet." The first rays were only just beginning to add a glow to the night sky.

Hardin shook his head. "No way someone's not awake. Irma should have half the sheriff's breakfast on the stove by now."

They moved quickly across the lawn and to the front door. Hardin took the lead, knocking loudly. "Let me do the talking."

Alex wanted to argue that point. What he wanted to do was grab the sheriff by his shirt when the door opened and slam him against the wall. Repeatedly. Until he told them where Jessie was.

Hardin must have sensed the man's thoughts. "We good?"

Alex bit his lip. "Yeah. Let's do this."

They turned back to the door. There had been no answer and no one seemed to stir within the house. Hardin knocked again. Still no answer. Finally, Alex leaned past him, reaching for the door handle.

Hardin stopped his arm. "I don't know how they do it in Pine Haven, but here, you walk into anyone's house you're liable to get shot. Especially the home of a police officer." Alex dropped his arm and pulled back. "Let me," the deputy said. He tried the handle and found the door unlocked. A push caused the door to creak open. "Sheriff Cormac, it's Deputy Hardin. I'm at your doorway and am stepping inside the house. You here?"

Silence was the only answer he got.

He ran his hand along the inside of the wall until he found a light switch. A click flooded the room with over-head light, illuminating the comfortable, but well broken-in furniture. Alex stepped around Hardin before he could be stopped. "Jessie? You in here?"

Again, more silence. Then, after a couple of frantic heartbeats, a shuffling came from the hallway off the living room. Both men turned, Hardin moving one hand to hover over his revolver as Roger slowly came into view.

His face was a mask of fear until he recognized deputy Hardin. A wave of relaxation rushed over his frame. "I thought...you were more of them."

Hardin rushed over to the frightened young man. "More of who, Roger?"

His eyes went wide and he gave a questioning look to the deputy.

"It's okay, Roger. Alex is a friend," Hardin said.

The boy stepped forward, wincing as he walked gingerly into the room. He made his way to the couch and dropped down. "There was a man and a woman here with my aunt and uncle. They made me go up to my room, but this time I stayed in the stairwell to listen. They were mad. Something about how things had gotten so screwed up with the doctor."

"Dr. Lindquist?" Alex asked.

Roger frowned. "I don't think so. I think they were talking about the other doctor that used to be in town. My uncle was telling one of the men that if he had shown some restraint then they wouldn't be in this mess. The other man replied something like...how was he to know the man had such a soft head. Or something like that."

The two men exchanged worried glances before Hardin spoke up. "Roger, did you see what the people he was talking to looked like? Did you recognize them?"

The boy shook his head, a flash of pain crossing his features with the movement. "No, sir. But I could tell he was big. Very big. The floors practically groaned under his weight. They took to arguing some more and then everything went really quiet. Someone else opened the door and came inside. They were dragging something with them." His voice trailed off and his eye began to well up.

That old icy feeling rose up inside Alex and began scratching at him again. "Roger...did you see what was being dragged?"

The boy swallowed and tears began to run down his cheeks as he squeezed his eye shut against the memory.

"Roger. What was it?" Hardin said, his voice catching in his throat.

The boy looked up at them with red, puffy eyes. "It was Jessie."

36

Just Incentive

The world seeped back into Jessie's consciousness like a slow-rising tide. A dull ache throbbed behind her eyes, each pulse a reminder of the darkness that had swallowed her. Her senses, dulled and disoriented, gradually sharpened, attempting to paint a picture of her surroundings. The rough texture of burlap scraped against her cheek, the fibers tickling her skin. Musty, earthy scents filled her nostrils, hinting at dampness and decay. Silence filled the space around her, broken only by the occasional creak of wood and the distant drip of water.

Jessie's heart hammered against her ribs as she tried to move, her muscles protesting the forced stillness. Her wrists, bound tightly behind her back, sent a jolt of pain through her arms. She was sitting upright, her body slumped against the hard back of a wooden chair. Panic threatened to claw at her throat, but she fought it, drawing on years of training to focus her mind. She didn't move but her thoughts were firing rapidly.

Assess the situation. Gather information.

She strained her ears, listening for any sound that might betray her location. The dripping water seemed to be coming from somewhere to her right, a slow, rhythmic *plink, plink* that echoed in the silence. That told her the room she was in was nearly empty of furniture or anything else that might absorb sound. To her left, she heard the faint rustling of leaves, suggesting an open window or door. A floorboard creaked behind her, and Jessie's breath hitched. She could feel the presence of another person, their silent approach sent a shiver down her spine.

"You awake?" A raspy voice, thick with age and tinged with malice, slithered into her ears.

Jessie didn't respond. Her mind raced to map out the tone and speaking patterns. The voice was unfamiliar, but the accent hinted at a thick, rural upbringing. It was someone local to the area.

Something nudged the back of her chair. "Don't bother trying to peep us, girlie," the voice continued, a hint of amusement lacing its tone. "Won't do you no good."

She felt the burlap pulled off her but the blindfold covering her eyes still crippled her. Why do both? Whoever had grabbed her wasn't taking any chances. Either they had done this before or they were aware of who she was and what she was capable of. She felt a surge of anger, but decided there was no point in keeping up her subterfuge.

Despite the pain shooting through her face, she tried to keep her voice as even as possible. "Where am I? Who are you?" She knew they wouldn't tell her anything. But that didn't matter. She needed to move her jaw, make sure everything was still working after the hit she had taken.

A dry chuckle filled the air followed by more of the raspy voice. "Told you not to worry about how hard you hit her. She's fine. Didn't holler and carry on like her friend did."

The mention of a friend sent a jolt of fear through Jessie. Had they captured Alex? Or were they referring to Dr. Lindquist? She carefully struggled against her bonds, testing the knots that held her. The coarse rope bit at her skin, refusing to give way.

"Save your energy," the voice chided. "You're gonna need it for what's to come." The drop in the tone didn't sit well with Jessie.

Footsteps receded, leaving Jessie alone with her racing thoughts. She took a deep breath, concentrating more on her surroundings. Musty air filled her lungs. The scent of decay grew stronger, suggesting she was in some kind of enclosed space, perhaps a barn or an old shed. Her mind flashed back to the one she had found on her first venture into Lost Cove. Instinct told her that wasn't where she was. That place was way too small to accommodate multiple people moving around.

She shifted in her chair, testing its stability. It was sturdy, unlikely to topple easily. The wood felt rough and unfinished, the edges digging into her back. A sudden wave of nausea washed over her, and Jessie realized she was hungry and thirsty. How long had she been unconscious? Hours? Days?

The sound of footsteps returned; this time accompanied by the clinking of metal. Jessie tensed, her muscles coiling in anticipation of what might be coming.

"You thirsty? I'm betting your throat is burning something fierce."

This time, Jessie had a better grasp on the pain coursing through her head. She tamped it down, not letting it mask her other senses. The voice belonged to a woman, although there was something about the deepness of the pitch, the raspy smoker's timbre that suggested the speaker might not be in the best of health. Jessie flinched, drawing her head back as she felt something cool and metallic pressed against her lips.

"Just water," said the woman. "You got my word on that."

Jessie tried to resist, but the burning in the back of her throat overrode her reluctance. She parted her lips and coolness soothed her. The water had a slightly unfiltered tang to it, but otherwise, it felt like velvet on her parched lips.

"There, that's better, huh?" said the woman.

"Why are you being nice to me?" She needed to get a feel for who was holding her captive.

"Oh, it's not for you. You're just incentive. So, I need you to be healthy when the time comes."

"When the time comes for what?" There was a shuffling behind her. Slight, almost muffled, but her body tensed as her head tilted to the side a bit.

"Whew. You really don't miss a thing, do you?" said

the woman. "You're hearing my friend. He's the one that brought you to me. And he's here to make sure you don't try nothing."

"Where am I?" Jessie asked.

The woman chuckled. "A place where the past ain't quite as dead as some might like it to be."

"Lost Cove." At least now she had confirmation. "And what about my friend? Jefferson Lindquist. Is he here as well?"

"The doctor? Yeah, he's here."

Jessie stiffened. She didn't like that the woman was so open and upfront. It meant she had no intention of ever letting Jessie taste freedom. Still, they obviously needed her. The woman had said as much. And if they didn't, Jessie knew she wouldn't still be breathing.

"So, here's the deal," the woman said. "We need your friend the doctor to do something for us. And we need him to do it fairly quick. My friend here wants to just smack until he complies, but the last time we did that it didn't turn out so good. Plus, I can't have some brain-rattled doctor trying to deliver babies." Jessie's thoughts came so fast she couldn't track them. "I mean, we could have just broken his fingers but what good would that do, right? But then it hit us. I'm betting he'd be a lot more agreeable if he had to watch us break your fingers."

Jessie felt hot breath on her face, accompanied by a rancid smell that nearly made her gag. The woman had leaned in close...inches from Jessie. Jessie controlled her urge to gag, and considered head butting the woman as hard as she could. If she could catch her square in the nose...but then what? She was still securely restrained.

She sensed the woman draw back, followed by more shuffling behind her.

The woman moved to stand behind her as well and Jessie could hear that she favored one leg when she walked. She filed that away. That might just come in handy later. There was a brief exchange of whispered voices. Whoever was speaking, kept their voices low and spoke rapidly. So fast that Jessie couldn't discern how many people may have been speaking. Silence... and then more shuffling. Jessie could smell the woman next to her.

"You sure?" the woman said. Jessie sensed that the woman wasn't speaking to her. The woman huffed. "Fine. But don't come crying to me if you get your pecker bit off trying it." A chill raced up Jessie's spine as she felt the woman lean in close yet again. "How old are you?" Jessie swallowed but didn't answer. "Cos it seems like someone seems to think you'd make good stock for us." The woman let out a phlegmy cackle. "Looks like we're going to have another use for you after all."

37

An Uneasy Alliance

The last gnarled branches whipped past Alex's face as he emerged from the dense under-growth onto a rocky outcrop. He paused, chest heaving, to catch his breath, before stumbling forward behind Deputy Hardin. The hike up had taken them longer than Alex had anticipated, but the deputy had been adamant taking the long way around was the only feasible option.

Alex breathed heavily beside him. "I thought you said they couldn't see well in the daylight. That we were safe."

Deputy Hardin placed his hands on his hips and stretched, relieving the aches marching up and down his back. "I said the really bad ones are impacted by sunlight. And they're not vampires. They can still come out, just can't see very well is all." He stepped forward to the edge of an outcropping and pointed down. "Anyway, another reason to come up the way we did is because it breaks onto this ridge, where we can get a look at the town without being seen. And it avoided any booby traps."

"Booby traps? You didn't mention those."

Hardin shrugged. "They are more for trapping food. But up here...some folks don't differentiate between what we would consider food and what they might consider food." He gave a nod in Blizzard's direction and Alex swallowed hard as he remembered Caroline's words.

"So how come you know so much about these... folks?" Alex asked. He eyed the deputy closely.

Hardin looked over, locking eyes with him. "Because Kerry used to tell me all about them. He said the day might come when I'd have to come up here and that I should be as prepared as possible. He said the sheriff knew everything about these parts, but that he would never speak about it. And he was right." He broke eye contact and swept his gaze down the ridgeline. "But if you're worried about me having their blood in my veins, don't. My family moved here shortly after I was born."

Alex just nodded but didn't reply. He wanted to take the deputy at his word, but at the same time he kept his guard up. He didn't know these people, and he wasn't about to turn his back on anyone. The words came out before he could stop them. "Do you believe Kerry killed Marley Shaffer?"

Hardin didn't look Alex's way and he didn't hesitate. "No. I don't. And I don't think he killed himself either." His eyes were trained in the distance. "The town is laid out pretty much in a curved line that follows the slope of the hillside. They didn't have equipment for excavating or clearing, so they built where the land allowed." He pointed. "See that? That's the old church. One of the first structures the original settlers of Lost Cove built."

Alex followed Hardin's gaze to a skeletal structure with a steeple that tilted precariously towards the sky. "I see it."

"If we get separated, or run into any trouble, head there. You can see the steeple from anywhere in town. It's the center of Lost Cove and the easiest place to get to. The abandoned houses and shacks look easy to navigate from here, but once you're down there in it...it's a whole different world."

"Do you think that's where they have Jessie?" Alex's tone was both fearful and hopeful.

A low growl emanated from Blizzard. Alex looked down as the dog's ears perked forward and his nostrils flared. The hackles along his spine rose as he stared down the ridge. Alex put a reassuring hand on his back. "I think he smells her."

Hardin nodded. "Dog's got a better nose than any human. If he says she's there, I believe him."

"What now?" Alex asked, his eyes scanning the town for any sign of movement.

Hardin crouched low; his face creased in concentration. His gaze slid over the scattered, rusted and patchwork rooftops littering the floor of the ridge. Scant movement at the far end of the town caught his eye and he pointed. "There. Makes sense that's where she might be. It's protected from any strangers or hikers wandering in because to get to it they'd have to walk through the town proper."

Alex nodded in agreement. "But I'm betting you know a way around all that."

Hardin exhaled sharply. "Nope. Not at all. But—" His gaze swept the backside of the ridge. "If we make our way down the south slope it will bring us out behind the town at that far end. Then, we try to find Jessie and the doc... if he's still alive." He turned his head to the sky, looking at the afternoon sun.

Alex didn't have to ask what the deputy was thinking. It would take them another hour, maybe two, to go around. The sun would start to dip at that point, setting early behind the mountain peaks that jutted upward around them.

They were going to be more vulnerable. But he quickly pushed that thought out of his mind. As they turned to plunge back into the overgrown thickets and foliage, Alex ran his hand over the gun at his side. His eyes were fixed on the back of the man in front of him, leading the way. For some reason, neither of the two offered him much reassurance.

In silence, the three figures—man, dog and deputy—made their way to the far side of the ridge where they would start their descent into the heart of Lost Cove.

38

A Vexation

The grandfather clock chimed six times, and each note hit Caroline's frayed nerves like a hammer. Back and forth she paced across an already threadbare rug in the tiny living room. Her mind was restless. No. It wasn't just her mind. It was her soul. She couldn't remember her grandmother's face, but her words were sharp in Caroline's mind.

If a thing weighs heavy enough and long enough on the mind, it can vex the soul. And when that happens, the only recourse is action.

The silence of the bed and breakfast, usually something she craved, was no help. Her chamomile tea sat untouched, its warmth dissipating into the emptiness of the house. She looked over at the needle point pillow lying in the chair and felt even more annoyed at her life. Was this what she had become after so many years? Someone she didn't recognize in the mirror?

She looked at her hands, now beginning to gnarl with age. At least she hoped it was age. Maybe it was the start of the malformations that had been passed down for generations to the women in her family.

No. Couldn't be that. That twisting of the bone and warping of the skin would have appeared at birth and she had been lucky enough to be spared that.

She sighed. She wasn't tired. Going to bed early wouldn't quiet her thoughts. If anything, the thought of climbing under the covers right now made her feel claustrophobic. A warm bath maybe. No. She feared she might let herself sink beneath the water and not climb back out.

Her mind flashed to the young woman, Jessie, and her friends. She knew they wouldn't come back down from that mountain. Her husband had probably already seen to that. It wasn't the first time this scenario had played out. Not even the second. But what made it different this time? Plenty of fresh-faced, dewy-eyed young ones had suffered the same fate. Caroline had been forced to turn a blind eye many times. So, what made these different?

Maybe that was it. The difference wasn't with them. It was with Caroline. Part of her had never really agreed with what happened up on the mountain, but at the same time, it was just how things were. How they had always been. Fretting over it now wouldn't change anything.

It was that darned dog. Why had that Alex fella taken him? She told him how much danger the poor boy would be in up there, and he hadn't cared. Or maybe his care for his friend overrode what he might have felt for the dog.

She cursed herself. Her plan to keep Blizzard had gone out the window.

Seeing that pup disappear out the door had struck something buried deep inside her. She made her way to her tiny prison of a bedroom and rummaged around one of the drawers of her dresser. She pushed aside her unmentionables and found what she was looking for. Clutching the framed photograph, she dropped down on the foot of the bed and stared at it.

She tried, but she didn't recognize the woman in the picture. It was so long ago, and so much had changed. It was taken a couple of days after she arrived in Bidonville. The woman staring back at her was hardened, but she still had something...a spark, a glimmer in her eyes. Caroline looked up from the picture into the small mirror above the dresser.

There was no spark anymore. That had been beaten out of her long ago. She glanced down again at the baby the woman was clutching and ran a finger over his tiny countenance. That child was gone too. Taken away like everything else.

She dropped the picture on the floor, not caring at the sound of glass breaking. She looked up into the mirror again and tried to summon that spark.

Her soul was vexed. And she needed to do something.

39

A Father's Teachings

The burlap sack scratched against Jessie's neck as she sat alone with her thoughts. The room they had her in was stifling and the stench of the coarse material that covered her face only added to her resolve to get free. The rope that bound her wrists was frayed but strong. She knew better than to waste strength trying to break it. But while it was sturdy, her fingers told her it was a simple overhand knot her captors had used. Given time, she would eventually be able to undo it.

But time was the one thing she was pretty sure she didn't have.

She had no idea why the raspy-voiced woman and the man had been talking, or why they left her. But she was fairly certain they'd be back soon. If she was going to free herself, then it had to happen fast.

And that meant she had a decision to make. Years of her father's training and his words flowed through her mind.

"The time will come when you're going to find yourself restrained. Tape, zip ties, handcuffs, ropes...hands, arms, feet... something will be used to restrain you in ways you can't now imagine. You're going to be afraid and think everything is hopeless. But it isn't. There's a way out of every tough situation. It's not pleasant, but I'm going to teach you. Word of warning; it's going to hurt and you're going to cry. But one day, you'll thank me."

He was wrong. She hadn't cried. But she had screamed.

There were two options. Neither one would be pleasant. She could either dislocate her shoulders in order to rotate her arms back and overhead so that she could then access her hood and blindfold. That would allow her to manipulate the rope with her teeth to untie the knot. Or she could dislocate her thumbs and worm her hands free of the rope.

A quick assessment of her situation told her which was more plausible. Part of her stretching and workouts were dedicated to conditioning and strengthening certain muscles in her shoulder that would allow her to dislocate them if needed. However, once she slipped them back into place, there would be a lot of weakness and instability. That would hamper her ability to defend herself and attack as needed.

That was not something she was willing to risk given the situation she was in.

So, thumbs it was.

She clenched her jaw, biting down hard against the pain, as she turned her wrists outward against the rope. When she felt the pressure against the base of her thumbs, she pulled outward and up, using the ropes to press against the joints until she heard a pop.

A cold sweat broke out over her body, and she exhaled slowly, controlling her breathing as she worked her hands against the ropes until she managed to slip one out, and then free the other. She grimaced as she brought her arms in front of her. Taking a deep breath, she assessed the direction her thumbs had been pulled from the sockets and then worked them back into place. She rotated each, trying to relax the ligaments supporting them that now screamed mercilessly at her.

The sack was rough in her hands as she removed it, and she felt instantly better having her skin exposed to the air. Next, she worked the blindfold down, giving herself the first glimpse of her surroundings.

The space she was being held in was a one-room shack, with misaligned, rotting timbers for walls, and a crooked window with no glass. That explained why she was able to smell so much of the vegetation. Behind her was the only solidly built piece in the entire structure.

A door.

A shadow approached it, followed by the rattle of keys. Pulling the hood back over her head, she quickly sat back in the chair and scooped up the discarded rope. Jessie draped it over her hands and placed them back behind the chair just as the door swung open.

Footsteps approached, the boards creaking slightly

under their weight. Jessie listened for signs that they might not be alone but could not make out the sounds of a second captor.

Good.

Jessie's head sagged on her chest and she didn't move. She kept her breathing as shallow as possible.

Whoever entered the room moved to stand next to her. Jessie could sense their presence but remained motionless.

"Hey." It was a man's voice. And there was something vaguely familiar about it. "Hey, lady, wake up. I'm supposed to take you over to meet someone."

Jessie didn't move, making sure her chest didn't rise and fall.

"Lady...you okay?" The man's voice trembled with excitement mixed with a touch of fear. He shook Jessie by the shoulders. Her body was as limp as a rag doll. "Shit... they're gonna kill me if you're dead." He shook her slightly again, and this time pulled the sack off her head, leaning in close to study her face.

Jessie's eyes sprang open. "Surprise." Her head rocketed forward, smashing into the man's face.

He grunted loudly, his hand flying to a nose that now spurted blood down his shirt. His eyes stretched wide as Jessie stood up quickly from the chair, free of her bonds. She crossed the distance between them and immediately recognized the man.

It was the same person who had attacked her and Deputy Hardin in the morgue. "You." She advanced as the surprised man backpedaled a few steps.

He opened his mouth to shout a warning, but Jessie

was ready for that. Her right hand stiffened and the tips of her fingers shot out, stabbing into his Adam's apple. A gurgle was the only noise that came from him as he grabbed at his throat.

Jessie pivoted, spinning and throwing her weight into an elbow strike that connected with the side of his head, stunning the man. As he dropped one arm, she grasped his wrist and shifted her weight, throwing him violently to the ground. She spun, snatching up the chair, and brought it crashing down onto his head, rendering him unconscious.

She stood still, her ears focused. She couldn't make out the sound of any footsteps rushing their way, so hopefully no one had heard the ruckus.

Moving quickly, she dragged the unconscious man to the far corner of the room where she used the rope to bind his hands behind him, and then used the cloth that had been her blindfold to gag him. He would probably be out for a while, but there was no need to risk him waking and calling out before she could find Dr. Lindquist.

A quick survey of the room, and a search of the man's pockets, yielded nothing she could use as a weapon. That was fine. She shook her hands to get the blood flowing and worked her thumbs in circles to delay the oncoming stiffness that could result from the dislocation.

She would need to rely on her own skillset to get through whatever might be waiting for her out there. Her father's words came to her again.

"You can't always rely on a prop. Weapons can be stripped away from you. but you always have your hands, your legs and your mind. No one can take those from you."

She opened the door to her prison just enough to peek out. Once she was certain there was no one else around, she slipped out into the night.

40

Contaminated Genes

"I'm telling you, if you want me to do this, then I need to do it the right way. My way." Dr. Lindquist kept his tone steady, fighting back any signs of the fear flooding his system.

A man, one he had seen before, stepped forward. He was short and built like a barrel. His eyes were wide set, his teeth jagged and misplaced. His hands were slightly webbed and seemed to be curled into a permanent half fist. He stormed forward at the doctor but stopped when the old woman held up her gnarled hand.

"You said you needed tools. We got you tools," she said.

Dr. Lindquist looked at the assortment of hand saws, pliers and rusty old garden sheers that were laid out on the makeshift exam table before him. They had brought in multiple building pallets and stacked them up to make an examination table, and placed the tools on an old door laid over two makeshift stools.

The old woman continued. "You said you needed clean rags and water and alcohol. Well, we got you the best drinking water we got, and the closest thing to alcohol we could find." She pointed at the jug of water and two glass jars of what the doctor could only assume were pure moonshine. The "rags" appeared to be some folded cotton shirt that he was pretty sure was anything but clean.

He cleared his throat, determined to stick to his guns. "You want me to examine that woman thoroughly, then I need my own tools to do it. And something appropriate for making sure she doesn't get an infection. Surely you can have one of your men bring me what I need from the office in Bidonville."

The shorter man shook his oversized head as he turned to the woman. "Don't do it. He's just stalling for time. Probably plotting up something against us." He turned his eyes on the doctor. "We been doing things this way for years now and we're all fine."

Dr. Lindquist arched an eyebrow. "Are you though?" He turned to the woman. "I don't know what you want with that young woman, but if I'm to make sure she stays healthy for you—"

The woman snorted and cut him off. "Oh, bullshit. You know exactly what we want with her. She's going to help us with a little problem we have called inbreeding depression. And you're here to make sure it happens." She gave him an evil smile. "Don't look so surprised. You thought I didn't know what was happening to my kinfolk?"

Dr. Lindquist had to admit that was exactly what he thought. The fact that she knew the medical name for her —and many around her—condition told him that she was more intelligent than he gave her credit for.

"Hmm," she scoffed. "Not the dumb hillbilly you took me for."

Dr. Lindquist decided to play along. He figured he was a dead man walking, so there was no need in placating the woman. "That remains to be seen. But, if you're so knowledgeable on the subject, then you must know that you can't repair the damage done to your genetics by a single infusion of fresh DNA from outside the contaminated pool, right? Impregnating that poor girl is not going to solve your problems in the least."

The woman frowned. "What makes you think this is a single infusion?" Her frown widened into a grin. "It takes time, but we've been at this for a while. We just need another doctor to help with the deliveries is all. Then we take it from there."

Dr. Lindquist again felt the chill of fear run up his spine. It wasn't for him. As the meaning of her words settled in, it was for all the young woman who had fallen victim to these people. And all the ones yet to come. "Well, like I said, if you want my help it will have to be the right way. Forcing me will not get you the results you want."

Her deep raspy laugh filled the room. "Oh, sugar. We ain't going to force you. You're going to want to help us. I got some insurance to make sure you comply." She frowned again and looked around the room before turning to the smaller man beside her. "Speaking of... where's that no-good brother of yours? He should be back by now with our insurance. Go see what's keeping him."

The man rumbled in exasperation. "You know Mikey. He's probably just lallygagging around. You know how slow he is. Why do I have to walk all the way over there?"

The woman leveled a look at him that made the man flinch. "You have to do it because I told you to. I don't remember asking you for your thoughts on the matter. Now get going." The threat was minor but explicit in her voice. The man cast his eyes downward and shuffled out the door.

Dr. Lindquist's head was swimming. While he might have been surprised by the woman's knowledge, he was certain she had gained it from someone else. Someone with a medical background. Perhaps the other doctor they had mentioned, the one that had practiced in Bidonville. "If you aren't going to give me the proper tools to work with, then I at least need as much light as possible." He gestured to the kerosene lantern. "Can I get enough light in here to adequately see what I'm doing?"

She squinted, looking from him to the lantern and back again.

"I am a doctor. No matter why you brought me here, I'm going to do the best I can to help any patient. Help me, to help you."

She nodded slowly. "I like that. Help me, to help you. I'm gonna remember that one. More light is the most reasonable request you've made. That I'll be able to do for you."

There was a commotion from somewhere outside the building and the smaller man came bounding back inside, the much larger Clint looming after him.

The woman frowned at the two men. "What's going on?" She looked between them at the door. "Where is she?"

The two men exchanged nervous glances.

"She's gone," said the smaller of the two.

Dr. Lindquist could see the woman suck in a breath and hold it before letting out what sounded like a bellow to his ears. "What do you mean gone? Where's your brother?"

The little man shook in genuine fear. "Mikey is out cold. Looks like she messed him up something fierce."

The woman's twisted eyes roamed around the room as she chewed at the inside of her jaw. "Find her. Fast. I'm betting she won't go far, especially if she knows he's still here." She turned to the gigantic man. "Clint, get some more light for the doc here, then go grab that girl out of the shed and bring her here. Stand watch over them both. Don't leave this room for anything." He nodded and stomped out. She turned to the smaller man, shaking her finger. "Go find that woman. Don't kill her but make her sorry she hurt Mikey. Round up whoever you need to help."

He nodded and made his way out the door. She turned her milky eyes on the doctor, her head cocked to one side. Slowly, she moved to follow the two men out the door. There was a click after she closed the door and

Dr. Lindquist knew there was no point in trying to escape.

Still, for the first time since awakening in this hellish place, he felt a glimmer of hope. There was only one person they could have been talking about.

Somehow, Jessie Night was in Lost Cove.

41

A Light in the Darkness

Every rustle of leaves, every snap of a twig, sent a jolt of adrenaline through Jessie's veins. The forest floor crunched underfoot, each step a calculated risk in the darkness. Her senses were on high alert as she scanned for signs that anyone could be following her. She moved cautiously in the dark, arms held out in front of her to protect her face from low hanging branches, weight centered low to help her quickly recover from any potential fall or trip.

The urge to run was strong, and she had to fight the surges of adrenaline. Running blind in the dark would be suicide. Plus, this was their world. For all she knew, there could be someone standing right in front of her waiting for her to fall into their arms. And she wouldn't even know it until it was too late.

She stopped, freezing in place. Something had registered. A sound in the woods that seemed vaguely out of place. She dropped to one knee and closed her eyes, head tilted to one side. Minutes passed and whatever had triggered her instincts was gone. If it was ever there.

Darkness and fear had a way of playing tricks on the mind.

Taking a deep breath, she stood, opening her eyes and scanning the darkness. Ahead of her, she could just make out the tiniest glow of light. Jessie realized her fingers had taken on a life of their own as she strummed her familiar pattern against one thigh as she stared at the light. Pros and cons of heading toward whatever the source of the illumination was flashed through her mind. It was risky. But she also knew that it was even riskier to stay where she was. What she needed was to find a phone, and while the odds of finding one in Lost Cove were slim, it was practically nonexistent that she would find one in the forest.

Taking a breath, she slowly headed in the direction of the glow.

It wasn't long before she could make out a structure through the tree line. It was a steeple, and the glow was now an orange flicker coming from inside the structure.

Candles. That meant someone was inside the church.

A cold knot tightened in her stomach. She crept closer, careful to stick within the shadows of the trees to get a closer look. Once the church was in full view, she stopped. It was as run down and weathered as everything else in the town. She wasn't even sure how it was still standing and able to support the weight of the visibly leaning steeple.

Still, there were no signs of movement inside, no shadows danced across the busted windows, no sounds came from within.

But someone had to have lit the candles.

Satisfied there wasn't an immediate threat, Jessie quickly left the cover of the tree line and crossed the distance separating her from the church. She crouched, her back against the side of the building. Her eyes scanned the foliage she had just left, looking for any sign of movement. Satisfied she wasn't being followed, she then turned her attention to the church. Slowly, moving in a crouch, she made her way to one of the blown-out windows. Taking a deep breath, she peeked inside, taking in everything she could about the space before dropping back below the sill.

As expected, it was basically one big room, with broken and splintered benches that had once operated as pews. They faced a raised dais with a rotted floor that faced a large, crudely constructed cross mounted to the back wall. There were candles in front of the cross that flickered in the darkness.

But there was no sign of who could have lit them.

Carefully, she made her way around the small structure, looking for any other entrances to the space that someone could slip in or out of the building. The church was comprised of the main structure, and a small, attached secondary building that butted out from the back. There didn't seem to be any windows or doors to the back structure, so Jessie surmised the only way into it was from within the church.

Her brief look hadn't revealed where the door might be. That meant if she went inside, she would be at an immediate disadvantage. Still, she needed to get out of the open and into a space where she could think. She needed to devote some serious brain power to what was happening, and it was hard to do that if she also had to worry that someone—or some*thing*—could sneak up on her at any given moment.

Decision made, Jessie crept to the corner at the front of the church. One last look around, and she slipped around the corner and into the opening. Once inside, she stood with her back pressed against the wall just inside the door. It took considerable willpower to steady her breathing while her ears strained for signs that she might not be alone.

She ventured into the open space, careful to keep from walking by one of the broken windows, and took a seat on one of the splintery pews. Her mind raced, recalling everything that had happened. At least now she knew the sheriff was involved. While she hadn't seen who had kidnapped her, it couldn't have been a coincidence that it happened as she was observing Sheriff Cormac in action. Plus, he had Dr. Lindquist's phone. She frowned.

Knowing about a disappearance, and being involved in it were two very different things.

Proving who knew what and who did what could wait. First thing she had to do was find out where the doctor was being held and get them both out of Lost Cove. Instinct told her the best time to do it would be before the sun rose, illuminating all the places she could use for cover. But daylight would also make it easier for her to navigate unknown terrain and see others who were undoubtedly already looking for her.

That triggered another thought, and she stood, making her way to the broken window, listening carefully. If they knew she had gotten free, wouldn't there be more commotion outside? The woman who had taunted her didn't seem like the type to just let someone they had tied up waltz out of town. She listened closely and then heard it.

A snap of a twig? No, the creaking and slight breaking of a rotted piece of timber. Someone was in the church with her.

A quick scan of the space around her showed nothing of use. She cursed herself for not making finding a weapon her first priority after getting free. She took a deep breath to steady herself, and curled her right hand into a fist as she slowly approached the only opening to the right of the raised altar. She knew it would lead to the space built onto the back of the church, but she had no idea who might be waiting for her inside.

For a moment, Jessie considered fleeing to be the better option. But the fact that whoever was in there knew of her presence made her discard running as a strategy. She didn't need someone reporting where she just was. That would only tighten the search grid around her.

As she passed the altar, she took one of the lit candles. It would help her see whoever might be in there, and in a pinch, it could double as a weapon if needed. Moving through the opening, the candle threw the barest minimum of light ahead of her. But it was enough for Jessie to catch the fleeting glimpse of something small scamper across the floor into one of the far corners of the room. Jessie's nose wrinkled. There was an odor in the space. Not entirely offensive but not exactly pleasant either.

Jessie shined the light in the direction of the movement and saw a tiny bundle clad in a dirty, off-white dress crouched before her. It was a young girl, no more than twelve. The girl sat on her haunches, bony knees hugged to her chest, face turned away from Jessie.

Jessie drew back, pulling the candle with her. "Hey. It's okay. I'm not going to hurt you." the girl tightened her grip on her knees, pulling them so tight Jessie feared they might break the child's ribcage. She held her hand up, palm out to show she wasn't holding anything. "See, nothing here to hurt you. Is this one of your candles? Did you light it?"

The girl slowly turned her head in Jessie's direction. "Yes. I was doing my job. Lighting the candles." Her voice was little more than a squeak.

Jessie gave her a nervous smile. "And I'm sure you do a great job with it. Do you have a name? My name is Jessie."

"I'm Clara Beth," the girl replied in a whisper.

"Clara Beth. That's a beautiful name. Are you from here, Clara Beth?" The young girl gave her a confused look. "I mean, do you live in Lost Cove? Is this your home?"

"I live in my house down by the creek. I don't live here in the church."

Jessie nodded. "Have you always lived here?"

"Of course. It's my home."

Jessie looked around in the dark room. "Can you tell me why it's your job to light all those candles out front?"

The girl nodded enthusiastically. "Papa said it's so that the angels can find the souls to take up to heaven."

Jessie frowned. "What souls? Are there...souls here, waiting?"

More nodding. "Sure. When you stop breathing, you go in the well and from there, the angels come find you and take your soul away."

A chill started up Jessie's spine. "Well, isn't that just great. So yes, you have a very important job. Do you know where the well is that the angels visit?"

The girl frowned and looked towards the wall to her right. "I'm not supposed to go in there. I just light the candles when it gets dark."

Jessie chewed her lip. "Good for you. Clara Beth, do your mommy and daddy know you're here by yourself at night?"

"Sure."

"And they aren't worried about you?"

Again, the girl looked confused. "Why would they be worried?"

Fair enough, Jessie thought. "Hey, I'm new here. I have a friend that's new here as well. A man. Have you seen a man here that you don't know?"

Her hair covered her face as she bobbed her head.

"Yep. He's a doctor. Papa said he's going to be my new doctor too when it's time."

The chill covered Jessie's body, raising the flesh along her arms. "Time for what, Clara Beth?"

"I...I don't know. He just said I need to be older to see the doctor."

"Okay, well that's good to know. Do you know where the doctor is?"

"He's at the old doctor's office. The fancy house. I can't wait to go cos I want to see inside the fancy house."

Jessie filed all this away, forcing a smile on the girl. "You know what, it's late. I bet you're supposed to be home by now. You can go, now that your job here is done."

She looked from Jessie to the glow out in the main church. "But I'm supposed to put the candles out after they burn halfway."

"Oh, I'll do that for you. That way, you don't have to stay so long."

The girl's eyes lit up and she smiled as she made her way to her feet. She started to walk away, and Jessie noticed how badly she limped. Her leg was turned outward at an awkward angle.

"Clara Beth," Jessie said. "This can be our secret. Don't tell anyone you saw me here. You don't want them to know I did your job for you."

Clara Beth giggled at her before turning and limping away.

Jessie turned her attention to the wall that Clara Beth had glanced at. Fear flooded her as she stood next to it with the candle, examining the surface. She found a hairline vertical crack in the wall, and when she held the candle close, the flame flickered, pulled in the wall's direction.

She pressed the heel of her hand against the wall, following the crack, until she felt the slightest pop. She pushed harder and the crack widened into a door that she was able to sneak her hand into and pull outward, creating an opening in the wall. She quickly covered her mouth and nose as the putrid air behind the wall nearly gagged her.

Taking a deep breath, she pushed the door, using the candle to light the darkness before her. Her legs nearly buckled at what she saw, and her own darkness threatened to close in around her as she dropped to her knees.

42

A Glimmer of Hope

Jefferson Lindquist was only half listening to the argument taking place outside the room where he was being held. Even though he could hear every word, and was certain it pertained to his future, the doctor was more intent on assessing the young woman with the terrified look on her face who sat before him.

"Tilley," he said, using the name she had told him. He placed his hands on her shoulders and gently rocked her. "Stay with me. I need you to keep focus." The doctor could feel the clammy wetness soaking through her shirt, soaking his palms. Her skin was pallid and cold to the touch. She murmured something, her eyelids fluttering slightly. "That's it. It's me...Jefferson." He watched her breathing closely. It was steady and strong. She was still hanging on. He pulled her body to his in a hug, whispering in her ear. "We're getting out of here. Someone's coming to get us. They're going to take us away from here, but I need you to stay focused so we can act when the time comes. Do you understand?"

Dr. Lindquist didn't know if it was the touch of his body against hers, the sincerity with which he spoke, or the caring caress that let her know she wasn't alone...but something seemed to reach the young woman. He felt life, a tiny tremble of it, flow through her body.

"Help?" she said. Her voice was so low that it was hard for him to make out, even pressed against her as he was.

"Yes, that's right. Help has arrived. And we have to be ready."

Outside, the voices grew louder. He could make out the raspy old woman, and the mountain-sized man known as Clint. The other voice he wasn't so sure about.

"Why the hell did you let her get the jump on you like that?" Clint was saying.

"I didn't know she was untied. She took me by surprise," came the pleading reply.

"She's a little thing. How come you didn't just smack her one and then tie her back up?" said the woman.

"It wasn't like that. She was fast. And hit hard. I ain't never been hit like that before. not even from Papa."

Clint huffed, stomping his foot. "You hush your mouth about daddy, God rest his soul. Did you even see which way she went?"

"I was out cold."

"I oughta cuff you one myself. But that's okay, we know how to get her back." Heavy footsteps echoed in the room as the three of them marched inside.

"Now, Clint, that won't work," said the old woman.

"The hell it won't," he replied, eying Dr. Lindquist. "All we have to do is make him scream loud enough and I'm betting she'll hear it and come running. She's hiding in the woods is all. I can make him yell loud enough that she'll hear him a couple miles away."

"We need him, you big buffoon. How's he going to doctor if you mess him up?" the woman replied.

Clint seemed to ignore her as he stalked towards the doctor. "He'll heal. I just need one of his hands...I'll leave the other alone."

Tilley started to scream as the giant reached for them, her voice piercing Dr. Lindquist's ear. The doctor panicked as well, starting to pull away from the man, but still using his body as a shield for the young woman behind him. He gritted his teeth and braced for the pain as the larger man forcibly took the doctor's wrist in his two hands. The doctor's arm looked like twigs in the hands of an angry child about to be snapped.

A commotion coming through the front door was all that stopped Clint as he turned to see an older man, doubled over with a severe hunch, shuffle into the room. Behind him he dragged a small girl with an obvious deformity of her leg.

"Mannered, what are you doing up here?" the old woman rasped.

The man gave the girl a yank and shoved her in front of them. "Go on now. Tell them what you told me when I asked what you were doing back so soon from getting your chores done."

The girl looked fearful, but stepped forward, hands clasped before her. "I did my chores like I was supposed to. But I didn't stay the whole time because the lady told me she would put the candles out for me so I could go home early."

The woman shuffled close to the girl, looking down at her. "What woman? She have a name?"

The girl nodded. "Yes. She said her name was Jessie and she was a friend."

The silence threatened to suffocate Dr. Lindquist as he felt the pressure on his arm relax. The big man turned his attention to the girl. "She was at the church? Where did she go from there?"

The girl lifted her boney shoulders. "Nowhere. She stayed inside."

Clint spun on the man next to him. "Go. Take a couple of the boys and find her." The man hurried out of the house, leaving Clint and the old woman to stare at the young girl. "What else did she ask about?"

The girl's eyes were wide as she slowly looked over at the doctor. "Him."

The old woman began to fret. "She's coming here. There's only one way up the path. Take her by surprise."

The giant looked over at the lights. "Should we put those out?"

"No. I want her to focus on the house. If she knows this is where her friend is, the lights will help draw her to us. She'll walk right past you."

Clint nodded and stomped out of the house. The woman turned to face Dr. Lindquist, malice in her eyes. She reached into the folds of her clothing and took out what looked like a long ice pick. She held it in front of her as she reached forward and snatched the young girl to her with surprising speed. "Mannered, get out of here. You ain't much of a use in what's to come. Go on home and I'll send Clara Beth to you soon."

The man seemed to hesitate a split second before complying, his crippled form following the giant out of the house. Once he was gone, the old woman turned Clara Beth in the doctor's direction. "Either one of you make a sound and I'll blind this girl." The tip of the ice pick hovered less than an inch from the terrified girl's eye.

43

Visitor in the Dark

The outskirts of Lost Cove consisted of overgrown vegetation, fallen trees and piles of discarded trash left to rot and rust, becoming an unwelcome part of the foliage. Alex and Hardin carefully made their way through the debris, Blizzard winding in and out of obstacles at their side, his padded footfalls nearly silent in the evening.

"So, the one thing we haven't discussed is what exactly we plan to do once we find Jessie," Alex said.

The deputy exhaled sharply. "We hope she's alone; we get her, and we get out. The less chance we have of a confrontation, the better."

Alex frowned. Right now he was very much in favor of confronting someone about what the hell was going on around here. "You know we can't do that, right? If even half of what I suspect is going on here is really happening, then a lot of people are going to pay."

Deputy Hardin glanced back at him. "And how will you make that happen? There are two of us, three if Jessie is still...here. Against who knows how many folks are in this town." He shook his head. "We get Jessie, the doc, and we head back down the mountain. Then, we involve whatever authorities are needed to deal with the fall out."

Alex stopped in his tracks. Something clicked in his mind. He now understood what it was about Hardin that had been pinging his radar. The evasiveness, the hesitancy and dodgy behavior. "You're afraid of these people, aren't you?"

Hardin stopped short, turned around and closed the gap between the two men to stand nose to nose with Alex. "You're damn right I am. And if you had half a brain you would be too." He sighed, running a hand through his hair and then down his face. "I'm sorry. I didn't mean to insult you. It's just...you aren't from around here. You haven't had to grow up in the shadow of this place. These...people, or whatever they have become over the years, are the boogey man and the thing that lives under the bed for all of us. Only, they aren't some made-up tales created to make kids mind their parents; they are warnings to help keep our children safe." He swallowed hard. "Especially the girls."

Alex understood and wasn't about to press the man for more details. "You're right. I have not lived your experience in the shadow of all this, so I had no right saying what I did."

They continued in silence before Hardin cleared his throat. "Nah, I get it. I've been where you are. I just didn't have the courage to come up here and do something about it." His voice trailed off and he swallowed hard. "Look, you should know that if things go sideways and someone attacks, don't try to reason and don't try to fight. They might look slow and crippled, but they're strong as hell and I am not even sure they feel pain. If you have to put one down..." He faced the detective and aimed his finger at his forehead.

Alex clenched his jaw and nodded before moving on.

"Also, as I'm sure you and Jessie found out, something changed about twenty or so years ago. When all the disappearances and dead women started showing up. Rumor had it that someone had risen among them. Someone smart and driven who was giving them directions. No one knows who it is, but that's when things became less random with the mountain folk and more... deliberate in whatever it is they're doing."

All this was sinking in when Alex noticed Blizzard stop in his tracks. The dog stiffened, his hackles up as a low growl rumbled forth. His eyes were glued to something ahead of them, in the shadows. His nose quivered and his ears twitched as he tracked movement. Alex and the deputy dropped low in the overgrown bush, trying to discern what had attracted the dog's attention.

Alex felt a hand on his arm and turned his head in the direction Hardin was pointing. At first, he didn't see anything. Then a shadow shifted. It was crouched low, hugging the base of a tree. Alex couldn't tell if it was facing towards them or away. He looked at the deputy who hadn't taken his eyes off the shape. Alex slowly moved his mouth next to Blizzard's and whispered.

"Down." Instantly, the shepherd dropped to his belly, unmoving.

"I'm going to circle around to the left. It's the only way for whoever it is to run when you head directly at them. Flush them out." Hardin's voice was so low Alex had to strain to hear him.

Alex swept his eyes along the terrain and saw that the deputy was right. If whoever was hiding ahead of them tried to run, there was only one unobstructed way. "What if they have a gun?"

"Then shoot first," Hardin whispered before heading into the dense bush to their left. In seconds the shadows had swallowed him.

Alex looked at Blizzard, suddenly wishing he had learned the silent hand commands Jessie had trained him with. "You stay," he said, before rising from his crouch to make his way towards the now still figure in the distance.

Once he was closer, Alex realized the figure was crouched and facing away from him, looking at the paths that led down to the broken houses laid out before them. The snapping of a branch underfoot alerted the figure to his presence and they spun briefly before sprinting off to the left, smacking into a waiting Deputy Hardin. Bouncing off the man, the figure was thrown to the ground.

Hardin had his gun in hand and pointed before him. "Show me your hands!" Just as quickly, he yanked it up and away from the boy.

"Roger?" Alex said. "You really need to stop popping up like this. How the hell did you get up here?"

The boy was frantic, his face dirty, his eyes wide and tearful. "My uncle brought me. He's angry. So mad...like I haven't seen before. He said it was time I learned about where my roots really are, or something like that. He has his gun, and said he needed me to see how things get handled when they get messy. He said it's time for a hard reset...or something like that." His eyes darted wildly between the two men. "He's going to kill your friend."

Alex locked eyes with Deputy Hardin. "Looks like we just found the mystery person in charge."

44

Everyone has to Breathe

Fatigue, pain and an overriding sense of disbelief flooded Jessie as she took in the horrific sight before her.

The candle she held illuminated more remains than she could count. Most were skeletal, nothing more than dirty bones wrapped in faded rags. They were stacked into the far corner of the room, spilling forward in a disrespectful pile. She had seen mass graves before and knew that those in front were the most recent victims.

Her eyes were locked on a male that had only just begun to decompose. His body was slumped over on its side, resting on a pile of bones. A grayish-white powder covered it, and Jessie didn't have to get close to recognize the scent of calcium oxide, or quicklime. Someone was trying to hasten the breakdown of the body. The man was dressed like the townsfolk of Bidonville, but as she held the candle closer, she could see that he was wearing comfortable, expensive loafers, and a gold watch gleamed on his forearm. She was pretty sure she was looking at the body of the town's physician.

But that wasn't the worst of what she saw. It was what was littered around the dead man and strewn among the numerous corpses piled around him.

More bones. Only these were smaller.

So much smaller that it made Jessie's heart ache. Some of the tiny bones were misshapen or broken...but there was no mistaking what she was looking at. Tears stained her face as she looked at so much life thrown aside. Cast away like someone's unwanted garbage.

And as she took in the carnage before her, a white-hot spark began to grow in her stomach.

Voices rushed to her, followed by heavy footsteps approaching the shabby church. Jessie blew out the candle's flame and pressed her back against the wall beside the door leading to the mass grave.

Footfall on the creaky wood flooring told her someone had entered the church proper, and she held her breath.

"What if she already left?" It was the man who had attacked her in the morgue back in Bidonville. The one she had left tied up and gagged.

"Well, first we clear the church then we start checking outside. She didn't get far." The second voice was the one from the room she had been held in.

The first man would not be a problem. He didn't have a taste for violence. But the second voice carried the promise of pain. This was someone who relished hurting others.

Their footsteps stopped at the same time, followed by a whispered exchange that Jessie couldn't make out. When they continued walking, their steps were lighter and slower. They had seen the open door in the wall and were heading towards her.

Fine. Anger fueled her as she slowly put down the candle. She hesitated for the briefest of seconds before gliding forward. "Forgive me." The hushed words left her lips as she reached down, running her hands over the dry bones around her.

Moving to place her back against the wall next to the door, she crouched and waited. A glow floated into the space. They had been smart enough to pick up candles of their own.

The first man entered the room tentatively, thrusting his light before him. He was short but stocky, and powerfully built. Most people when entering a room look to the left and right, but rarely look down and to the side. He didn't see Jessie crouched next to him until he was already in the room.

She was holding a broken femur bone and swung it like a club, connecting with his knee cap. He grunted, dropping the candle as he bent forward. Jessie swung again, this time using the bone to strike him with an uppercut that connected with his chin, sending him sprawling backwards into the church.

There was a grunt as his flailing body collided with that of the man behind him. Before either could react, Jessie was on them. Surprise barely registered on the face of the man she had left tied up before the toe of her hiking boot connected with the side of his head with a crunch. He went down, a puppet with cut strings.

She pivoted in time to see the stocky one charging at her. It barely registered that the knee she struck should not allow him to stand, let alone run, before he was on her. He barreled into her with a grunt, driving her across the room. He had strength and momentum on his side. Strength Jessie knew she couldn't match. But his momentum? Now that she could use against him.

Rather than try to counter his charge, Jessie gave into it. She let her weight drop down, her body going limp. As expected, the man began to stumble forward, still maintaining his grasp around her waist. He released one hand from around her, instinctively seeking to break his fall. When he did, Jessie threw her hip into his midsection and rolled, bringing him crashing down face first onto the floor next to her.

Once he was on the floor, she twisted from his side, taking control of the arm he had attempted to break his fall with. Wrapping her legs around his arm, her feet braced against his chest, she arched her back, straining until she heard the tell-tale pop of his shoulder dislocating. Releasing the man, she rolled away, landing in a crouched position.

To Jessie's surprise, the man didn't scream, or roll over grasping his shoulder in pain. Instead, he scampered to his knees, his face red and blustery as he stood. He went to swing at her with his damaged arm, looking down in surprise when it didn't follow his mental commands.

"What'd you do to me, bitch?" he demanded, still trying to make his arm reach for her.

45

Yep, She was Here

"Where's Sheriff Cormac now?" Deputy Hardin asked.

The quartet of three men and a dog were making strides into the heart of Lost Cove. They moved at a fast clip, no longer worried about what attention they might attract as they labored ahead. They could hear voices coming from the distance, but the trees and vegetation muffled the sound too much for them to make out words.

"He's at a cabin near the back of the settlement," Roger answered. "He told me to wait for him outside, but he was so mad...I didn't know what he was going in there to do. So I ran."

"How did you get up here?" Alex asked.

"He has an old four-by-four that made it up most of the main trail. Then it was just a twenty-five-minute hike or so into the town."

Hardin turned to him. "He drove up in that old Blazer of his?" The boy nodded. Hardin turned to Alex. "That truck of his has an old CB radio as well as a wide band police issued radio. There's a chance it could get a signal out. One that could reach the state troopers."

Alex stopped, his mind racing as he considered the deputy's words. He turned to Roger. "Which house is your uncle at?"

The boy pointed ahead and to their right. "It's the first one that sits back from this path as you round the bend. Only one lit up with lanterns."

Alex looked in the general direction, then back to Hardin. "I'm going in. I need to find Jessie and the doc. You go for the radio."

Hardin turned to Roger. "Can you show me where the Blazer is?"

The boy nodded and turned to head off the trail. Hardin nodded at Alex and then headed after him, plunging into the darkness.

Alex turned back towards town and the distant voices and picked up the pace as he marched forward. Blizzard stopped at his side, lifting his nose as he sampled the air. "What is it, boy?" Alex looked around nervously, checking for any movement in the patchy shadows. "I don't see anyth—"

The dog gave a short, sharp bark, and then plunged ahead, running along the barely trodden path they were on.

Alex sprinted after the dog, struggling to keep him in view. He pushed branches out of his way and powered over broken vines that threatened to send him sprawling before emerging from the forest to see Blizzard giving the ground some hard sniffs. The dog walked in circles a couple of times, and then proceeded forward, nose glued to the ground. This time, he moved at a more manageable pace for Alex, who followed close behind.

The shepherd stopped just before the church that Hardin had pointed out from the ridgeline. Blizzard was circling the dirt near the entrance. A low, anxious whine emanated from the dog as he wagged his tail hard, looking from the church to Alex.

"It's okay," Alex said, squatting down beside the dog to comfort him. "She's in there, huh?" He listened quietly for a moment, watching Blizzard's body language. If anyone were outside the church, looking to surprise them, Alex was certain the big shepherd would have alerted him.

He took a deep breath, stood tall, and drew his gun. Making his way into the church, he stayed close to the wall, hugging the shadows created by the candles' dwindling flames. Immediately, his eyes locked on the two bodies. Carefully he approached, weapon at the ready, but quickly saw that they were both incapacitated. He studied them for a second before turning to Blizzard. "Looks like Jessie put quite a whooping on them."

But Blizzard wasn't looking at Alex or the unconscious men. His amber eyes were focused straight ahead at an opening in the wall near the makeshift altar. His ears flattened against his head and his hackles were raised. Alex gave him a reassuring pat as he carefully crossed the space leading to the door. He gathered up a candle in one hand, and entered the space, his gun at the ready.

The site that greeted him made him dizzy and nauseous. He quickly swept the room, looking for Jessie, then breathed a sigh of relief when she wasn't among the macabre sight. Backing up, he motioned for Blizzard to follow him out the door where he gulped a lungful of the fresh, cool air. The dizziness faded as he headed back to the foot trail that would lead him closer to the house Roger had described.

That was where the sheriff would be.

That was where Jessie would be.

Holstering the gun, he plunged ahead into the foliage and the shadows.

46

Bad Punches

Jessie crouched in the darkness, watching the play of the dim light coming from the broken window of the shack and the darkness around it. She had gotten off the main path and approached the house from behind. The terrain was treacherous in the dark, and with each step she had half expected to hear the sound of one of her ankles snapping or ligaments tearing from stepping on a loose rock or into a crevice she couldn't see.

Nothing moved. But she knew a trap when she saw one. There were no sounds coming from inside the run-down cabin. But then why would a lantern be lit? Also, as she approached, the front door, such as it was, was sitting ajar. Almost inviting her to walk up.

Her knees ached as she squatted. But then she saw it. Movement in the bushes to the right of the footpath leading to the sagging porch. Someone was waiting for her to pass.

The question was, how many someones were waiting?

There was only one way to find out. She stood and started to take a step away from the protection of the shadows when a familiar sound stopped her in her tracks.

Barking. Blizzard's barking. It was distant, in the direction she had come from. That meant he was tracking her. Which meant Alex was most likely in Lost Cove as well.

Glancing back at the figure hiding off the path, she saw stirring in the darkness. She wasn't the only one that heard the barking. She reacted quickly. Feeling the ground around her, she picked up the largest rock she could comfortably hold and heaved it in the direction away from the barking. The rock hit and rolled downhill a bit, crunching branches as it went.

Jessie watched a large shadow peel off from the undergrowth and quickly head away from the path in the direction she had thrown the rock. Wasting no time, she sprinted for the cabin door.

Immediately, she locked eyes with an older woman holding an ice pick to a young woman's face. "What the hell?" Jessie recognized the raspy voice at once, her eyes narrowing on the woman who had held her captive. "Clint!" The raspy cry rattled out of her chest.

Her arm dropped slightly, just enough that the startled woman she was holding was able to push her hand aside and throw herself away from the woman. That was when Jessie noticed the man standing to their side.

Dr. Lindquist.

The old woman lunged, trying to grab the young girl. Jessie moved to intercept her, but the medical examiner was already in motion. Dr. Lindquist moved between the old woman and the terrified girl. The shocked look on the woman's face grew as the doctor drew back his fist and slammed it into the side of her head, dropping her instantly to the ground.

"Ow! Damnit!" he cried, wringing his hand in pain.

Jessie was at his side, taking his hand in hers. She frowned, examining it. "You've sprained your wrist. Who taught you how to throw a punch?"

"Old episodes of CSI," he replied, sheepishly.

"Well, as soon as we are back home, I am correcting that form." Jessie dropped his hand and threw her arms around his neck. "You have no idea how glad I am to see you."

He slowly raised his arm around her and patted her on the back. "Not as happy as I am to see you." He pulled away and motioned to the young woman cowering in the corner. "It's okay. This is the friend I was telling you about." He turned back and smiled at Jessie. "The one I knew would come." The girl took a tentative step closer to them. "This is my friend Jessie. Jessie, this is Tilley." He gave Jessie a hard stare. "Tilley Cormac. She's the daughter of Sheriff Cormac. And she's been held here against her will for a couple of months now."

Jessie looked from the girl to Dr. Lindquist, unable to hide the sense of shock she was feeling. "Tilley. I'm sorry we're meeting under these circumstances. But...how did you come to be here...?"

Dr. Lindquist was shaking his head. "We don't have time to get into all that. Is Alex with you? Tell me you have a car to get us out of here."

The look she gave him deflated the man. "I was captured and brought here, same as you. But I heard Blizzard off in the distance. If he's here, then Alex can't be far behind." She looked around, taking in the shabby arrangements. "Maybe we can secure this place until he gets here. I'm sure he brought help."

Again, the doctor shook his head. "No way. This place can't keep out a stiff breeze. Let alone that hulking monster working with her." He jabbed his chin in the unconscious woman's direction. "We can't stay here, Jessie. These people...you don't understand. This is some kind of breeding colony. Or something like that. The isolation of living in the closed-off community has depressed their gene pool. So much inbreeding has occurred that without a new influx of DNA, they're in danger of going extinct. So, they've been...taking young girls and...and..." He didn't have the strength to finish.

Jessie swallowed hard. "Well, it stops now. I promise you that. What can either of you tell me about who's left that's part of this? Is it all of Lost Cove?"

Tilley shook her head. "No. There are some genuine nice folks here. And there are kids. I haven't seen many, but there are some. This all seems to be the work of a select few. They're following the lead of a really mean one..." Her voice trailed off, pained by unpleasant memories. "I mean, he's really bad. The things he does..." Tears welled in her eyes and Dr. Lindquist took her hand in his to comfort her.

"Well, we need to get out of here before this bad man, or anyone else, shows up. I heard Blizzard in the direction of the old church I came from. If he and Alex are coming this way, we can maybe meet them halfway." She looked at the doctor. "Stay close to me. If anything happens, both of you run."

"Jessie, you can't fight these men. Years of inbreeding have changed them...they'll be bigger and stronger than most."

Jessie nodded. "They also don't feel pain. At least not all of them." She pointed to the old woman on the floor. "Anyone else with her? Who was that Clint person she called out to?"

There was a creaking of the floorboards as a massive shadow filled the open door. "That would be me, pretty thing. And you ain't going nowhere."

He smiled, all crooked teeth and cracked lips. Then he clasped his hands together and cracked his knuckles, before advancing on Jessie.

Cat's out of the Bag

Jessie took a small step back, part of her hoping the floorboards couldn't support the mammoth man's weight. That they would snap, opening to swallow him whole.

But that was just wishful thinking.

Somewhere in the distance shots rang out. A volley of them, and then silence.

Clint gave her that evil grin. "Sounds like my people just finished off your friend." He made a fist, cracking his knuckles once again. "I've always been told that it was wrong for me to delight in hurting another person. And I've taken it to heart. They told me I was just too big and didn't know my own strength. That accidents happen. But you know what? That's not true. I always knew what I was doing. I knew when a slap was just enough to rattle some teeth, or when it was just enough to split a skull." He looked over to Dr. Lindquist. "Like what happened to the doc before you. But don't you worry. I understand the need to keep you in one piece. For now, at least." He stood tall, rolling his head around on his neck as his gaze wandered to Tilley. "And you. Deal with your daddy is over from what I hear. That means we can use you any old way we want."

Something in his voice made Jessie snap. "Is that what you did to Marley Shaffer? Were you the one who hurt her?"

The sound of the woman's name brought out a lascivious grin on the man. "She couldn't give us a new child for the Cove. That's all we wanted. So, she wasn't any use to us anymore."

"That's because your own DNA is so corrupted it will probably never take. Any offspring you produce will be an abomination," Dr. Lindquist said, his voice pleading. "But there are things we can do. Genetic treatments and detection scanning that can help your people."

The monster pointed at the doctor. "You were already told what to do. What your place is here. When I'm finished with your friend, you will get little Miss Tilley here ready to conceive. Or I'm going to twist your foot around till it comes off."

A sneer crept across Jessie's features. Anger bubbled inside her. As the man had been talking, she was sizing him up. Trying to take him head-on would be suicide. She also doubted that attacking the usual vulnerable areas on the man would work.

But that just meant she would have to get creative.

Images of the bodies in the back of the church flashed through her mind. The doctor. The bodies of children and those that should never have been brought into this world.

And finally, the image of Marley Shaffer, and what she had endured at the hands of this monster. Everything fed the fire that howled inside her.

She didn't resist. Didn't try to quell it. For the first time, she let it build. Let it add to the anger she had always kept under lock and key. The man standing before her was evil. The kind that shouldn't exist in a decent world.

She didn't want to kill the monster before her. For the first time in her life, she wanted to hurt someone.

"And to think I had thought about keeping you to replace Caroline. She's gotten way too old and mouthy lately. Something tells me you would have been fun to break in."

And that was the nail in the man's coffin. Jessie's eyes narrowed as she remembered the bruises on the older woman's face.

Clint stormed at her, throwing a haymaker right cross at her face. She easily ducked under it, coming up beside him. He turned, facing her and once again attempted to punch her. When that didn't work, he lunged, both hands aimed at her throat. Again, Jessie dodged the man, this time dropping down and quickly striking at his solar plexus before sliding out of his reach.

As she expected, the blow didn't have much effect on the man. But that was okay. She was gauging his speed and response times. They were painfully slow. He was used to relying on his brute strength to abuse older and slower opponents.

Clint frowned as he stormed close to her once again. Jessie knew that she couldn't avoid him forever. At some point he'd corner her and get his hands around her neck or, even worse, swoop her up in a bear hug. She saw him drop his arms to his side before starting to raise them again. And that was when she moved.

She dove at him, spinning around so that her back collided with his massive chest. He was surprised and lifted a hand to grab at her, but he wasn't prepared for how fast Jessie was. She grabbed his hand before he could clench it into a fist. She grasped his pointer and middle finger in one hand and his pinky and ring finger in the other. She quickly ripped her hands apart, tearing the fingers away from their housings in his knuckles. At the same time, she slammed the back of her head up and back, catching him in the bridge of his nose.

He howled, stepping back from her as she spun away from him. Clint looked down at his now mangled hand. Shock quickly turned to rage as he wiped blood from his face with the back of his still functioning hand. Hatred flared in his eyes. But behind the anger there was something else.

Caution.

Jessie maneuvered around the room, turning her side to him, her eyes locked and anticipating the smallest of moves. Clint's hips shifted and she knew he was about to charge. The man came at her like an enraged bull, head lowered, intent on scooping her up and smashing her against the wall of the shack.

Jessie remained calm, letting him come dangerously close to her. At the last minute, just before he could make contact, she bent down, spinning on one foot to sweep her other leg out and back, connecting with Clint's ankles. The speed of her move caught him off guard and the man tumbled face forward onto the floor. Instantly, Jessie rolled onto her back next to him, using her momentum to drive her elbow across her body and into the back of his head, smashing his face even harder into the rotted floorboards.

Clint reached around with his undamaged hand, trying to grab her, but Jessie was already in motion. She rolled, coming up on her feet in a crouch next to him. She grabbed Clint's forearm as he tried to grasp her. Standing quickly, she pulled his arm into the air, and then dropped her knee onto his shoulder, driving her entire body weight into the joint. No matter how strong he may have been, he couldn't counteract the force of physics.

Had he been on his feet, she could never have mustered the force to hurt him. But with the aid of gravity, she heard the shoulder snap as the ball was torn free of its housing.

Then, continuing the same motion, she swung one leg over his arm and performed the same maneuver on his elbow. The report of the bone snapping filled the space like a gunshot.

She stood and moved away from the man. "Stay down."

He grumbled, spitting blood on the floor as he somehow managed to drag himself to his feet. Dark eyes flared as he realized that he only had use of half his body. "Bitch. I'll die before I get beat by a woman."

Then he smiled at her and turned to launch himself at Tilley and Dr. Lindquist.

The doctor moved to place himself between the madman and the screaming young woman. Clint threw his arm with the crippled hand around the doctor's neck, pulling him close as he lifted his knee and drove it into Dr. Lindquist's midsection, dropping him in a breathless heap on the floor. With no one to impede him, he took a lumbering step toward the terrified woman.

Jessie dove at the floor, scooping up the ice pick the old woman had dropped when Dr. Lindquist had punched her. In one fluid move, she came up behind the lumbering Clint and leaped for his back. She wrapped one arm around his throat as both legs clung to his waist. Her right hand became a blur of motion, stabbing at Clint's exposed side. She drove the ice pick between his ribs twice, puncturing his lung, before bringing it up and driving it into the base of the man's skull.

He crumpled to the floor without a sound, landing face first with a thud.

Jessie bent to help the doctor to his feet. He gasped for breath holding his side. Tilley stood motionless staring at the gigantic form of the man now dead at their feet.

"It's okay, Tilley," Jessie said. "He can't hurt you anymore."

Tilley stared at the man, then Jessie. "I've never seen that man before tonight. He has never touched me."

Jessie frowned. "Wait, he isn't the one you were referring to?"

"No. The one who kidnapped me from my home and

uses me to get to my dad is..." Her voice trailed off and her eyes widened in terror. She lifted a trembling hand and pointed over Jessie's shoulder. "That's him."

Jessie turned in time to see Roger step into the cabin.

"Well," the boy said, "looks like the cat's out of the bag now."

Age is More Than a Number

Jessie wasn't sure what stunned her more. The ear-to-ear grin that spread across the boy's face, or the fact that he was holding a gun to Alex's head.

The detective had a trickle of blood flowing down the right side of his forehead and stood to Roger's left, both hands raised in the air. Alex locked eyes with Jessie, and then gave Dr. Lindquist a slight nod. "Jessie. Doc." He was rewarded with a blow to the head from the butt of the revolver Roger held.

"I told you not to speak," Roger said with a sneer.

"Roger...what is going on? How can you...I mean, you're just—" Jessie began.

He interrupted her with a snarl. "A what? A boy? A child?" He spat to his side. "Fuck you. I'm forty-five years old. But I still look the same as the day I saw my sixteenth birthday." His eyes wandered around the room, stopping on Clint's body. "Well. Looks like you fucked him up something bad. He dead?"

Jessie kept her eyes on him as she nodded. "He is. He tried to hurt my friends, and he left me no choice."

Roger stared hard at the body. "Well. I guess he finally found himself in a situation he couldn't solve by punching." His eyes lingered and then wandered over to the old woman lying not far from him. "You kill her too?"

In response, a soft moan escaped the woman's mouth, and she stirred slightly.

Roger nodded. "Good. Cos I need her. And if she had been dead, I was going to shoot one of you in the head." His gaze flitted across them. "Still might. Toss that out the door," he ordered, nodding toward the pick. Jessie complied, throwing the ice pick out into the dark. He placed the barrel of the gun to his head and scratched.

Jessie held her breath. This was something that villains often did in movies, but in real life it usually ended with the perpetrator blowing his own head off. She looked from Alex to the door, her eyes searching.

"You looking for that beast of yours?" Roger said. "He ran off into the woods. I got a couple shots off at him. Might have even winged him I think."

Jessie felt her blood boil. "Roger, what do you think this is going to accomplish? What are you going to do? Keep us all chained up here? Kill us? Do you think we won't be missed? Half of Pine Haven knows where we are."

The twisted smile dropped from Roger. "Yeah. So I'm gathering. And that has put me in quite the spot. But as long as I have her—" he nodded in Tilley's direction, "—it will keep the sheriff in line and doing what I ask. Hell, he let me stay under his roof while we were figuring out what to do to clean this mess up. You should see the looks he gives me sometimes."

"And Hardin? Is he in on this?" Jessie asked.

He laughed, staring at her. "That idiot had no clue. He thought we were all family. Everything was fine until you showed up."

Jessie let out an exasperated grunt. "Fine? A woman was murdered."

Roger grinned. "Actually, she was kidnapped, tortured, *then* murdered. Although technically, if Clint here hadn't killed the doc, she might still be alive."

"And the baby?" Jessie questioned.

Something—a shadow of emotion—moved across his features. "Was not viable. They've been escorted to heaven by the angels."

Hearing this monster speak of anything holy made Jessie's blood rise. "Oh yeah? I saw what that church is being used for. Don't you dare play reverential with me. Tell me something, were you the baby's father, or was it him?" She motioned to Clint's body.

He hesitated before his sneer returned. "Oh, that one was all mine. Each of the ones he created turned out worse than the one before. There are so few of us left. Our culture, our way of life...our families...they are all dying off. Not to toot my own horn, but I knew we needed more. More like me. I wasn't born like the rest. Other than the fact that I look like a fucking baby...I can pass for anyone in any town or city. We needed more. And I tried...but something was broken. And the doc...he couldn't fix it."

"It can't be fixed," Dr. Lindquist spoke up. He winced through his words, still holding his side where Clint had kneed him. "What has happened to your family here is the result of too many generations of inbreeding. The recessive genes you carry are too deep. I'm sorry, but in a case like this, life cannot find a way. We can test you and anyone else from here. Try to isolate what is happening to you on a genetic level...but reproduction for you is off the table. And I think you know that."

Roger's lip drew up, and he stomped forward, hissing at the doctor. "That's a damn lie and you know it. We just haven't found the right stock." Hateful eyes landed on Tilley. "But she will work. I can feel it."

Jessie moved to block his view of the girl. "That's not going to happen, Roger. You know it's not."

Alex nodded at the boy, holding a hand to the side of his head. "The state troopers will be here soon."

Roger laughed. "You mean the ones good old Deputy Hardin was going to call? Newsflash. He didn't quite make it back to the truck. Appears this dangerous mountain has claimed yet another poor hiker who shouldn't have been out in the dark."

Jessie could feel Alex tremble with rage. She gave him the subtlest of movements letting him know the time wasn't right for him to try anything. She needed to buy time to think. "Did you have Kerry killed? Was that your idea?"

He laughed again. "Of course I did. Took some doing. The old geezer put up a hell of a fight. He was the one that gave me the shiner and busted my ribs. But when he realized what I'd have Clint do to his brother, his tone changed quick."

"He sacrificed himself because he loved his brother," Jessie said. "You can't manufacture that kind of love, Roger. That's what you're after, right? You have to see that."

"And what will you do when the child you force on Tilley doesn't survive?" asked the doctor. "Because I'm telling you, it won't."

Roger's words came out as a snarl. "Then I find another. And another after that if needed." His breathing was forced. "You don't get it. You just say it so casually... telling me that my family is going to be erased out of existence. How is that fair? Since I came into this world, I was told we don't matter. That to everyone else, we don't even exist. And that once the last of us were dead and gone, no one would even remember us. But why is that okay? This —" he spun, sweeping the gun in an arc, "—might not seem like anything to you. But this is my home. Why is it so wrong for me to want it to continue? Why can't...why can't I have something to love and cherish and watch grow up?"

Jessie swallowed hard. "Roger...it's natural to want all of that. But there are laws—"

He cut her off by jabbing the point of the gun in her direction. "Don't you talk to me about laws. The only laws that exist up here are the ones we make. The ones *I* make. Look at me. I didn't come out all bent and twisted. If I'm okay, then I can make more like me. I just have to keep trying."

Dr. Lindquist cleared his throat. "But you aren't okay, Roger. You have to know that deep down. You're smart. I've seen that. You know this isn't going to solve anything."

Roger huffed. "What am I supposed to do? Just accept the fact that my people are dying off and there isn't anything I can do about it? No. I refuse to accept that. I studied genetics. I know. I just...just need to find the right combination. I can make more of us. I can save my family." He leveled a look at Jessie. "But you're no good to me. You're too old. Too..." He looked at Clint's body. "Too dangerous." He raised the gun, aiming it at Jessie's chest.

"Roger, no!" cried Alex. Before anyone could react, he was already in motion, his body in front of Jessie's, his back to Roger as he shielded Jessie from the bullet.

He tensed; his body stiffened. But the sharp bang they expected to echo through the shack didn't happen. Slowly, he turned, moving away from Jessie so they both had a look at Roger.

His face was a frozen mask of confusion. Eyes stretched wide. His mouth hung open as if he were about to speak. A small pool of frothy blood appeared at the corner of his lips and ran down his chin.

There was a protrusion sticking through the front of his shirt in the center of his chest. He looked down at it just as the gun clattered to the floor. Slowly, he spun around, shock settling in as he took in Caroline's tiny form standing behind him.

She backed away, letting go of the ice pick lodged in Roger's back.

He reached for her, but not in a menacing way.

"Mama? Why?" And then he collapsed, landing in a heap next to Clint.

"He always was too mean for his own good," Caroline said. Tears streamed down her cheek as she sat down on the floor next to her child. She took his hand in hers and held it gently. Then, slowly, as if she were in a dream, she picked up the gun he dropped and brought the barrel to her temple.

Jessie lifted a hand to stop her, but before she could, a white blur moved through the door. Blizzard padded to Caroline's side, his bright eyes locking with her teary ones. He whined softly, moving to place his head against her chest.

Caroline hesitated, but then reached up a hand and scratched his ears. Her body convulsed as she put the gun down and took the shepherd's head in her arms, her sobs filling the cabin as she buried her face in Blizzard's soft fur.

49

All Are Welcome

It was midday when Jessie and Alex finally sat down on the front porch of the bed and breakfast. They were sore, battered and bruised, but the wooden rockers were surprisingly comfortable. The plate of fresh baked cinnamon buns sitting on the small table between them also helped ease the last day's pain.

They sat quietly. Even though the morning bustle had slowed, there was still a lot going on around them. The screen door was taking a beating with the foot traffic in and out of the house. Each time it slammed, Caroline's voice could be heard echoing throughout the house. "If you break that door, you're going to have to fix it!"

When she had brought Jessie and Alex the cinnamon rolls, she had joked about it. "It is going to take time. When you were raised in a barn, sometimes all you know is what the animals taught you."

Jessie had taken it as a joke, but the more Jessie

thought about it, the more she was convinced Caroline had been serious.

Alex watched another child, not much older than seven, run into the house, only to run back out again and stand in the front yard, looking around in wonder. "I gotta give it to her. This was not a decision I saw coming."

Jessie nodded. She had talked for most of the night with Caroline, making sure the woman understood the enormity of what she was doing.

Caroline had smiled. "This is something that should have been done long ago. A need that should have been dealt with. But from a place of love, not fear. I was always afraid of Clint. Hell, I was afraid of Roger as well. Can you imagine what it's like to fear your own child?" Jessie hadn't spoken, because it wasn't something she had ever considered. "And for too long, I stood by and let that fear rule me. I knew what was happening to those poor people up in the mountain. I didn't know about the women being used, but I knew the life that the community up there suffered. That was my life too for so long. But then I came here, and...I'm ashamed to say this... but I didn't want to go back. No matter how many beatings I had to take from Clint, I'd rather that than life in those hills. But when I saw you...that you were willing to do whatever it took to find out the truth about that Marley girl...well, I knew it was time I took a stand. Even if it meant my death. I couldn't be silent anymore."

Jessie had reached over and covered Caroline's hand with her own. "There are no words that can describe what you're offering. But there is not one person that would blame you for wanting to take some time to be by yourself for a bit. To get to know who you are."

Caroline smiled warmly. "Jessie, some of the loneliest times I've had have been when certain others were right there in the room with me. I've been alone for too long. As for getting to know who I am...well, maybe being around people more will help me figure that out."

Jessie nodded, drawing back a bit. "And I know it doesn't change things for you, but I want you to know that I am sorry about what happened with Clint."

Caroline's eyes narrowed. "Don't be. The only thing I'm sorry for is the fact I wasn't there to see it happen."

Jessie took in a deep breath and hoped she didn't appear too awkward when she redirected the conversation. "Still, taking in the children from Lost Cove? That's a big undertaking."

Caroline gave her a large, genuine smile. There aren't many of them. They deserve better than what will happen to them if they stay on the mountain." Jessie nodded, thinking of Clara Beth. "Also, their parents will be welcome here in Bidonville as well. Many will opt to stay because they're caring for kinfolk and parents that aren't in any shape to make the trek down the mountain. But when things settle, they'll be welcome as well."

"I heard that Tilley Cormac is going to move into Kerry's home. She's offering to take people from Lost Cove in as well."

Caroline nodded. "That's right. That girl is made of steel. She knew Kerry wouldn't want George going off to some group home, so this way he can stay in his house, and she can use the extra space to help with the children and adults I can't take in. The whole town's coming together to make a change for those people."

When Jessie had relayed everything to Alex, she could tell that he was as moved as she had been.

"I just worry about the trauma those poor people in Lost Cove have been through. Apparently, most of them are just now realizing what Roger, Clint and that old woman were up to. They weren't complicit in any of it. The only thing they were guilty of was believing the word of a few bad seeds," Jessie said.

"What will happen to her? That old woman?"

Jessie exhaled sharply. "She'll spend the rest of her life in prison I imagine. With Clint and Roger dead, she confessed to everything. Backing up what Roger had said. Turns out those two brothers she coerced into helping were her children. I don't see any judge going lightly on that family. What did you find out about Sheriff Cormac?"

"He's turning himself in," Alex said. "Throwing himself on the mercy of the courts. He honestly believed that if he did everything they asked, it would keep the peace between Bidonville and the Cove. And once they kidnapped his daughter, he was helpless to do anything that might have compromised them. Roger had him in his pocket at that moment. Your arrival threw everyone into a panic. Including the sheriff. But he's telling the courts everything that happened in order to shield his wife. He says she knew nothing about any of it, but who knows." He shrugged his shoulders. "From what I heard, Irma's already planning to put their house on the market. Roll the money she gets from it into paying off Kerry's place and possibly doing an add-on. Hopefully she'll be just fine after all this."

"Who will take over the police department?" She was thinking of Deputy Hardin and the cruel fate he had met at Roger's hands.

"There's an acting sheriff from the next county over who has agreed to step in until they can get a new police force up and running. Seems like all the towns in the immediate vicinity are doing what they can to help. Or keep things quiet. I'm not really sure which."

Jessie sighed. "You were right. This is a completely different world up here. I can't tell you how much I am looking forward to getting back home to my own bed."

Blizzard came trotting out of the house and nosed at the cinnamon buns before Jessie pulled them out of his reach. He huffed his annoyance but settled down at her feet.

The door opened again, and this time Dr. Lindquist stepped through.

"Hey, Doc, how's things going in there?" Alex asked.

"Slow," the examiner replied. "For the most part, the children I examined are malnourished and some are bordering on dehydration. But my biggest worry is the fact that no one from Lost Cove has been vaccinated. At all. For anything. I'll start with the basics and work my way up. But...they're happy. That will go a long way."

"You're sure you want to stay up here?" Jessie asked.

He smiled at her. "It's only for a couple of weeks until they can get a new doc in town. Apparently, there is already someone a few towns away planning to make the move." He looked at a couple of the children standing in the parking lot staring at the parked cars. "They need help. And that's what I'm here for." He looked at Alex and squinted. "Of course, had you relayed the message the lab in Pine Haven had sent, we could have avoided all of this."

Jessie swiveled her head in his direction. "How so?"

"I sent them Roger's blood on a whim, along with the blood samples you found in that shack, and what I extracted from Marley. They ran them all and found that Roger's blood not only had many of the same genetic markers for deep inbreeding, but that they were also a match for Marley's child. He was the father."

Alex slapped at his knee. "Well, if you hadn't gotten yourself kidnapped, you'd have been here to get the message for yourself. And maybe next time, I won't risk my neck to come save you. You're welcome, by the way..." His voice trailed off as he stood and escorted the doctor back inside the house, their voices trading quips as they headed towards the back of the small bed and breakfast.

Jessie sat alone, as Blizzard raised himself to his haunches, placing his head on her lap. She smiled, scratching between his ears.

"Well, boy, we solved our first case together. Might not have been the ending anyone wanted, but we got answers."

Clara Beth ran by, chasing after one of her friends, her limp barely noticeable as she stopped and waved. Jessie returned the wave and watched the girl continue whatever made up game she had been playing.

Jessie marveled at how tough and resilient children were. She hoped some of it would rub off on her over the next few days, because she knew this case was going to leave scars.

But scars, like memories, were designed to fade for a reason. She survived. She would live to take on another case. And maybe, just maybe, she'd be able to give someone else comfort in knowing that she'd be on their side.

Even if no one else was.

50

Good Hunting Grounds

The midday rush was in full swing at Angela's Bakery. Pushing through the lunchtime doldrums meant getting that boost of caffeine and the sugar high from the delicious baked goods on display.

It was a nice day on the green, and many of the patrons were opting to get their treats to go, finding a bench or patch of grass in the expansive town square where they could take in the sunshine and the unmatched beauty of a Carolina blue sky.

No one really noticed the tall man who entered the bakery with the large duffel bag slung over his shoulder. He wore his hat with the brim pulled down over his features. The brown duster, baggy button-up shirt, and loose-fitting jeans obscured his build, making nothing about him memorable.

He adjusted the bag on his shoulder as he studied the

glass display before ordering a morning glory muffin and a large black coffee. The girl behind the counter smiled as she handed him the coffee and said she'd bring the muffin to him if he wanted to take a seat. He selected a table next to the large storefront window that allowed him to take in the foot traffic along the bustling, picturesque main street.

The coffee was hot as he sipped it, carefully watching the patrons as they entered and exited the shop. No one really looked in his direction or paid him much attention. Even the people that came in alone, picked up their order, and walked out the door without really looking around.

That was good.

He had always imagined that in these small towns, everyone knew everyone and was hyper aware of strangers in their midst.

Thankfully, that didn't seem to be true. It made doing what he planned that much easier.

"Here you go. Sorry it took a bit longer. Fresh batch was coming out of the oven and I figured you might like a warm one."

The man looked up and smiled. Her name tag read Julia, and she seemed extra bubbly. "Why thank you kindly, Julia. It smells heavenly."

"Can I top your coffee off?" She held a pot in one hand.

"That would be nice, thank you."

She set about pouring the coffee, glancing quickly at the duffel bag at his feet. "Haven't seen you in here before. What brings you to Pine Haven?"

Of course. The patrons might mind their own business, but the service industry workers were the same everywhere. Overly friendly, always asking questions. He kept his hat low, only glancing up quickly at the woman. "Oh, I'm just passing through. Taking in the beautiful sights, might do some hiking and a little hunting."

"Well, you'll love the hiking here. All kinds of scenic routes that overlook the lake. And if you're into game hunting, you won't find better than Pine Haven."

For the first time, he looked the woman in the eyes and smiled. "That's what I've heard. I'm really looking forward to finding out for myself."

Julia nodded and headed back behind the counter to take care of the next customers.

The man took a bite from his muffin, then looked down with a frown.

At his feet, the zipper of the duffel bag had opened slightly. He smiled, seeing the different lengths of rope all coiled neatly within. In addition, there were numerous rolls of silver duct tape and a set of white zip ties.

The handle of the X26E taser was barely visible, peeking out from under one of the coils of rope. He practically salivated looking at the specialized carbon grip on the weapon. The opportunity to try it out had not yet presented itself.

Soon.

He reached down, feeling inside to make sure nothing had potentially fallen out.

Satisfied, the man continued munching on his muffin and sipping at the cup of coffee. He grinned to himself as he looked out the window once more.

This was going to be fun.

BOOK FIVE IS COMING VERY SOON and is now available for pre-order!

Dead Of Night- Jessie Night thriller Book Five

Also, if you'd like to stay up to date on all new releases, including the third book in this exciting new series, join the author's mailing list, at:

sendfox.com/emberscottauthor

ABOUT THE AUTHOR

Ember Scott is an author of thrillers and mysteries living in the great state of North Carolina. He is a lover of dogs, mountains, lakes...and some people.

He loves to create tale about very bad people that do very bad things and ultimately get their comeuppance.

If you like fast paced thrillers that are built around unforgettable characters, then this is the author for you.

He can be reached at:

emberscottauthor@gmail.com

ALSO BY EMBER SCOTT

Made in the USA
Middletown, DE
24 August 2024

59673494R00213